WHO
WE WERE
IN THE
DARK

JESSICA TAYLOR

DIAL BOOKS

DIAL BOOKS
An imprint of Penguin Random House LLC, New York

First published in the United States of America by Dial Books,
an imprint of Penguin Random House LLC, 2022
Copyright © 2022 by Jessica Taylor

Dial & colophon are registered trademarks of Penguin Random House LLC.
Visit us online at penguinrandomhouse.com.
Library of Congress Cataloging-in-Publication Data is available.
Printed in Canada

ISBN 9780735228146
1 3 5 7 9 10 8 6 4 2
FRI

Design by Jason Henry
Text set in Adobe Garamond

For all the girls who have found themselves
and all the girls still searching

WINTER: NOW

CHAPTER 1

There are places you know, and then there are places that know you. Donner Pass, the high point over Truckee, where the elevation made Donner Lake spread like deep blue ink throughout the dip in the valley—that was somewhere that knew the sound of my footsteps, the smell of my frozen hair, the rhythm of my heart.

Inside the cabin, the *plink plink plink* of the kitchen faucet needled my ears. I tossed my keys onto the cracked tile counter and flipped off the water. It had been left on by someone to keep the relentless cold from freezing the pipes solid. Our cabin wore the signs of a year without me. Cobwebs trailed down the staircase spindles, a layer of grease caked the stove from the year before, and the once-white sink was stained with rust spots and limescale.

I used to miss these walls and woods when I was suffocating between locker-lined hallways. I'd wait for summer and winter and spring—three times a year when Kevin's Jeep would climb up, up, up through the twisted hills. As the oxygen thinned, I could finally breathe.

Here in Truckee, high above Donner Lake, the air tasted like pine, like lake water, like fresh snow. Here, I'd hear my brother's whoops as we tore through the forest at night, feel Rand's kisses vibrating against my throat on the hotel rooftop, relish the hollow clink of Grace's glass against mine, her eyes going bright as she raised her drink to the night and the summer and *us*.

Back then I didn't know that I'd have to hold Grace's silence too. How that absence of sound would be the loudest of all.

Donner Pass didn't just know me. It knew them too. Now, after a year away, without me and without us—our wonderful and wretched foursome—I wished this place could forget.

SPRING: YEAR ONE

CHAPTER 2

There was a story Scotch-taped to my bedroom wall back home. Frayed edges, torn from a spiral binder. The ink was gel and purple from a too-nice pen I'd borrowed from my math partner last year and forgot—kind of—to give back. Inside that shimmery, violet universe, a girl was trapped in a box. One day, the girl tunneled through the side and reached out for a perfect world. A bright, sunlit life her fingers couldn't quite touch—

A jerk of the Jeep made my eyes snap open. Mountainside trees whirred past, giving way to the bright flash of a quick-flowing river.

Kevin and Wesley were listening to the game on the radio—A's vs. Cardinals. I'd lost track of the score.

From the back seat, I stared at the sleeve of Kevin's Cal T-shirt as he shifted gears on the old Jeep and cornered the tight mountain turns. The college tee didn't go with the gray at Kevin's temples that peppered its way into his half-hearted beard. That was the real giveaway that he had decades on Wesley and me. A forty-year-old former frat boy who had inexplicably sprouted a conscience.

The A's batter struck out and Wesley bit his knuckles.

He was an A's fan—we both were. My brother liked that they were a small team with no budget who turned it all around. Our mom raised us on the roar of the A's stadium and hot dogs that snapped between our teeth. That was back when we had extra cash for games, before Mom got sick.

The constant stream of the announcers' voices and the occasional roar of the fans were enough to drown out the silence in the car.

"Yeah!" Kevin yelled when the Cardinals hit one out of the park, which was probably the eighth word he'd said since we left Gridley two hours before. I didn't know why he'd root for them, a team from Missouri. I didn't know why, because I didn't know him at all.

Wesley hugged the headrest behind him as he looked back at me. "Nora, you got your stuff out of the dryer, right?"

He'd already asked me this twice, first while we watched the front window for Kevin to pull up—half an hour later than Kevin had said—and again before I went back inside to leave a fresh glass of water next to the pill bottles on Mom's nightstand while she slept. The back of her hand had been curled up over her eyes, blocking out both the midday light seeping through her blinds and the phantom from her former life idling his Jeep in our drive.

"Forgot," I said as I propped my bare feet on the center console and wiggled my toes against Wesley's arm. "I guess I'll be sockless and pantsless all week."

"There's a Target in Reno," Kevin said over his shoulder. "I don't mind detouring."

Wesley exhaled and faced forward. "She's being a smart-ass."

Kevin chuckled, tightening his hand on the steering wheel and letting it go loose. "The smart-ass gene runs rampant on my side of the family, Nora." He scratched the scruff on his chin and flicked his eyes to Wesley. "Your, uh, mom says you play baseball."

"Yep." Wesley shifted his long limbs around in his seat, knobby knees bumping the glove box. "Just JV, though. They don't put a ton of freshmen on varsity."

Kevin squeezed Wesley's shoulder, and I noticed the carburetor burn from Wesley's after-school job had turned an angrier shade of red. "Next year," Kevin said. "You'll make it next year." In the rearview mirror, he gave me a questioning look. "Nora, you, um, play too, yeah? Eighth grade. You gonna try out for JV next year?"

The seat belt chafed my neck. I zipped my sweatshirt to my chin and sat up straighter. "There isn't a girls' team next year. Not at the high school."

The dizzying pull of the roadside river's current churned through my stomach.

Spring breaks were for sleeping until lunch, climbing up on the roof to see the stars, and staying over at any house that found itself parentless for the night.

Our mom had just moved us into a smaller apartment that put my brother and me into a new school district. Everything I'd known for basically all my life was being carried away from me, whitecaps on a roiling river.

The trees pulled away from the wide blue sky as our wheels

hit the lookout point at the top of the hill. Kevin rolled down the driver's-side window. The air slapped against my face as the car climbed higher. It must have been twenty degrees cooler than back in the valley.

"Lots of history in these hills," he said. "You can feel it."

Wesley bumped his head up and down in a little nod. "Sounds cool."

He was approaching this "vacation" like it was another day of work at the shop, a thing to go along with, a duty to fulfill.

"You'll feel it when you're up there, Nora," Kevin said. "The air, the lake, the pines—you're going to love it." He glanced to Wesley. "Both of you."

All I could feel was the humming of the radio speaker against my leg and the certainty that my brother and I should not be hurtling up a mountain with a stranger.

My short story was far, far away, flapping under the ceiling fan I probably left on. I should have brought the pages with me. A year ago, I'd started it. It still needed an ending.

The announcer on the radio called the game for the Cardinals. The A's lost. Kevin's fist punched up in the air. Wesley cringed a little but smiled at Kevin and said, "Go, Cardinals."

These two, my dad and my brother, they were both strangers to me. Just in different ways.

Kevin said less and less again the closer we got to Truckee. Occasionally when he had to change lanes, he lifted up in his seat and craned his neck to see over the luggage blocking the back window.

My brother and I spilled onto the dirt driveway like puppies, blinking in the mid-afternoon sunlight, muscles tight from the long drive. I hadn't realized I'd expected a taste of the luxe life until I was staring up at the cabin. I felt myself sink a little.

It must have been built in the seventies and never updated. Every cabin we'd passed on the way up had seemed nicer, newer. But they all had to have been built around the same time. So not newer, but fresher, maybe. More lived-in. More loved.

A nice cabin wasn't somewhere Wesley and I belonged anyway.

Nice cabins were for kids who didn't worry the electric company would turn off the lights again because that little red notice in the mail went unanswered, or that their gym shoes were too tight around the toes to climb the rope to the tip-top, or that the school would give them a different lunch than the other kids—only half a sandwich and an apple—because their lunch account was short by twenty bucks.

Holding my backpack in front of me, I walked inside and stood in the middle of the carpet, watching dust float across the sun-streaked air.

Kevin tossed the keys on the tiled kitchen counter and swept his hair off his sun-freckled forehead. He glanced around the musty room. "This is, uh . . . it."

Do you remember him? I'd asked Wesley the week before, sitting on his bed and trying to make him talk to me. He'd just shaken his head. Wesley must have been about eighteen months old when Kevin took off. Me, just days.

Our mom said he'd died. A quick answer in the drop-off line at school while Wesley and I sat in the back seat clutching backpacks as big as we were. It was the week before Father's Day, and Wesley had wanted to know where to send the card he'd made during craft hour the day before.

But our dad was very much living. He had not one but two mailing addresses, when we could barely pay the rent on a tiny two-bedroom duplex.

Wesley came through the front door behind me, my duffel hanging from his long arms. He took in the framed baseball paraphernalia hanging on the wood-paneled walls.

"Let me." I reached for the handle of my bag.

Wesley heaved it farther into the room. "I've already got the thing inside."

I'd always looked a lot like my brother—our matching dark hair, pale skin, and pink-tipped noses that sunburned too easily. Only I was an inch shorter than his five ten, had a meatiness to my structure he lacked, and my jaw was softer, not so square.

Now that I watched Kevin in profile, I knew where my soft jaw had come from.

A darkness filled me up, even as sunlight rippled in through the tattered curtains. I picked at the edge of one and curled it between my fingers.

Kevin cleared his throat behind me. "Those were your grandma's. This place was hers."

"Our grandma," I said. "She's—"

"Gone," he said.

"Sorry," I said, at the same time Wesley asked, "When did she die?" Under the unease, there was still that polite interest in his voice, almost cheeriness.

"Just this last year. Your grandfather the year before that."

A sadness settled over me then. We could have known them.

I picked up my bag and held it close to me. Inside it, there was a king-size bag of M&M's and two books—enough to last me approximately two of the five days we were trapped between these walls. "What, um, what are we going to do all week?"

"Well, I guide," Kevin said, gesturing toward the back window. I guessed that was the direction of the lake. "Fishing tours during the on-season. For tourists, I mean."

My backpack was making my arms ache. I let it thud against the carpeted floor. "What do you do in Boise?"

"Lodi," he said. "I haven't lived in Idaho since I was in my twenties. I work at a hardware store, off and on."

A flush rose up Wesley's neck, settling in his cheeks. "Lodi?" When the most recent version of the truth had come out, Mom had said our very-not-dead dad lived all the way in Boise, Idaho. "That's, like, three hours from us."

I blinked hard.

Three hours in the car and he could have reached us, found out we were not okay. Now I understood why *dead* was the kinder lie.

Kevin swallowed and rubbed his chin. "I'm—" He threw a wild look out the window in the direction of the lake we hadn't yet seen. "I need to get down to my slip, check on the boat."

He could have told us ten different lies about why he'd never come and we probably would have doe-eyed nodded. Because even if we'd known he was full of shit, it was what we needed—a reason. So we'd take the lie. But Kevin didn't even offer that. Kevin didn't want to try.

So I wasn't going to either. I wouldn't try to ask hard questions that'd only get me silence. I wouldn't try to "bond" or whatever. I wouldn't try to undo fourteen years of dead or not dead or who cares anyway he just wasn't there.

Wesley grabbed the handle of my duffel, knuckles going white.

"Wesley," I said. "*Wesley.*" Hoping he'd say something to make this a little bit okay.

In the month leading up to this trip—and even now—I kept waiting to catch my brother in a look, in some kind of shared understanding. We had a dad. He wasn't dead. He liked the *Cardinals*. And we were spending a week with him somewhere around Donner Lake. If there was ever going to be a time when Wesley and I got each other again, it should have been this.

But there was a panic in his eyes I'd only seen when Mom was spinning out.

I heaved my luggage away from him, high in my arms, and headed up the creaking stairs.

The pines shuddered in the breeze outside. Every room, closet, and cabinet felt like they hadn't been opened in years. But the March air was cold, and Wesley pushed past me, struggling to close the window I'd opened in the bedroom.

"Stop," I said. "It's broken."

He fought it, the tendons in his neck popping out.

"Wesley, stop," I said, stepping closer. He was too quick to get mad, and I didn't want this to be one of those times.

The window wouldn't budge. The frame was bent. I'd fix it later.

He let go and sank down to the worn carpet. "Stupid-ass thing," he said. "Everything in this hole is broke or busted."

I smiled. "Same thing."

Wesley, clutching the back of his neck with both hands, met my eyes. "I guess." His body relaxed against the wall.

"And we're luckier than most—two live parents and *two* broke and busted houses."

Wesley hmphed, not really a laugh.

A pine needle blew in. I picked it up and sat down on the end of the bed. "How was Mom?"

I didn't know for sure he'd called her, but I knew he'd been worried she'd forgotten to walk the rent check to the mailbox.

"Fine. I guess." Wesley tossed his hands up, dropped them. "Or maybe her voice did a good job of fooling me. She paid the rent at least." He was quiet. "Thing needs some oil." He nodded toward the window. "Won't glide. I'll see if there's any around here."

"Hm," I said.

He looked over at me, eyebrows drawing close.

I thought about Mom, what she might be doing at home without us.

We'd been apart from her one week the summer before, when our uncle Dan took us to Fort Bragg. Her headaches were worse while we were away. The day we got back, she'd begged Wesley to get her to the hospital—he couldn't even drive yet.

Fifteen minutes of jolting brakes and too-fast turns, and he'd pulled up to the hospital.

This trip was just a week long; the next one would be all summer. Mom couldn't make it all summer without us.

"How do you really think she is?" I asked.

"Good." Wesley stood and tried to shimmy the window again. "Bills we could prepay are prepaid. Sticks are in the casings of all the windows—no one will be busting in."

"That's not what I mean."

He tugged at a loose strand on the fraying, rust-colored carpet. "The neighbors are going to look in on her."

I said, "Fixing things, Wesley—it isn't going to actually *fix* anything."

He sighed. "I know that, Nora."

The pine needle crumpled in my fingers and I let the pulverized pieces drop to the carpet. "It's . . . complicated."

"Complicated," Wesley said dryly. "You have no idea."

CHAPTER 3

SPRING

The gray full moon was high in the sky after I'd unpacked my stuff upstairs. We'd had a family dinner, sort of—some burgers Kevin threw on the grill and let burn. I was no stranger to hunger, but I couldn't eat mine. Wesley scarfed his down, said he was tired from the drive, and disappeared into the bedroom next to the one I'd chosen. It had been two hours, and I could hear the theme for *Finding Bigfoot* humming tinnily from his computer speakers through the wall.

The distance wasn't too different from home—me in my room and him in the living room that served as his bedroom.

Still, I wished he'd come out, do something, even just walk through the woods with me.

But Wesley and I hadn't really been friends since two summers before, when he'd turned thirteen and decided to focus all his energy on whatever would put extra cash in our pockets—mowing lawns, clearing brush, tossing newspapers onto dewy morning lawns. He'd disappeared.

One sweltering August night before school started up, Mom had been sprawled on the couch while I traded cold washcloths for colder ones, pressing them to her scorching forehead.

Wesley had come in the back door. The refrigerator opened and I heard him pouring a glass of milk. The tension that had gripped me like a fist loosened. Wesley would talk to Mom this time, know the right thing to do, make it better somehow.

But he froze as he came into the living room. His long arms, tanned from a summer outdoors, went slack at his sides. Milk sloshed from his glass. He looked from Mom on the couch to me cross-legged on the floor, then back to Mom. Her breaths were sharp, her freckled cheeks pink beneath the washcloth covering her forehead.

Over the raised brim of his milk glass, Wesley met my gaze.

I looked at him, waiting, hope making me float a few inches off the floor.

He took a drink and shook his head, then padded in his grass-stained socks across the carpet to his room, the one he still had back then. The door clicked shut behind him.

I half expected things to change the morning Mom sat us down—clear-eyed that day, not bloodshot like nights when the headaches kept her up. She told us about these breaks—these springs, summers, and winters we'd be spending in the mountains with our bio dad. The one who wasn't dead after all.

Wesley had just spooned through his cereal until his corn-flakes, bought with his own money, dissolved. He'd finally looked up, but all he had for me was that same absent stare.

Now I opened my window to the Truckee night—Wesley had spent the afternoon fighting the thing and cussing at it before I'd nudged him aside and straightened the bent frame with a pair of channel locks I'd found in the woodshed.

Outside, the mountain air was a million degrees cooler. Only one house stood close by, a few hundred feet up and across the road, away from the faraway black expanse of shiny Donner Lake. Everything was quiet and dim inside. No signs of life.

Lights salted the windows of a few homes across the lake. The houses were as small as tiny lanterns from where I stood watching from the window. Our cabin—Kevin's—it must have looked like a dollhouse to the people on the other side. I wondered if I was small enough that they couldn't even see me.

A creak rippled through the wind. In the sole nearby home, an upstairs light flicked on. The window opened.

I ducked behind the drapes.

A heave and huff from a small voice made me peek out into the night. A scuffle from between the curtains, and one jean-clad leg swung out. Then the other. A girl scaled the tree branch and slid down the trunk.

She tucked her copper hair behind her ear as she touched down on the ground. She wore it in a messy, slept-in way that would have made her look like an extra in the cast of *Les Mis*—a wretched street waif with style.

"Hey!" she said into the night. She stomped down the road, closer to Kevin's cabin. Closer. She looked right up at me. "Hey, you."

15

My fingers froze to the windowsill. I'd moved out from behind the curtains without thinking. I opened my mouth, but no words were there.

"You going to keep standing there or you going to come out with me?" she asked.

I'd snuck out once before, one night when I couldn't calm Mom down. Wesley'd come after me, freaking out at me the whole way home.

"I—"

"You shouldn't. You can't. You couldn't possibly," she said. "Those are the words standing between you and the night of your life. Ask yourself this: What will you regret more at sunrise—coming with me or staying here?"

Her words were a lit match.

"I'm . . ."

"You're what?" she asked.

A thousand things—pissed off, jealous. Alone. But none of them the answer I wanted. Nora Sharpe, what was I?

The lit match tipped.

"I'm . . . I'm coming."

And as I lifted the sash higher, something inside me ignited, unfolding in a silent burst. I had one leg out the window before I'd thought it through. I didn't care. I didn't *want* to have regrets at sunrise.

The ten feet standing between me and owning my own life were a problem.

"The trellis," the girl said. "Use it like a ladder."

My biceps ached within seconds of grabbing hold of the thing.

The toes of my shoes almost didn't fit in the gaps. I pulled away from an exposed nail, and the sawing rip of fabric filled my ears.

I finally clattered to the ground, where the girl gave me the up-down. "That climb was iffy," she said. "But you really stuck the landing."

I huffed out a laugh.

The torn pocket of my jeans flapped open. I tried to tuck it in, thought of the money I'd need for a new pair, the Target in Reno that Kevin said he'd drive me to, and the greater cost of letting him do something for me after all these years of nothing.

"Come on," she said. "We can't stand in the road all night, Nora. It's Nora, right? We've got a friend waiting."

"Yeah, Nora." I stuffed my hands into the pockets of my hoodie. "Wait, what are we—we're meeting someone?"

A quick glance and a smirk, then the girl's steps were brisk as she pointed herself up the road toward the top of the hill. I jolted after her.

Her flats were a light gold leather that winked as she walked under the one streetlamp illuminating the mountain road. The jeans she wore were an expensive brand I'd tried on at the mall once—only on a whim. I could have bought three months' worth of school lunches for that price.

These cabin kids. They had money.

I glanced at her, but she gave away nothing.

"I'm Nora," I said when we were well past Kevin's cabin.

"We covered that." She smiled—she had two sharp eyeteeth that gave her a fierce, mischievous look—and pointed to herself. "Grace Lombardi."

The freedom felt good. I liked it out here—traveling the road cut through the forest, under the sway of a new stranger who also liked to sneak out late at night—tethered to nothing, not Mom, not Kevin. Not Wesley. Breathing in the cool pine air, clear and deep enough to fill any emptiness inside me.

CHAPTER 4

SPRING

"There," Grace said, pointing way high up the mountainside.

Rising at the top of a hill, the gray back of a building at least ten stories high jutted toward the sky. We made it to the parking lot, our feet crunching fast through pine needles scattered across the asphalt. Against the starlit backdrop, a gold sign: THE HONEYRIDGE LODGE.

We rushed past a delivery truck with an open roll-up door, cloth bags overflowing with white linens. At the farthest end of the building, a steamy door opened and someone tossed a cardboard box into the dumpster before returning inside.

Grace froze, gripped my arm as she glanced around. "Someone's following us."

We ducked behind the dumpster. Grace held her finger to her lips as if I might talk and give us away. I would never have done that—I was trying to not even breathe.

The footfalls stopped and Grace's hand rose, pointing at the figure ahead.

The shape came into focus.

Wesley stood in the blast of the hotel's floodlight.

He must have been awake in his room beside mine when I'd made my escape.

My heart still jumping, I braced myself against the dumpster and stood up.

He focused on me, then sighed, all weary and long-suffering. "You can't do this, Nora."

Behind him, Grace moved slowly, catlike, before she stepped into the light.

Wesley's head snapped around. He focused on Grace, her arms crossed, her hips thrust slightly forward, an elegant slouch, her mussed hair an amber halo in the lamplight. He stood up a little straighter. "Who's this?"

She lifted her hands and pointed both thumbs at herself. "*This* is Grace."

"This is just my brother," I said.

"Hello, Brother," she said. "Does adventure run in your DNA too? And do you happen to have a name other than *Brother*?"

"Wesley," he said, a smile flickering on his face that made him look momentarily dopey and happy and unlike I'd seen him look in basically forever. "I'm Wesley."

Instead of answering, Grace stared far across the parking lot. "Gang's all here."

A small figure moved across the asphalt toward us, jacket hood pulled down low against the cool spring night.

As the figure got closer, I realized he was probably close to my age, but the kind of boy who could still pass for ten. Under his coat, he wore a fuchsia button-down shirt with a turquoise collar. He moved into our little circle of light, and I saw dark hair that swept down over his forehead. He pushed it back, eyes settling on me.

"You've collected," he said to Grace, and there was something about his mouth when he spoke, and the fullness of his smile—there quick and then gone—that I liked. "Excellent. The cult is coming along nicely."

He was too beautiful for reality. He and Grace both.

Wesley gave him a look, but maybe the kid wasn't joking. If Grace wanted to lead a cult, I already knew she could gain a following.

"Nora and Wesley," Grace said, pointing to each of us. "Or, I should say, Indoctrination Candidates Two and Three."

"Good evening, Two and Three," the boy said. "I'm One, but you can call me Rand. Rand Elliot." He had an English accent. His tongue rolled over the *a* in *Rand*, stretching it clear into the next day.

"You are a love," Grace said as she bent down and kissed him on the cheek.

Grace's boyfriend then. He belonged to her and she to him—they made sense.

Rand looked up, to his left. Quietly, he asked, "Is someone over there?"

Grace's ears seemed to perk like a cat's and she held her finger to her lips. She waved us behind the dumpster. The press of the others' bodies around me made me aware of my own, thicker than anyone else's, taking up space. We barely fit, the four of us, but somehow we did.

The back door to the hotel closed with a thunk as two girls made their way to the parking lot. One looked around, then leaned against the front of the delivery van. The second girl joined her. They couldn't have been more than three years older than us, one with long dark hair in a messy bun, revealing an undercut, and the other with a short, blond pixie.

"And I can't take this with," the girl with the undercut was saying, sliding something—her phone, I figured—from her pocket and staring at its dark surface. "My parents can trace it."

She tossed it into the dumpster. It clanged against the side and Rand jumped. He noticed me watching and sent me a sheepish smile through the dark.

The other girl slipped her hand into her friend's in a way that made me realize they were more than that, and said something low. Her eyes were wet. They glinted as she pointed across the parking lot to a set of headlights jumping across potholes and heading in their direction.

It pulled up about ten feet away, a mint-green sedan with a vague figure at the wheel.

"That's my ride," the dark-haired girl said, rising, slowly letting their hands break apart.

The other girl caught her wrist as they moved toward the car, partially under the floodlight. Something about the way they stood, not quite facing each other, not quite turned away, made my throat tighten.

Damp swimsuits under their clothes left wet patterns soaking through their sweatshirts.

"There's a pool, huh?" Wesley whispered. "Can we swim?"

I shot Wesley a look.

Grace said, "It closes at eight p.m."

"They're killing me." The dark-haired girl ran a hand over the close-cropped hair at her neck, eyes roving as if trying to avoid eye contact with the other girl. "It's like death by a hundred thousand paper cuts—like I'm bleeding out so slowly, and if I stay, everything I like about me is going to die."

Her words sliced into me. Death by a hundred thousand paper cuts.

Grace was softly shaking. With one hand, she steadied herself against the dumpster.

"But what's even out there?" The other girl flung a hand out at the night. "What's there, Candace, that's not here?"

The girl—Candace—smiled, and it looked familiar for a second in the light—sad but sort of determined. Maybe a smile like Wesley's sometimes.

"Freedom, my own . . . thing—I don't know," she said. "Maybe I don't even know what I need. Maybe that's what I have to figure out."

The girls wrapped their arms tight around each other. Candace pulled back, then leaned close and touched her lips softly against the other girl's.

One quick turn—like if she didn't go right then, she never would—and Candace moved across the parking lot like she was floating on air, like a fairy across a black lake of night-damp asphalt.

The blond girl followed, earthbound, and passed her a duffel bag. Candace tossed it into the seat and slid in after it without looking back. The door thunked closed.

Alone now, the other girl walked back to the hotel, using a slide card to unlock the door and pull it open. Caught in the wedge of light from inside, she turned and looked as the car revved and rolled forward. At the far edge of the lot, Candace was swallowed by the night.

When I turned back, the hotel door was closed. Both girls gone.

Grace's eyes, unmistakably green in the floodlight, shone with tears, and Rand was holding her hand. Death by a hundred thousand paper cuts. Maybe Grace felt it too.

She let Rand's hand drop and, bringing her voice high, said, "I hereby propose we exit the trash heap and reenter the world."

Rand raised his hand. "Motion seconded."

"Thank you, Professor," Grace said.

Wesley stared at Rand, then Grace. "You two talk like aliens from another planet."

"Interesting aliens, though," I said quickly. I didn't want to offend our new friends. "The kind who'd want to cohabitate with us on Earth, not vaporize us before stealing our planet."

Grace stared at me for a second. There was the quick flash of a smile. "We're very selective about who we vaporize," she said.

Rand nodded. "The residual cryogenic liquid gets everywhere."

The clang of a heavy door popping open again cut through the quiet, and we all jumped.

A boy stood in the doorway, dangling a key. Two or three years older than me, blond hair against tanned skin, and clear blue eyes.

His lips slid into a smile that would have been perfect except for one inward-turned front tooth.

"It's about time," Grace said. "Thank you, Neil."

I glanced at her. I didn't talk to boys like him. I didn't even know boys like him.

"Just don't fuck anything up," he said. "Or if you do"—he gestured at the three of us—"blame one of them."

Grace walked over and tried to get the key from him, but he held it higher, out of her reach.

"No reward?" he asked.

Grace smiled and took his face in her hands. She reached up, and at the last second before their mouths connected, she turned and pecked him on the cheek, a loud smacking kiss.

Then she snatched the key from his hand and flew through the door. "The night is wasting away!" she called.

Wesley huffed when I angled past Neil and followed Grace in. But it wasn't three seconds before his heavy steps fell in behind me.

Inside, Wesley and I stilled under the glow of the overhead lights. Ahead, Grace and Rand were both halfway down the hall already. They looked like extensions of this place, guests hoping the concierge could recommend a boating excursion or give directions to the best boutique shopping.

Wesley looked at me and I looked at him. I took a step back toward the exit.

Grace unlocked a door beside the elevators. She held it wide open. "Ladies first."

And then I lurched forward, down the hall, and my feet hit the

25

stairwell. Below me now, Grace poked her head around the door. "Aren't you coming, Brother?"

Wesley sighed but followed. A few steps up, he said, "Why aren't we taking the elevator? Couldn't Mr. Vineyard Vines get you a card for the elevator too?"

"No cameras in the stairwell," I said. "The elevator's a different story."

Grace paused against the railing, smiled as she squinted at me. "I knew I liked you."

Stair after stair, we climbed. We passed the seventh floor, and the backs of my thighs burned. We reached the eleventh, and everyone except Grace was heaving for air.

I bent to catch my breath, and Grace's voice echoed down the stairwell. "Just one more."

I don't know why we followed. Some promise, some hope of whatever waited at the top.

My breath was tight inside my chest from the dust, the exertion, the exhilaration, when the door flew open and the breeze off the rooftop hit my skin. I stepped out from the lit stairwell into the dark night and blinked fast, my eyes adjusting to a sky full of moonlight. It was small above us but bright.

"Wow," Wesley said, then quieter, "Wow." He smiled—a flash of white teeth.

So high above the town, it felt as if the mountains across the skyline were at our level.

Behind me, Rand stayed far from the edge.

The breeze caught the exposed skin on my chest, and my body

exploded into a million little goose bumps. I went to stand beside Rand, zipping my sweatshirt to my chin. "It's even colder up here."

"It's balmy compared to a Donner winter," he said. "Everything moves a bit slower, every sound a bit lower. Winter feels like dying, but not fast."

Was he quoting something? Or was this just how he talked? "So . . . you feel a kind of way about the seasons," I said, nodding.

"But summer." He smiled into the distance as if recalling something magnificent, as if he could feel the sunburn on his cheeks, the lake lapping his feet. "Summer is my favorite."

Grace looked back at us. "Rand!" she called. "I haven't asked—what the hell have you done since Christmas?"

He tapped his finger to his chin. "Went public on my Internet start-up," he said, "broke the world record for bench-pressing, and received my acceptance into NASA's space program."

"Same," she said.

"You, Wesley?" Grace asked.

Wesley shrugged. "Skipped some classes. Worked at the shop."

"Never mind," Grace said. "Nora?"

"I—" Glancing between Rand and Grace, I knew what was true, and then I knew what I was supposed to say. "I—discovered the cure for migraines."

Wesley gave me a sad look that melted into a small smile.

"It's permanent," I said. "No side effects. I wrote a book about it in a weekend and it was an instant best seller. And I—uh—I swam the length of Great Barrier Reef."

Wesley took a couple of small, slow steps closer. "Let me go again."

"Have at it," Grace said.

"I hit five home runs in game one of the season," he said, as if testing each word carefully. "Then I hot-wired my principal's '71 Corvette and drove it all the way to Fort Bragg. I—"

"Bigger," Grace whispered.

"Then I"—he yanked on his hoodie strings—"I robbed a bank and used the money to buy my mom's house from the landlord. And then I bought out Disneyland for a day and had the whole place to me and my sister."

For just a second, Wesley came into focus again. I pictured riding Magic Mountain with him, getting Dole Whip brain freezes on Main Street like we had that one time, years ago.

Grace beamed at him. "It's good to know you haven't bored yourself to sleep."

My brother seemed to stretch a little taller.

"Are you hungry?" Rand asked me as he gestured to the space behind him.

Silver hotel trays billowed steam across the starlit night. Grace flitted over to them and removed the lid of the first, the second, and the third. Tiny steamed sea creatures in shells—I didn't know their names—in the first, and some sitting atop their open shells in the second, and warm, crusty bread in the last.

What was all this? It felt strange and luxurious—the meal and the night. Like I'd dropped into a glittery star-filled world where Mom wasn't sick, where Wesley and I ate fancy food on hotel rooftops. Like a world from one of my stories, except real.

"The caterer deserves a tip," Grace said.

I wasn't sure if she was joking, but I smiled.

Grace and Rand stretched out on the rooftop and Wesley did the same.

"How old are you even?" Wesley asked. "Who's paying for all this?"

"Sixteen," Grace said. Wesley's age.

"Fifteen," Rand said. A year older than me.

"You seem older," I said. "Both of you."

Grace got up, tore off a chunk of bread, and dipped it into the sauce around the seafood before sitting down again. "We get that a lot."

They were like something out of a magazine or a movie or Instagram. They tossed the wiggly contents of the shells down their throats, scattered empty shells across the rooftop. I picked out a couple of the cooked things and did the same.

"Bullshit. It's all about not caring too much," Wesley was saying to Grace. "Two weeks of acting like I didn't care and everyone wanted to know me.

"I had baseball too," Wesley added. "That helps. I made varsity."

He'd told Kevin JV. I turned to see him shrug, all casual, and was startled by the smoothness of his lie. But then he looked at me, a bit of panic in his eyes, and I kept my mouth shut.

"What if that's not it at all, though?" Grace asked. "What if the key to surviving it is having something else? Something to escape into."

"How are you doing with it?" Rand asked, turning to me. My confusion must have been visible. Because he added, "Descending into the ninth circle of Dante's Inferno in the fall. I'm a freshman now. Glad I'll be a sophomore next year."

"Oh, right. I'm . . it's supposed to be this exciting thing, right?"

29

I looked at him. "Maybe there's something wrong with me."

"Only if there's something wrong with me too. So, yes, definitely. There's something wrong with both of us. And I hope it's contagious." Rand motioned to the food. "Have you had oysters before?"

"Of course." I picked up my first one from the ice, the gray and white parts jiggling.

He leaned close enough that the puff of his breath moved my hair against my cheek. "You kind of have to pretend to eat them. For Grace's sake."

I almost did—pretend. But this opportunity to try them was maybe a one-time-only thing, so I emptied the contents into my mouth. The blob was slimy against my tongue.

Rand's eyes went wide and then he smiled and lowered his voice. "Don't chew it. Just let it slide down the back of your throat."

It tasted like the ocean, only wigglier and probably less salty. But when Grace handed me another, I drank it down too.

"Impressive," Rand whispered.

"What is this even?" Wesley's eyes crinkled into a smile as he looked out into the night. "What are we doing?"

Grace looked amused. "Do you have to define everything? Eat an oyster. Wait for the sunrise. Have another oyster. They're ours, the oysters. Like the world." She stretched her neck to see Rand. "Rand, isn't that some kind of saying?"

"I believe you're thinking of *The world is your oyster*. Which is the kind of fake positivity that's slowly killing us. As a society, I mean."

Wesley walked to the edge. "Everything looks so small down

there. Or maybe we just feel bigger up here." He flushed and rubbed the back of his neck. "Sounded stupid."

"No," Grace said. "Up here"—she spread her arms wide—"we are gigantic."

Past the parking lot, the ski runs, and the farthest line of trees, the elevation rose into a steadily climbing mountainside. Splitting the mountain in two was a jagged bright line made by a stream of traffic.

"Even the headlights are pretty from here," I said. "What is that? The highway?"

"That's the road leading to Donner Pass and the abandoned railroads," Rand said. From here, the cars almost didn't look like cars. More like glowing little embers popping from a fire. "Donner Pass," he said. "You know about it?"

"Not this again," Grace said, but her laugh was soaked in something—excitement, expectation. "*History.* Ugh. I'll never understand the obsession with talking about things that happened a million years ago."

"You're saying it's not worthwhile to know history?" Wesley asked.

Grace turned to him. "Are you a history buff?"

"Yeah," Wesley said. "I like *MonsterQuest, Finding Bigfoot, Ancient Aliens.*"

"So, *fake* history?" Rand said. "I wonder if fake history also repeats itself. Interesting."

Wesley's gaze jumped between them. "But what are we even talking about?"

"The Donner Party," Rand said.

I'd heard a little about the Donner Party. Partly that it had to do with cannibalism but mostly that there was a store on an episode of *The Simpsons* called Donner's Party Supplies.

"In 1846, this group of families—it was more than just the Donners—they were all trying to migrate from the Midwest to California. Better life and all that." Rand shrugged. "But mountain roads were socked in with an early blizzard—they missed the clear weather by a day—and they couldn't make it out of here. Out of eighty-seven pioneers to end up stranded that winter, only forty-eight survived."

"And the ones that lived"—Grace sat up on her knees—"survived by *eating the others*."

"Well," Rand said, "they were starving to death, and as members of the party died, they, well, they ate the only meat they had available."

"Anyone still hungry?" Grace asked, motioning to the food.

My stomach turned over and I held my hand over my mouth. "Stop."

"Hmm." Wesley filled his mouth with a couple of the cooked things and chewed. "I mean, I get it, though. Don't you?"

"Cannibalism?" Rand asked. "No, I can't say I do."

"It wouldn't be my first choice," Wesley started to say.

"I'm with you." I turned to Rand. "I don't think I could do that, even if it meant dying."

Rand crossed his arms and rested his chin on his fist. "But—feed on someone else to nourish ourselves. Maybe we all do that. Not literally. But in a way."

"Like how?" I asked.

"Like—" Rand waved his hand through the air, then smiled. "If you don't know, maybe you're the rare exception."

Wesley sighed. "All I'm saying is that if we were ever in a situation like that, live-or-die kind of stuff, and I kick it first, then you've got permission."

"Permission?" I asked.

"You know, you can eat me."

"Well, thank you for that," I said. "I'll try not to have nightmares now of hacking you up and roasting you for dinner." I laughed, glancing sideways at Grace. She was quiet, studying Wesley.

He tilted closer to her. "It would be nice if one of you returned the offer, just in case."

"Practical." Grace leaned back on her elbows, crossed her legs. "You always like this?"

"Like what?"

"All *Breakfast is the most important meal* and *Take your gummy vitamins* and *You can eat me first.*"

A corner of Wesley's mouth turned up. "Don't you take your gummy vitamins?"

The ground under me felt harder, and I shifted against it. In the hours since Grace had tripped into our world, she knew my brother better than I did.

"Not that I don't like how you think," Grace said, flicking her eyes to Rand and me. "Hey guys, when you finish feasting on Wesley, I'll be dessert."

Rand scratched his head. "I feel like we've drifted into weird territory here."

I shuddered.

"This scares you?" Wesley asked me. "The Donner Party? Really?"

"It doesn't scare me. But, you know, it's gross."

"When you're trying to survive, lots of things are gross," he said. "What about people who drink their own piss? I mean, I wouldn't do that just for shits and giggles, but if it meant living to see another day, I'd give it a shot."

"Duly noted," Rand said, inching back from the steamer trays. "The story of the Donner Party maybe wasn't that simple. Nobody knows what really happened. Was everyone even dead before the decision was made that they would be—"

"Dinner?" Wesley asked.

"Or breakfast." Grace winked at Wesley. "It *is* the most important meal of the day."

Wesley laughed and everything about him seemed to loosen.

Rand sighed and focused on me, the only one legitimately interested. "Think about that. If it's true, then they had to pick. Or someone had to volunteer."

"Well, the choice is easy," Grace said. "Wesley has *already* volunteered." She snatched his arm and pretended to bite his biceps. "Mm. Tender." Her smile flashed pointy eyeteeth.

The night dimmed. The oysters were eaten. We all gradually made our way to the edge of the roof, Rand hanging back.

I dangled my feet over the ledge, my shoes swimming in air as the sun rose over the lake below. Beside me on the ledge, Wesley yawned and put his arm around my shoulders. I held myself as still as I could, afraid of losing a weight I didn't know I'd been missing. The lake water reflected back the coral sunrise as Grace sat down on the other side of me, Rand standing several feet behind her.

"Okay, tell me," Wesley said to Grace, who had stolen his sweatshirt and was wearing it like a cape. "What's the deal?"

Grace tugged the string on the hood, making the fabric bunch tight around her hairline. "Our parents drag us here, year after year, only to bore us to the very brink of death—"

"Not the slightest amount of exaggeration or privilege in that statement," Rand said.

Grace ignored him. "We needed something beautiful but . . ." Her hand floated through the air as if she were plucking the right word from it. "I don't know . . . uncomplicated."

My brother pulled away and looked at me, his brown eyes shining. It was the look I'd been waiting for forever. He cleared his throat, straightened up. "Let's stop thinking so hard. You're making my brain hurt."

"Really, Grace. Oysters on the rooftop are anything but uncomplicated," Rand said.

"The pulling-it-off part takes some finagling," Grace admitted. "But the other parts are easy. This perfect night. Our shiny new friends."

"Indoctrination Candidates," Rand corrected.

"So you come up here a lot?" I asked. "I just noticed—you didn't get short of breath on the climb."

"Oh," Grace said, fidgeting with the zipper on her jacket.

Rand laughed. "Parkour and free running are her hobbies."

"Really?" I asked.

"Um, no," Grace said. "But let's just say I'm used to climbing up stairs, out windows. I like being near the top of the sky."

Wesley slipped his prepaid phone out, his fingers moving fast over the screen. "What did you say your last name was?" he asked Grace.

She laughed then, and pulled her hair over her shoulder, really focusing on him. "You really have to look me up? I mean, I get it. If you need that."

Wesley lowered his phone. "You mean you don't want to look *me* up? I'm insulted."

"I don't have to," she said. "Your perfectly posed selfies and funny little videos aren't going to tell me anything I don't already know. They'd probably tell me less."

Wesley slid his phone into his pocket. "Okay. Yeah. I don't need to either."

Rand tensed, his throat bouncing as he swallowed.

"Good," Grace said. "I like that. How about you, Nora? Do you need to look us all up?"

I thought about the online version of me—it was way closer to reality than this. All the backgrounds of pictures I should have filtered: drought-dry grass beside rusted metal fencing, our kitchen countertops scattered with pill bottles and bent soda cans.

I laughed. "I'm good."

The real world wouldn't devour this perfect night.

After Rand fell asleep with his back to one of the rooftop's tall air vents, Wesley made breakfast out of the last of the bread, leaving

36

Grace and me on the ledge with our feet kicking through the air.

Her gaze traveled to the faraway mountains. In the dim morning light, only the occasional car traveled the road. I thought about the girl we'd seen running away, and how many miles she might have put between herself and the lodge by now.

"Where do you think she was going?" I asked. "That girl."

"Candace?" Grace's small smile gave way to a look that was uncertain and then gone.

"Did you know her?" I asked, secretly hoping for some thrilling detail. "I mean, you come here a lot, right?"

"What does it even mean to *know someone*?" Grace's hands waved. "Or something?"

"So you . . . did?"

Grace gave me a glance. "No, I didn't."

I felt my shoulders dip a little. "Oh."

Another car passed on the far-off road. I thought about who might be inside it. "Where do you think she is right now?"

"Hm?" She glanced at me. "Oh, I don't know. Maybe . . . she's watching the snap of early-morning headlights rise over Donner Pass. Or maybe lifting her thumb to the wind and watching the southbound lane for a car with an empty passenger seat." Grace raised her chin and held her arm straight out, thumb lifted.

"But it's not a car that stops, is it?" she added, after a while.

I cocked my chin at her. "It's not?"

"It's a bus—well, kind of—a fancy air-conditioned motor coach carrying a folktronica band on their U.S. tour."

I nodded. "Their muse. Inspiring whatever the hell folktronica is."

"The guitarist," she said. "She'll fall for Candace. And they'll dye each other's hair and scream-sing the loudest, most-perfect lyrics. The drummer will fall for her too. And he'll start to feel like he can only hold a beat when she's in the room. But they won't make her want to stay."

"No, they won't," I said. "Because it's not people—a person— that her life is missing."

The orange pulled away from the mountains as it turned a pure blue that stretched over the lake.

Wesley yawned and a look passed between us. Daylight was chasing. It was time to depart this strange, starry world.

We left Grace and Rand on the rooftop, not knowing if we'd ever see them again. I hoped we would. This swept-away feeling, I wanted to feel it again.

A few steps past the hotel, Wesley nodded toward the morning-damp forest. "C'mon, let's take a shortcut."

One breathless mile or two later, he had to listen for the sound of cars to find the road again. I smiled. "You're totally lost."

He laughed as our shoes slipped over dewy moss. "No, *you're* lost."

When we finally tiptoed up the stairs to our rooms, Wesley stopped at his door and gave me a small, closed-lip smile, as if no bills were unpaid, our mom wasn't sick, and our dad hadn't decided our entire childhoods weren't worth knowing.

Nothing could be as terrible, because now we'd had this— oysters and mussels, stories and truths, a cold spring night on a rooftop with strangers we knew.

CHAPTER 5

SPRING

Two days had gone by.

I stared across the road and green pines between Kevin's cabin and Grace's, trying to see through the space in her curtains and not feel creepy about it.

She'd led us through the nighttime forest all the way to the glittering top of the Honeyridge Lodge. I couldn't just knock on her door and ask if she wanted to come over and stream Netflix.

The breakfast table wobbled as Kevin cut his eggs with a knife and fork, sunny-side up and covered in Tabasco. I thought he was looking in my direction, but realized his attention was on the TV behind me, blaring the news in the living room.

What's changed? Why now? That's what our mom had asked him over the phone when all this started. I couldn't hear his end of the conversation. By the way Mom brushed her hair from her forehead and blew out a long breath, I knew the answer couldn't have been satisfying.

Kevin chewed methodically, still staring past me. Tomorrow I'd sit where I could at least see the screen for myself.

He hadn't said a word about us sneaking out. He either didn't know or didn't care. Mom, if she'd been there, if the headaches weren't agonizing that day, would have known and definitely would have cared.

Wesley reached for his milk as he glanced at the TV, his fist bumping the glass and flooding the table with milk.

"No prob," Kevin said, half standing to grab a fistful of dish towels.

I pushed my chair back to help. But Wesley still gaped at the TV.

Bright and glowing on the screen was a picture of the dark-haired girl from the hotel.

"Candace Hurst," the announcer said. "Candace was last seen wearing hot-pink sunglasses, a green anorak, and jeans."

That wasn't what she'd been wearing at all. Her swimsuit that night had made a triangle pattern through her white sweatshirt.

Information for an anonymous tip line flashed across the screen.

"Wow." Kevin had stopped to watch too. "I should call them. Help with the search. They'll probably want people who know these woods."

Wesley gave me a wide-eyed look.

"You two have an interest in missing persons or something?" Kevin asked as he continued to mop up the milk.

"No," I said. "It's just—she's not much older than us."

"Wes?" Kevin said. "You okay, man?"

I thought of Candace on that tour bus Grace made up, the

folktronica band. The guitarist and drummer, two points on a love triangle, her the third. She'd inspire a song before she'd give them a wave and head for a new destination, miles of road and sky ahead. If they found her, she'd have to come home. She'd never breathe free.

"Yeah." Wesley glanced at Kevin and crossed his arms. "Was just thinking Nora should stick close to me. I mean, there could be some creep snatching girls."

I snorted but turned it into a strangled sneeze.

Wesley stole a piece of bacon off my plate, looked me in the eye.

He'd let Candace drive on. He'd keep the secret.

After Kevin slipped out the back door, Wesley threw himself across my bed with his laptop in his hands. It was as thick as a dictionary and gun-metal silver. Ancient. If it ever died, we couldn't replace it.

The cabin's landline phone was hot against my ear as Mom said, "This is good for you. To know Kevin." Her voice sounded far away, no pain cutting through, only the medications that made her words slur. "He seems so different now. Gray in his hair. Serious-looking."

I wanted to tell her that he was rarely at the cabin so far, that Wesley and I were kind of on our own, that burgers on the grill and eggs around a breakfast table didn't make him a dad.

But I didn't want to cause a ripple that could turn into a wave that would wash this week out early. The way Wesley and I had chased the sun back to the cabin two mornings ago, the cold sting of the air in my lungs—those weren't things I was ready to leave behind yet.

Wesley narrowed his eyes at his screen. "They think some psycho got her or something."

"Hey, I gotta go," I said into the receiver. "We're, um, all going fishing."

"Okay," she said. "Nora, wear a life vest."

We said our goodbyes, and I dropped onto the mattress beside Wesley to see the screen. "That's what it says? What kind of news are you reading?"

"It doesn't have to say it. They're looking for *persons of interest.* That's what it means."

"Well, they're not going to find anybody. Candace took off. Her choice."

"*We* know that, but the cops don't. Her parents don't. They gotta be so fucking worried."

His words were like fists tightening around my lungs.

I should have known the new Wesley wouldn't last.

More annoying: He was right. But so was Candace. And I was pulling for Candace.

I closed the laptop. "Where's Kevin anyway?"

Wesley traced the crisscross pattern stitched into my comforter. "Fishing. Guiding. Getting ready to go do one of those things. Something like that."

Wherever he was, he seemed to care more about what lived in Donner Lake than the two half-grown kids he'd suddenly dragged to its shores.

I couldn't figure out why he wanted us around at all. He never had before.

Wesley sat up, glanced over his shoulder at my door. "That girl.

Grace." He said her name as if she were a secret. "Do you think she told anyone about this? Or that little kid who was with her?"

"I doubt it," I said. "And his name was Rand. The guy, I mean. Her boyfriend. He's older than me by a year."

Wesley looked surprised. "He was her boyfriend? He looked like he was twelve."

Something thudded against my window. I flinched.

Wesley jumped up from the bed. "What the fuck was that?"

"A bird, maybe?" I said.

I threw back the curtain. Down below, squinting up through the sunlight, was Grace.

She was hopping along with one bare foot in the air, trying to fish her sandal out of the bushes beneath my window.

"Oh good," she said behind her. "It's her window and not the parentals'. Lucky guess."

Rand stepped out from the shadow of trees that lined the road, arms crossed and wearing a pair of red Ray-Bans that really did make him look like a kid playing dress-up.

"Your presence is requested," she said. "Your brother's too."

Wesley poked his head out beside mine. "When and where?"

"Can you meet us at the lodge? The restaurant?" Rand asked. "We need to talk."

"We thought we might, um, check out the lodge at the top of the hill," I said.

We stood on the porch, hands in our pockets, as Kevin tied fishing lures.

"Someone said— We read it's kinda cool," Wesley added.

Kevin glanced in the direction of the lodge, as if he could see it from this far down the hill. "Yeah, just, uh, let me finish up with my tour this morning, then—"

"We got it. We kind of wanted to go now," I said. "We can walk."

Kevin slipped Wesley a crinkly twenty. "For both of you," he said. "Do you need more?"

Wesley stared at it a long time like he didn't know what to do with it. He and I were too used to filling in the space between what our mom should do and what she could do. He'd forge her signature on hot checks and send them off to the electric company and the landlord—the landlord getting the electric company's check and vice versa. Anything to buy a little time until we could get money into the account. He'd clean rain gutters and get food on the table. I'd call the school for him and make my voice sound convincingly adult.

"Maybe one more twenty," Wesley said.

The restaurant in the lodge wasn't the sit-down kind. It was counter-style and similar to the cafeteria at school, with trays you carried yourself from station to station. But the bars that held the trays were gold and the tabletops granite and the food, at a glance, way better.

Grace and Rand were halfway up the line that wound around the counter, deep in conversation and looking very much like they belonged.

Wesley glanced around intently, obviously looking for her.

"They're over there," I said. We got in line and I leaned in. "The soup in the bread bowl is the cheapest." We weren't about to waste all forty dollars on one lunch.

Wesley chose chili and I picked clam chowder. When we got to the front to pay, I pulled out one of the twenties, wondering if I should have tried to pass for twelve and ordered off the kids' menu to save a couple dollars more.

"Your friend already got you," the cashier said.

"Our friend?" I asked.

He nodded across the room. "The red-haired girl."

Grace sat across from Rand at a table by the windows, wearing giant white sunglasses even though we were indoors. Her bedhead red hair was an elegant mess. Out the bright window, the ski lifts were still against the snow-tipped mountains.

We grabbed silverware and crackers for our soup and made our way across the room. Wesley practically dove for the seat beside Grace, so I sat next to Rand.

"Thanks for paying," I said.

I didn't know what it meant that she'd paid. I waited for her to stare at my clothes or my hair, my uneven nails. I waited for her to say something, to give me a pitying look.

But Grace only shrugged and removed her sunglasses. "Don't mention it."

Sleepy green eyes, a froth of mussed hair, sharp angles, and wiry arms tucked inside wrinkled clothes—maybe Grace always looked like she'd just woken up.

She folded her arms over her chest and leaned across the granite table. "Here's the deal. We didn't invite you here for the view." She smiled at Wesley. "As much as we enjoy your company, there's one small issue. So maybe don't tell anyone about sneaking up to the roof that night. Or being at the Honeyridge at all."

"I won't," I said. "I swear."

But Wesley sat back from the table. "Why?"

Grace picked a strawberry off Rand's plate of chicken and waffles and bit into it. "Because we enjoy not going to juvie for criminal trespass."

Wesley gave her an incredulous laugh. "Is that really why?"

Rand sighed and raked a hand through his hair. "Give it up, Grace. He's seen the news. The *girl*—"

"Candace," I said.

Approval flashed in the serious look Grace shot me.

"Shouldn't we do something, though? Tell someone?" I asked.

Wesley leaned forward, lowering his voice. "Could we get in trouble over it?"

"Yes." Grace turned back to Wesley. "We'd get in trouble if we admitted we were there."

"But her parents," I said, remembering Wesley's earlier words. "They could be thinking she was dead or that someone kidnapped her. Maybe we *should* tell."

"Who?" Grace asked. "The disbelieving cops? Her parents who were so shitty, they made her run away?"

"I don't know," Rand said. "We *could* call. It's not the worst idea—an anonymous tip."

I nodded, but then stopped. If they knew she'd run away, they could figure out where she'd gone. Her chance to escape would be over.

"Anonymous?" Grace asked. "What do you think this is, Rand?

1995? Are you going to find a pay phone? Hang up before they can trace the call? There are cell phone pings and GPS and security cameras. Your call would be anonymous for all of two seconds." She looked at him. "And then you'd be a suspect."

"What about a letter," Wesley said. "Just so her parents could relax a little. So they wouldn't worry."

Grace took a sip of her iced tea. "Maybe they deserve to worry."

Rand shifted in his chair and the legs made a scraping sound against the floor. "She could have talked to them," he said. "Instead of just running."

Grace spun her tea, letting the ice clink against the glass. "Maybe she knew that wouldn't get her anywhere, that whatever they were offering wasn't the open road. Parents disappoint."

Rand stole back the rest of his strawberry from her plate. "But sometimes—"

"Sometimes they make us feel like a mistake," she said.

I tried to catch Wesley's eye, but he seemed unaffected by whatever tension was rippling across this conversation.

Casually, Grace angled her chair toward Wesley. "Why do you think she left?"

He ruffled his hand in his hair. "I don't know. Like, what was she running from? Maybe you're right. Maybe she'd earned it— the run for it she was making. Doesn't feel right, though, to make her family worry for nothing."

"Nora," Grace said. "What do you think? Should we tell?"

"I—" I imagined Candace floating across the parking lot as if she were skating over ice. She hadn't even known I was there, crouched behind a dumpster. I wanted her to have a chance. "I—

No," I said as I met Wesley's eyes. "And I don't think we should do anything if we can't all agree."

"Fine." Wesley tore off a hunk of his bread bowl and shoved it into his mouth. "Whatever."

"It's settled then." Grace pulled a dish that looked like an omelet in a pie closer to her and picked up her fork and knife. "Let's eat."

I raised my spoon to my mouth, relieved the conversation seemed to be over. The oyster crackers were buttery, soft and crunchy at the same time, cracking between bites of creamy clam chowder.

"I need more napkins," I said as I pushed away from the table.

At the counter, I grabbed a wad of napkins with one hand while the other stuffed my pocket full of oyster crackers.

"You're a criminal," a voice said behind me, but when I turned, it was only Rand. He looked right then left and leaned against the counter as he filled his own pockets with oyster crackers. "Let's double your haul."

We settled back at the table, and I couldn't take my eyes off him—the way he casually stared out the windows at the ski lifts while each shift of his body made the plastic in his pockets crinkle. I looked over at Grace. She was watching me with cool, green eyes. I cast mine quickly down at the table.

She rose abruptly. "Come on," she said to Wesley, and, I think, to me.

We stumbled out into the watery sunlight and far enough into the woods that before long I could only see a sliver of the Honey-ridge sign through the trees.

"You two hike?" Grace asked over her shoulder. Her gold flats straddled the yellow dotted line in the middle of the road. They weren't hiking shoes at all.

"Sure," Wesley said.

Grace hopped from the edge of the asphalt to the pine-needled ground beyond. From the forest shade, she waved us along. "Then hurry up."

CHAPTER 6

SPRING

We wandered through the shadowed pines of Donner, and it was easy to pretend I was like Candace, escaping a cramped existence, popping out on the other side, lungs full.

"Doesn't matter if we get there today or tomorrow or next week," Grace said as she looked past us to Rand. "It's still going to be there!" she shouted down to him.

Rand stopped completely. "I'm not going to Zion Ledge, Grace. We've already had one high-up adventure this week."

"Wait." Wesley slowed. "What's Zion Ledge?"

Grace smiled. "Let's just say you won't see it in any Donner Summit guidebook. The Boating Club wouldn't hand out such dangerous information to tourists."

"Too much liability," Rand said, finally catching up but not looking happy about it.

"You'll be fine," Grace said. "I promise. And you know I always keep my promises."

A branch slapped Wesley in the face. "Is this even a real trail?" he asked.

"A virgin," Grace said to Rand. "Can you tell?"

The shade was cool but a wave of heat rose up from my chest and flooded my face.

"A hiking virgin," Rand said. "Of course I can tell."

"Speak for yourself, bro," my brother said. "I am a virgin of no kind."

My mouth fell open, but I clamped it shut. If there were girls, they were a secret he kept far away from our house.

Wesley stared at Grace as if her reaction mattered to him.

She side-eyed him. "Samesies."

Rand fell back and paced his steps with mine. When Wesley and Grace were a ways ahead, he said, "They're both full of shite."

"How long have you known her?" I asked Rand. We'd fallen pretty far behind. "Grace."

"Two winters ago, she rescued me from literal hell."

"Literal hell? You should know better than that."

Rand smiled that lovely smile—a flash and then gone. "Trapped in a cabin with my depressed, bickering parents for the season. Their natural state is pessimism. Yet they thought simply buying this place would bring us closer." He laughed.

"And Grace's fantastic adventures saved you?"

He focused on Grace, far ahead. "The adventures weren't so fantastic. Not back then."

Before I could ask more, he walked on. Leaves that looked sharp felt like velvet as I brushed past them. The pounded-down ground became softer under my steps, less traveled.

With his ridiculous sunglasses halfway down his nose, Rand scanned through the trees and up the moss-covered cliffside I kept touching for balance. Wesley had stopped too. "Did, uh, anyone happen to see what direction Grace hiked?" Rand asked.

"She ran ahead." Wesley cupped his hands to throw his voice. "Grace! Where the hell are you?"

Into the woods, Rand called, "If this is an attempt to thrill and delight, I'm feeling sadly underwhelmed, Grace."

I stared up at the blue-gray sky as if Grace might have grown wings and flown away. It felt like a game.

But as time slipped by, the shadows started to feel like they could swallow a girl.

"Lovely as you are, Grace, we're not waiting all day and night for you," Rand called.

If Grace *was* playing a game, I had an idea. "We're going to head back if we don't find you," I said. "We'll go home and—"

"Yet another new world awaits," echoed through the forest.

Rand rolled his eyes.

The sound came from a small opening in the mountainside hidden by a fallen branch. I didn't know how Grace had spotted it in the first place.

"Where've you been, weirdos?" Grace wiggled her fingers, her arm snaking out far enough that the sunlight danced across her silver rings.

I sighed. Wesley shook his head.

Lowering down, tucking my knees to my chest, my head barely cleared the top of the mountainside hole. The walls were so close that my hips ground against rock as I pushed myself in. Wesley, tall but skinny, slid through. Rand slipped in easily.

I shivered in the cool dry shade of the cave. The soles of my sneakers cracked against the ground—it was frozen. Clear icicles hung from the cave ceiling, sparkled in the streaming-in light, despite the fact that it was sixty-something degrees outside—well above freezing.

Wesley's teeth chattering as he pulled his hoodie close. "What the fuck is this?"

"An ice cave." Rand's hand shot overhead to touch the dripping icicles. "Ice caves are part of the Donner Pass Summit Tunnel Hike. Not too far from the old train tunnels. But somehow I don't believe California State Tourism includes this one on the tour."

Grace's phone camera flashed as she took a selfie.

"A new profile pic?" Wesley teased.

"Please," she said. "This is for me and only me."

I lifted a hand to touch the tip of an icicle. "Do you think we're the first to find it?"

"We're definitely the first to spelunk it."

Rand bent to pick something up and flashed it at Grace. "So much for that. It's a silver dollar." He flipped it over to read the date. "From the year 1983."

Grace took it and shelved it on a small jutted-out section of cave wall. "In case the ghosts from the eighties return in full regalia. Parachute pants and all. They'll need something lucky."

"I'm amused and disturbed," Wesley said to Grace.

She took his hand. "My favorite combination."

Wesley looked down at their interlaced fingers. "What are we doing in here?"

"Falling into a different world." Grace let go of his hand, squinted up at the cave's ceiling, then returned her gaze to me. "Haven't you ever wanted to do that? Be someone else?"

She was talking to all of us, but I felt those words for me and only me. I'd already fallen into a different world, here in Truckee, one Grace and I could escape into.

"What kind of hedonism is calling your name?" she asked. "Nora?"

"Interesting that you should say *hedonism*," Rand said.

"Oh, *do* philosophize us, Rand," Grace said as she crouched beneath the place where the ceiling sloped down. "Please." She smiled up at him.

Rand's fingers skimmed the slick gray walls. He touched his tongue to the center of his upper lip, then said, "Epicurus was a Greek philosopher. He had this theory. So, we're alive for eighty to a hundred years, give or take, but every day we know we could die tomorrow. Don't we have a moral obligation to live each moment to its fullest, maximizing our joy? Happiness?"

"Rand was a famous philosopher in a former life," Grace said. "Or just named after one."

Rand shrugged. "Bertrand Elliot after the late, great British philosopher Bertrand Russell. One of my parental units—my father—is a professor of philosophy. At Oxford. At Pepperdine now. The meaning of life is regularly programmed dinnertime conversation."

"Enough. Enough," Grace said. "Don't ruin this with our at-home realities."

Rand cast his gaze to the ceiling.

Grace picked up a piece of shale from the cave floor. "We should leave something—something that'll still be here after we've lived our epicurean lives to their fullest."

She walked to the farthest cave wall and scraped the stone against rock. When she backed away, I saw she'd written her name. She passed it to me, and one by one, we all did the same.

"After we're gone, this will still be here," she said. "When we're rotting in graves or ashes on the wind, people like us will wander into this cave someday and they'll find this."

"They'll know this place was ours." I nodded.

"And that we existed." Grace stepped back to admire her work. "And they won't know anything else about us."

We pushed our way back into the sunlight and followed a narrow path cut between the brush. Up here, the air was thinner. The deeper I breathed it, the more alive I felt. We crossed the shallow run-off from the lake, slick stones under the soles of our shoes.

Ahead of me, Grace stopped, hands on her hips. A few steps closer and we'd run out of ground. One by one, Grace, Wesley, and I lined up at the edge of the cliff.

We'd reached Zion Ledge.

"Holy shit," Wesley muttered as he stared down into the clear, still pool below, blue as a springtime sky.

Directly in front of us was a small half wall made of concrete. My knees pressed into it as I looked out at the sun-sparkling water below. It was about thirty feet down, a shadowed, quiet cove, widest closest to the shore where we stood. The trees along the narrow coastline shot toward the sky, protecting the view of it from the rest of the lake. We could have only been seen by someone on a boat past the small opening where water fed in from Donner Lake. The water beyond was shallow and blue and vast, but not nearly as inviting as the private cove below and the small beach that spooned it.

Behind us, Rand stood under a line of trees set back from the bare expanse of ground at the cliff's edge.

"Rand," Grace said. "I hope you realize this gift is for you."

He swallowed, his face losing some color. "You really, really shouldn't have."

"Come on," Grace said. "Get closer to the edge. It won't kill you."

"But the fall would," Rand said.

"Is he, like, afraid of heights or something?" Wesley asked.

"You're quick," Grace said.

"Fear of heights—see what Darwin had to say about that, and survival of the fittest," Rand said as he inched deeper into the trees. "Those fearful enough of heights to avoid them tended to live long enough to produce offspring and continue their lines. Acrophobia is actually one of the most common fears."

"I thought you were afraid of *heights*," Wesley said.

"You're thinking of arachnophobia," I said. "Fear of spiders."

"This bothers you more than the roof, man?" Wesley asked.

"Not keen on the roof either, but the roof has a wall around it almost as tall as me," Rand said. He nodded to the edge. "That barrier is knee high."

"Come on, Rand," Grace said, holding her hand out to him.

"Do what the at-home version of Rand would never do. Walk to the edge with us for one tiny second, and I promise I'll never bring it up again. It'll be good for you."

Rand shook his head.

Grace leaped back across the ground until she was at Rand's side. "Take deep breaths." She looped her arm into his, yanked him along with her. "Visualize yourself standing at the edge. It's beautiful, I promise."

Wesley laughed and got on the other side of Rand. He hauled on his arm and dragged him a few feet, enough that Rand's shoes made track marks in the dirt.

Rand glanced at me, brown eyes wide and reflecting the sunlight.

I took a step toward them. "Wesley, stop. He said no."

But my last word was drowned by a scream that cut the silent day.

I whipped around. Grace, mouth open, yelling.

"Stop!" she screamed again.

Wesley let go of Rand. He stared at Grace. "I thought you wanted him to walk to the edge," he said.

"Not like this—not like that," she said. "It has to be his choice, his decision to be someone new here, someone who isn't afraid."

"Well, what he's choosing is to park his ass on the sideline over there," Wesley said. "If it's his choice, just let him choose."

Grace tilted her head, looked at Wesley with something like respect. "Okay," she said. "Let's try something different." She dropped her bag onto the dirt and unzipped her sweatshirt.

She threw one leg over the concrete wall, and then the other until she stood on the narrow dirt ledge, twenty feet of sheer cliffside directly below her, and the pool of blue water beyond that.

"You know there's a tunnel underneath the lake, right?" she asked us.

Rand groaned.

"A secret place used by smugglers during the gold rush," she said. "I wonder if I dove down far enough if I could find it."

Rand took a step closer. "Grace," he said, a warning.

"Relax. If she jumped, she'd just hit the water," Wesley said. "That drop doesn't really look like it'd be enough to hurt anyone."

Never breaking eye contact with Wesley, Rand took another step. "There are rocks under the surface, Grace. Even if you managed to land in a deep spot, the cold would hit you so fast, you'd barely be able to swim. You could drown."

"Grace, come on," I said quietly. "Just swing a leg back over."

I didn't believe she'd jump. Not really. It was pretty clear Grace was a performer.

Rand shook his head. "I can't come any closer, Grace. I absolutely can't. This is not something I can mind over matter. It's not the choice you think it is."

"I can see the rocks from up here," Grace said, a smirk teasing her lips. "I'd know where to aim."

Rand shifted closer, his hand reaching out to her. "It would take less than two seconds to hit the water from this height, but it would feel like a full minute."

"Grace," I said, making my voice bright. "Let's go back to the cave. I want to see—"

Wesley came up behind her, hands closing around her biceps. "Stop fucking around."

Grace lurched, pulling herself and Wesley nearer the drop.

"Let go," she said.

"I'm not letting go," Wesley said.

Grace squirmed, almost lost her balance. Wesley's hands tightened on her.

"Hey!" Rand leaped across the dirt. He launched himself between them, tugging Grace until she fell backward into the dirt, legs still bent over the low concrete wall.

Grace went entirely still. Then:

"Look," she said, standing, brushing off her pants. She straightened; smiling and draping her arms over Rand's shoulders, she spun him toward the expanse below. "You're at the edge. You're doing it. You've *done* it. This isn't some posed picture of you on Instagram, pretending like you're close to the edge when you're not. You're here for real. Fear conquered."

"What?" I said.

Rand, breathing heavily, beads of sweat freckling his forehead, didn't say anything. Neither did Grace. Rand's throat made a clicking sound as he swallowed.

"Yep, beautiful," he whispered. He dodged Grace's touch and backed away from the edge. "Really spectacular."

He walked to the cover of the trees, then grabbed ahold of his knees and threw up.

Grace retrieved her sweatshirt from the ground and knotted it around her waist. She sighed, shoulders sinking. "I wasn't really going to jump."

I could see Rand's pulse tick against the skin of his neck. He raised his head, his gaze now hardened on Grace. "That wasn't cool," he said.

"But you did it." Grace straightened up and held her chin high. "Just like that."

"Dude, you're fine," Wesley said. "Besides, facing your fears is healthy, right?"

I turned fast. "That wasn't cool." But I wasn't looking at Grace. I rounded on my brother.

"You're making too big a deal outta this," he said. "It's not even that far down."

Rand's face was still gray as he moved into the dappled sunlight. "That's not quite the point," he said. "A phobia—I can't—it's not—"

"And you overcame it," Grace said. "You—you *here*—you can be who you want."

Rand whipped to face her. "This isn't something else you can bend to your will."

"Relax, guys," Wesley said. "Come on."

I turned to see my brother shrugging off his shirt. He kicked off one shoe, then the other.

"Wesley," I said. "What are y—"

One running leap and he'd sailed over the wall and into the empty air.

I reached the edge in time to see a spray of clear white water explode into the air below.

Beside me, Grace shouted, "I don't see him!"

"No," I heard Rand whisper. "No. No. No." He stood just behind me. My heart pulsed in my ears, eyes on the circular wake where Wesley had dropped, waiting for him to resurface and laugh.

"There!" Grace said.

A few feet from the bank below, Wesley's wet head surfaced. He shook water from his hair and tromped up the embankment to the shoreline. "See!" He shivered. "Not that high!"

Grace whooped and lifted both arms toward the clouds.

My heartbeat leaped faster.

Grace backed up toward the trees, looking at Rand, who now stood inches from the edge. Her mouth shifted into a smirk. "Mind over matter," she said.

With the sun setting over the lake and the temperature dropping, we made our way back to the cabins. I looked over my shoulder at Wesley and Grace. He shivered and grinned, looking irritating and hilarious in Grace's too-small sweatshirt. I kind of hoped he'd freeze.

Grace practically skipped along beside him. I couldn't tell if she was giddy that he'd proved her point—at least she thought he had; Rand might have had another opinion—or excited he'd made the day into something bigger than she'd planned.

"Don't stare," Rand said, our steps falling together. We walked at least twenty feet ahead of them. "You'll just encourage her."

A queasy unease churned through me. What she'd done to Rand was horrible, and what Wesley did—it could have killed him. But here they were now, happy, unscathed, walking and bantering, trying to impress each other. I didn't know how to feel about anything.

"What did she mean back there? I asked. "Some posed picture?"

Rand sighed. "I may have once used the magic of Photoshop to put myself somewhere I'd never actually be. Grace has a hard time letting things go. Obviously."

"Is it always like this?" I asked, meaning is *she* always like this. "Since you got together?"

"Together?" Rand gave me a funny look, his dark eyebrows drawing close. Then his face opened up and he laughed. "We're most definitely not together."

Something electric hummed in my chest.

"Oh," I said. "I called that one wrong?"

"Eh, yes. What made you think—?"

I waved my hand in a vague way. "You guys just have a—like, a connection. An unspoken thing. You get each other."

He considered this. "We do," he said. "But not in the way you're thinking. We're kind of like a mash-up—like that one LL Cool J song and 'Come On Eileen.' Two things you wouldn't think go together but make the most incredible sound when combined."

I didn't know that song. And I wasn't totally sure what he meant. I remembered the tension between them in the restaurant, when we were talking about Candace.

"Why are you frowning?" he asked, lightly touching the space between my eyebrows.

"What do you think about people who run away?" I turned to him. "Are they scared?"

Rand side-eyed me. "Like running away to the roof of the Honeyridge or like taking off in the night for the vast unknown?"

"Both."

He smiled. "I think they're brave."

I smiled back at him then, hoping I could someday be some version of brave.

And when I looked up again, we were in front of Kevin's cabin.

"This is me. I'll, um, see you later?"

He gave me a nod as his feet shifted away. "Oh, wait," he said, coming back. "Your loot."

He pressed a handful of single-serving oyster cracker bags into my open hands.

"Rand." I caught his wrist as he started to move away again. "Why do you think she ran? Candace. Really."

He toed the dirt trail with his sneaker. "I don't know. Maybe she felt like a burden."

"A burden?"

"Tired of feeling like her parents were doing her a favor by having her around."

The words cut through me. My home life wasn't family dinner at six, homework at the kitchen table, and falling asleep next to the sweet old basset hound. But I'd never felt like that.

And I didn't think he was talking about Candace or Grace. "Rand . . ."

"Or, you know, who knows?" Rand said. "Could be anything." He pushed his hair off his forehead. "My place—it's that way." He nodded toward the lake, the nicest cabins closest to the water. "Responsibly harvested redwood siding. Recycled aluminum roof. We're reducing our carbon footprint while trying not to kill each other."

"Rand." My throat felt stuck. I swallowed. "We're going home in a couple of days, and I—I hope I'll see you again."

He smiled, and it lingered longer than usual. "You most certainly will." He laughed to himself. "Grace won't let the last night of spring break go uncelebrated, I promise."

He raised his hand in a wave and I raised mine. As he shrank into the curving trail, Wesley jogged up. Grace was gone. I looked around—she hadn't even said goodbye.

"You really shouldn't have done that," I said. "Jumping. Even if Grace loved it."

Teeth chattering, he blew a breath into his palms, grinned. "But you're kinda glad I did."

"No," I said, "I'm not." I watched him shiver in Grace's tiny sweatshirt. "But your new outfit is a dream." Wesley laughed.

"Seriously, though"—I shoved him lightly—"you could have permanently hurt yourself. What if you'd broken your arm and couldn't play baseball? What if you'd broken your *neck*?"

Wesley scuffed at the pine needles. "Uh, that wouldn't have been a problem."

I squinted at him. "What does that mean?"

"Getting hurt wouldn't have been a problem for baseball." He met my eyes. "I didn't make the team. Not even JV."

"Wait. But what about what you said to Kevin in the car? And to"—I gestured to the trail we'd just come down.

He shrugged, looking out at the lake. "What about it? Just a little storytelling. You get it."

And I guess I did.

CHAPTER 7

SPRING

On the last night of spring break, Grace led us down the trail all the way to the lake. Without even the light of a cell phone, our eyes adjusted to the dark. And our feet didn't stray from the path she set for us.

"Breaking and entering." Grace thumped her fist on an old wood-sided building at the end of the dock. "Do you think a judge would take pity?"

Rand fiddled with the lock. "On you, Grace? Certainly," he said dryly.

Wesley stood back from the door, his arms folded against his chest and his knuckles pressed to his teeth. "We could totally get busted for this. Just saying."

Home was still a sunrise away, but he held himself back now like he was already there.

Grace looked up at the galaxy-strewn sky. "Wesley, how many stars do you think?"

His eyes seemed to focus then, like he was waking up from something. He watched her, tilting his head slightly as if a sideways version of her could possibly make more sense.

He shook his head. "I'm not that good at science."

She raised her eyebrows. "But you can count, can't you?"

Wesley didn't reply, and Grace's eyes, drifting downward, settled on me, and lit up. She moved close and whispered, "Candace is probably on a long stretch of starlit highway right now. Hair freshly dyed, blowing out the rolled-down window."

"She's driving fast," I whispered back. "Too fast, but she has to because she barely makes her plane. She leaves her hat behind at the ticket counter, but she'll buy a new one when she gets there."

"Where's there?" Grace asked.

The possibilities filled me. I felt myself float a few inches off the dock.

"Morocco," I said. "The French Riviera. Thailand. Pompeii. Where *isn't* she going?"

Grace was smiling, breathing my story deep, her inhalation pulling me back to earth.

"Abracadabra, ladies and gentleman." Rand backed away from the cracked-open door.

Glittering starlight reflected across the lake's still surface as Grace slowly pushed us into another new world. I entered with my hair afloat, electricity in my veins.

Dusty paddleboats were everywhere—at least a dozen—all draped with blue tarps. Creaking boards buckled under my feet as I moved deeper and stared up at the rafters hung with spiderwebs, and the metal-and-wood roof beyond them.

My veins cooled and hissed, my skin dulled, my hair fell flat.

After dinner on the rooftop of the Honeyridge, the ice cave, Zion Ledge, this was . . .

"Don't look like someone just ran you over, Nora," Grace said. "Don't you know by now that I always provide?"

She tossed back a crinkly blue tarp, sending up a cloud that made Wesley sneeze about a hundred times. She fiddled for something, and as she moved, I realized she'd already been in the boathouse. The production she'd made of Rand breaking in was all for show. I raised an eyebrow at him, and he shrugged, smiling, a little embarrassed.

Grace pulled something into the light. "Ta-da," she whispered.

In her hand was a green bottle with a gold label.

"Champagne all around." Only she said it like the French do. *Shahm-pahn-ya.*

"Does anyone have a corkscrew?" Wesley asked.

"This is champagne, my love," Grace said. "No corkscrew needed."

It was dark inside the boathouse, but I noticed a blush on his cheeks that I didn't think was from his sinus explosion.

"Where, pray tell, did you acquire that?" Rand asked.

"Bought and paid for," she said.

I liked seeing what money could do. People always said it couldn't buy happiness, but it could buy something.

Grace twisted the wire from around the neck of her bottle. She wedged her thumbs around the cork until it popped free with a loud whoosh. Bubbles spurted from the bottle. Wesley grabbed it fast and let his mouth fill as if he were glugging from the old garden hose back home. I'd never known him to drink before. Not even once.

Grace passed the bottle to me, but with my fist squeezed around the icy neck, I hesitated.

I'd only tasted a sip of a beer once.

Rand stepped closer. "You don't have to, Nora." When I didn't say anything, he took the bottle, drank some, paused long enough for me to take it back if I wanted, then gave it to Grace.

"One drink," Grace said as she pressed the bottle back into my hands. "Just enough for a buzz, to feel like you're flying—or at least floating."

My hands froze around the sweating bottle. "I won't like it, and I'd probably just waste it." I held it back out to her. "You guys go ahead."

"One drink," she said. "For the end of spring break. For the person you become when you're here."

I lifted the bottle, but Rand said, "Don't make her."

"I'm not making her." Grace turned to him. "Nora"—she faced me again—"do you think I'm making you?"

I didn't necessarily want to drink it, but I wanted to feel that special something, whatever it was. I wanted to feel connected to them.

"I'm good," I said to Rand. "I want to." And I tipped the bottle back and drank.

The bubbles rushed down my throat. All that was left was a bitter taste on my tongue.

When I came up for air, I didn't feel like I was flying. I wondered how many bottles that would take. How many bottles to make me feel as if my head were floating away from my body. How many bottles before I'd be as magnetic as Grace.

"Making that your own personal property?" Wesley asked.

I opened my eyes. My fist was still wrapped around the bottle neck.

Wesley held out a hand for it. "Man, one drink and my sister's already a lush." He fake clinked the champagne bottle against Grace's imaginary glass. "To Nora's rehab."

I laughed and felt the warm hum of the bubbles inside me swirl. A joke between us—that was a thing that happened now.

Three more passes among the four of us, and the room began to vibrate. To steady myself, I took off my shoes and sat on the boathouse floor. The boards above had slats, some with spaces between them that showed the underside of a steel roof.

The ground creaked beside me, and I turned to see Rand, sleepy-eyed, sitting next to me.

"Have your parents had enough R&R, Nora?" he asked, but he said it like it was a joke. "Are they ready to travel back to their dull old nine-to-fives?"

Maybe that was life for Rand and Grace. They had cabins because their parents needed an escape from their day-to-day. What Rand had told me—that his parents bought the cabin to bring them closer—made me wonder what had driven them apart in the first place.

"Not really. It's just my dad here. I—" I didn't want to talk about my at-home life and ruin this perfect moment. I smiled. "They hate that they have to set alarms for Monday morning."

I shifted and saw Wesley staring at me.

I stared back, demanding something, until he gave me a blank look and turned back to Grace. She was trying to convince him that she could see the sky up through the cracks of the boathouse ceiling.

"Come count the stars," she told him. "Believe in the universe and it will believe in you."

Rand groaned. And I laughed. But her words, however cheesy, made me feel something.

She led Wesley away to the far corner, where a tiny sliver of night sky salted with stars managed to shine through. She pointed to it and Wesley reached up and intertwined her fingers in his. Then he was kissing her.

I looked away because—of course. It was way too weird. He was my brother. But my eyes wandered back—to the way he held her chin as his mouth moved softly over hers.

I shifted on the boathouse floor. Tried to focus on Rand. I wouldn't have expected Wesley to kiss anyone like that, slow, relaxed, like he knew something about this.

Rand cleared his throat, nudged my cast-off sandal with his foot. "You, um, want to take a walk?"

I stood up fast, teetered, and braced myself against the wall. As we made our way out, I glanced back at Grace, pointing at a thoroughly solid part of the ceiling now and convincing Wesley he could see the moon. Then I took my sandals from Rand and moved through the door.

The two of us settled at the edge of the dock. A fishing boat thumped occasionally against the pilings. I could hear crickets chirping through the brush. And I remembered what Rand had said about him and Grace being this incredible mash-up. I wondered if whatever this was, with Wesley, would change that.

The bottle of champagne was still in Rand's hands. Remembering Grace's words, I asked, "Is that for the person you become when you're here?"

He smiled with the bottle inches from his lips. "As my parents drive the winding road off this mountain, the person I am tomorrow will very much hate the person I was tonight when I drank all this."

My fingers closed around the neck of the bottle and I moved it past his reach. "Who are you, back home?"

He reached for it and turned it over, showing me it was empty. His dark eyebrows caught the moonlight and arched. "Maybe I'm just me. Maybe I don't have the capacity to be two different people, here and there."

In the boathouse, I heard Grace's soft laugh. "Does Grace?"

Rand frowned and I pressed two fingers to his forehead, like he'd done to mine the other day.

"If she does, she's erased all evidence," he said.

"Huh?"

His smile was a little sloppy. "When I met her," he said, "Grace was quieter. Almost shy. Nothing like the Grace I googled, a wild and wicked version quite similar to who she is now. Here. But a few months later, her entire online presence"—he made a *poof* gesture with his fingers—"gone."

"That's . . . really weird. What does it mean?"

He inched away from me, like maybe he'd said too much, then shrugged. "Maybe she became who she always really was. Maybe that's why we're here."

"Do you believe that?"

"Maybe. What do you believe in?" he asked.

I looked up at the sky. Lights from the faraway houses across the lake had gone dim, making the moon seem brighter, more real, the craters deeper and the light spots full of glow.

Grace's words crept back in. "Can I believe in the universe?"

Rand leaned back on his elbows, following my gaze. "What do you believe about it?"

"That it's big—bigger than our lives back home, huge enough to be full of infinite possibilities for all of us." I sighed. "Maybe that's what everyone believes."

Rand laughed, his smile white against the night. "I don't think most people believe there's much outside their current existence. Myopia—tunnel vision. People mostly only see what's right in front of them."

Had that been true for me? I knew about bigger things now, people and places like this.

With my eyes champagne-heavy, I leaned into Rand and stopped fighting my sleepiness.

I liked being alone with him almost as much as I loved the four of us together. Grace came with Rand, and he came with her. They were a strange duet, full of possibility, and a ticket into a world where I could be anyone.

My eyes opened to clean, wet air, the edges of dark blue waters burnishing gold.

"Sun's coming up," I said.

Rand rubbed his knuckles into his sleepy eyes.

"Nora!" someone yelled.

I twisted around. Wesley stood at the bank, motioning for me to follow.

Kevin was packing up to drive us back today. He could have gotten up early. We could be caught.

I got to my feet fast, scanned and searched for Grace. But the dock was empty except for the boys. "Where is she?"

"Gone." Rand combed his hands through his sticking-up hair. "Her parents always take off before sunrise."

My heart started to pound. I hadn't said goodbye. "But—"

"It's okay. She does that. *This*. You'll see . . ."

"Nora!" Wesley cupped his hands around his mouth. "We're gonna get busted."

Rand and I reached out to hug, our hands knocking together. Then I bent and his arm hooked my waist and held me in a quick squeeze before letting go.

He handed me my sandals. "See you in summer."

"Summer," I whispered.

I didn't know what that meant—when exactly each of us would be back and if those moments would collide—but there was enough hope in that one word to fill me to the brim. *Summer.*

While Wesley and Kevin checked the locks on all the windows, I walked past the packed Jeep in the drive, and followed the yellow-dotted line on the asphalt.

This place, just five days before, had made me feel strangled. Now my feet slipped easily down the road, one in front of the other, until I found myself at the water.

At the end of the dock sat Grace.

"You're still here!" I rushed toward her. "I thought I wasn't going to get to say—"

Her eyes were bleary, ringed with eye makeup, even though the rest of her face was bare. She didn't look anything like the Grace from the night before.

"Grace, I—what's wrong?" She didn't respond, and I backed up a step. "Or I could—go."

"Sit." She wiped her tears on her black T-shirt. "But only if we don't have to really talk."

I hesitated. I wanted to really talk. It seemed Grace *needed* to really talk. I opened my mouth to say more—then clamped it shut.

Really talking . . . about Gridley and Mom and Kevin. I didn't want that.

I sat beside her. Silent.

We were small beside the water that stretched out wide before us. The dock made hollow sounds as we kicked our feet against it, our toes dangling a few inches above the calm surface.

Grace ran her fingers through her hair, which made it puff out in a wild way that looked on purpose. "At the lodge," she said, "you never said why you thought Candace ran away."

Neither did you, I thought. Rand did, but just to me. Wesley had been the only one to say, openly, why he thought she might have done it.

"She must have felt trapped," I said. "She said as much." *A hundred thousand paper cuts.*

"How do you think she was getting by?" Grace asked. Before I could answer, she said, "Maybe she couldn't keep telling stories to herself. The stories weren't enough for forever. She had to breathe new air, swim in real salt water, live something that was hers and only hers."

My own story, the girl locked inside a box, was waiting for me at home, flapping under the ceiling fan—Mom wouldn't have thought to go in my room and turn it off. The girl in that story didn't have a face before, not really. She could have been Candace or Grace or me.

Grace glanced up the hill toward the cabins, then watched her feet swing back and forth from the dock. "We all have one, don't we? A monster."

I laughed and looked into the water. "What good lake doesn't have a monster? Sharp teeth, long claws, probably feasts on children."

Grace stared me down, her incredulous look shifting into a smile. "Everyone knows about it." Her hand waved over the lake. "The monster. But it doesn't take someone every season. It's smart that way. It plans and it waits."

My feet still hung beside Grace's, and I pulled them up under me.

"It sees the sunlight filtering down but never reaching its own dark depths. It must be lonely down there. It must be like living in another world."

"Stop it," I said, forcing a laugh. "Stop it, really. This sort of thing freaks me out."

"It stares up at the legs kicking inside donut-shaped water floats. Bobbing skiers waiting for a motor to start. Fishermen with fragile lines that can hold only a meager catfish or trout."

I inched my hips back, away from the edge, and threw a look over my shoulder in the direction of our cabin. "I need to go, Grace. Wesley and Kev—my dad—they're waiting."

Grace's black-ringed eyes blinked up at me when I stood. "Yeah, you better go. It's a Friday," she said, getting to her feet and giving me a too-loose hug. "Traffic is murder."

I squeezed her hard before I let go. She felt both slight and substantial in my arms.

"You're coming back, right?" she asked, squeezing her arms around herself. "In summer. You promise."

"Yeah," I said. "Of course."

"Good," she said. "You okay?"

"I'm fine," I said. "Absolutely." It was Grace who didn't seem fine.

Back up the center of the road, following the dotted yellow line, I stopped and looked back at her, still unmoving at the end of the dock.

WINTER: NOW

CHAPTER 8

When the heart stops beating, it's not necessarily the end. Not yet. Even once the heart stills, full of un-pumped blood and never-going-to-open valves, the brain can stay alive for a few seconds more. Sometimes I used to think about it. I imagined living—even a moment or two—beyond the beat of my own heart.

Standing in front of the cabin's kitchen window, watching the gray-black-green world outside become frosted white, I knew that, after a year away from Donner, that's what I'd been doing with this place—living past the end, waiting.

Four days would be enough, I'd decided.

Plenty of time to pack up every dusty inch, clean the worn fixtures and tiles.

Plenty of time to figure out what happened the night Grace vanished.

When the cabin was officially under new ownership, when I

knew what had happened to my friend, I'd begin a new life, heart pumping once more.

Sponge in hand, I poured Comet into the sink. Blue powder clouded the air—or maybe it was my breath in the cold. I zipped my coat to my chin. The pilot light on the heater was out and I couldn't get it relit. My fingers didn't want to bend, they were so freezing, but I forced them to claw away the grime. Everything was fixable or cleanable; nothing would affect the sale.

In the living room, the Weather Channel hummed on the old TV with news of the blizzard that was hours away from hitting Donner. I wasn't afraid of a little snow and wind. The harshest storms we'd faced in these mountains had nothing to do with weather.

Behind me, the front door blew open.

Wesley swatted away the blue cloud before planting his elbows on the kitchen counter. "It's as cold in here as it is outside. Aren't you freezing?"

"It's fine. I'm fine." My teeth chattered. "I'll build the fire if you'll bring in the wood."

"Yeah, that's a problem," he said. "Someone stole the wood, Nora, every last stick. Busted the lock on the woodshed. Door's all chewed up with axe marks."

I glanced at the unmoving thermostat in the hallway. "Kevin needs an HVAC guy out here. He'll need to buy wood before he leaves town. I'll text him." I dried my hands on a dish towel and pulled out my phone.

Kevin had dropped us off at the cabin before heading to the Costco in Reno for groceries. All that remained in the cabinets were dented cans of Campbell's, weevil-ridden oatmeal, and stale chips. Kevin hadn't been back here much either in the past year.

"And now he needs to pick up new hardware for the wood-shed," I said, finishing the text and facing Wesley. I noticed his coat hanging off his body.

He'd lost weight since he'd last worn his winter clothes. It was more obvious now, stiff waterproof fabric hanging loose above his thin legs. My own legs were big for the rest of my body, thighs muscular, built for powering through snow or hiking to Zion Ledge or climbing a dozen flights of spinning hotel stairs once upon a time. Now they were mostly for running cross-country at school, something that was never the escape it was meant to be.

Wesley's eyes caught mine. His blue irises were sunken and sadder.

His feet rocked forward on the vinyl flooring, making the wood boards beneath creak. "Is it weird for you?" he asked. "Being back here?"

I plunged my hands under the faucet's icy water, pretended it was the cold that made me wince. "Why would it?"

Wesley looked at me, then seemed to decide something. He moved toward the door. "I'm going to chop what's left of that ponderosa pine that fell last year. Maybe it's dry enough to burn."

My mouth opened to tell him to be careful.

A blast of air burst in as Wesley opened the door. "A new heater," he said. "That's really going to cut into your bottom line." There was an edge to his voice. "Wouldn't want the property value to take a hit. Not before you and Dad can get this place sold."

The door slammed and rattled the walls, the windows, something inside my chest.

79

Through the yellowed lace curtains my grandmother had hung at least forty years before I was born, I watched Wesley pick up the axe. It carried a shine as he swung—new and razor sharp. But he missed the wood, sinking his axe into the block beneath, fighting to free it.

He wouldn't accept that the ownership of the cabin didn't matter, that after that night, the secrets he and Rand had kept, everything we'd done to each other, the cabin was already gone.

The scratchy side of the sponge was worn through. In the pantry, between a stack of brown grocery bags and a yellowed phone book, I found a new one—and the flash of something familiar.

My hand grabbed for it. I knew she wouldn't leave us empty-handed.

I pulled out a framed picture of Wesley and me, him grinning and me looking like an uncertain pickle in my neon-green life vest. Flipping it over, I pried off the back. It was the perfect place for her to leave a message—a sign, the answers I desperately craved.

Nothing was inside.

I sighed. Kevin must have framed it sometime in the last year and forgotten it.

Three hard knocks juddered the front door. I slid the picture back onto the shelf. I hadn't heard the rumble of Kevin's Jeep, and he couldn't have made it back that fast anyway.

A coldness sucked deep down inside me when I opened the door, and it had little to do with the snow.

"Nora." Rand tugged off his gray beanie and balled it in his hands. The white backdrop shone starkly against his inky hair as his smile fell away. "You're back."

My mouth formed his name, but no sound. His dark hair fell across his forehead and into eyes that were dim in winter, brighter in spring, sparkling in summer. His lips, the soft bow that he touched his tongue to when thinking, and the bottom lip that pushed into a pout when he was feeling gloomy, I knew their warmth.

Seeing him here—it was the swirl of familiarity and also completely new. He was tall and solid, so far from the boy I'd first met, so far even from how he'd looked last winter.

"I saw the Jeep out front earlier." Rand gestured to the driveway. It was empty now except for a snowmobile. Rand's. A brand-new version of the one I'd ridden for the two winters before. "I thought it was just Wesley. Like over the summer . . . I didn't think you'd come back."

I rested my temple against the doorframe. "Wesley and Kevin were lonely up here."

"Was that it? Or was it the for-sale sign out front?"

The question took me by surprise. I didn't do a good job of hiding it.

"What are you doing here?" I asked.

His breath made translucent shapes in the air. He turned to the tall white fir trees, already bending under the snow. "I wanted to see if you needed anything. With the storm coming in."

"We don't."

"They say it's going to be bad," he said.

"It's never as bad as what they say on the news."

"Do you have plenty of bottled water? In case they're right?" His shoulders angled closer, his eyes peering past me.

I stayed planted, a barrier blocking his way. "We've got enough."

Rand touched the back of his gloved hand to his nose—always sensitive to cold. That wasn't where our differences began and never where they ended.

"Enough for what?" He knitted his fingers together. "Three days? A week? What about wood? That heater was on its last leg two winters ago."

I remembered what those fingertips felt like. I said, "We're fine."

He nodded to the west, the lakefront five miles away where the priciest cabins stood, including his own. "If you need anything—"

"I'll ask." We both knew that wasn't true.

"I've missed you, Nora. Us."

Us. I didn't know who or what I missed the most. There was him and me. Messy, exhausted, blissful, Rand and me. And then there was the four of us.

The hinges creaked, door wheezing as I started to close it between us. "I missed us too."

Rand's brown treaded boot caught the door. "Did you stay gone because of me or because of her?"

Maybe Grace was what kept Wesley away at first, but she wasn't what stopped me.

"Neither," I said. "I stayed gone because of me."

Rand reached out, his fingers brushing my wrist. "Grace wouldn't have liked it. You not coming back. Us falling apart." He looked toward the woodshed, the sound of Wesley chucking logs onto the concrete floor. "All of us. Before that night. Those questions—"

He looked out over the snow. His eyes flashed back to me. "They still don't know anything. After all this time."

My shoulders sank, and I found myself leaning toward him, giving in to the ache, the relief of sharing the air with someone who had loved Grace too.

But the air between us was murky with the memory of Rand staring at me like he didn't know us, Wesley and me. Rand, conspiring to hide from me the one truth that might have made our foursome the thing I needed us to be—real.

I straightened up. "Bye, Rand." And I shut the door.

I pressed my back against it until the whirring of my brain calmed, my heart still a clenched fist in my chest.

The questions that night ripped at our seams, but it was hearing each other's answers that severed the threads. *That girl,* they said. *Where is she? When did you see her? People don't just up and vanish. Who had something against her?*

That girl. The way they said it—she was just another face on the news. They barely used her name, just made her a headline, there one moment, gone the next, swallowed by a dark Donner night. Grace wasn't real to them. Maybe she hadn't been real to us either.

SUMMER: YEAR ONE

CHAPTER 9

My story kept going, this time onto crisp printer paper with no lines. This time written in a serious black ballpoint pen. The box kept rebuilding around the girl, smaller and smaller. My story was there at the end of eighth grade. Specks of glitter clung to the pages, remnants from the CONGRATULATIONS! sign Wesley held for me in the gym bleachers at the awards ceremony that Mom had been too sick to attend.

Then the gray spring and the end of middle school rolled up, and in rushed the gold and glimmer of a sun-soaked summer. Wesley and I hadn't talked about Grace or Rand once since we walked home from the boathouse that chilly spring night. We didn't avoid it, exactly. It was more like we were polishing a secret with our silence.

I googled them once—Grace and Rand—even though I said I wouldn't. Thousands of Grace Lombardis showed up, only a few Rands. None of them mine.

Searches for Candace Hurst only brought up those first local headlines, nothing new, a private Instagram page with twenty-six followers, and a barely used Facebook.

Since we'd come home from spring break, Wesley had spent most of his time out of the house, mowing every overgrown lawn he could for quick cash. Once, though, he actually helped me block the bright early summer light from Mom's bedroom windows.

Maybe it was my imagination, but I saw the way he looked out the window, past the yellow lawn, down the potholed road, to something beyond.

I passed behind him one morning, his cheek smashed into his hand and cereal getting soggy as he stared at his laptop screen. Glowing back at him was Donner's ten-day forecast. He glanced over his shoulder at me. A feeling of urgency passed between us. Nine more days.

On the last day of school, in mid-June, the morning before eighth-grade graduation, my backpack bounced against my hips, loose without the weight of textbooks. I walked by the philosophy classroom and thought of Rand.

See you in summer.

I'd hoped it was true. But I didn't know when they'd be coming back. After that first spring, I didn't know when *I'd* be coming back, or for how long.

Mom and Kevin had a hushed conversation a few weeks before school let out. My mother's end of the conversation started with "That's so long" and ended with her waving her hand vaguely and saying, "Maybe it'll be good for them to spend some time away from here." He still didn't give her any reason—not that I knew of—about why he wanted us there.

Wesley said we should just ask him, but I wouldn't give Kevin the satisfaction of knowing I cared. "Ask him if you want," I'd said, and had gone back to writing my story.

Turned out Wesley would have plenty of opportunity.

It was decided we'd be at Donner three times a year—two weeks after Christmas, one week for spring break, and all of glorious summer.

The promise of that word—*summer*—had a kind of spark. It wasn't flying down the highway between the drummer and the guitarist of an up-and-coming band or watching out a plane window as the wheels touched down on a sunrise-lit Moroccan runway. But whatever glowing, oxygen-bright existence Candace was living, I'd have a glimmer of it too, this summer.

That first day back, I checked Grace's cabin every hour for any sign of motion.

The Lombardi cabin sat up the hillside from ours a few hundred feet, and if I arched myself out the window far enough, I could see the very tip-top of the huge quaking aspen that grew out of Grace's front yard, bright yellow leaves in a dark green sea.

I would have been watching for Rand too, except I didn't know exactly which lakeside house was his.

Wesley kept catching my eye as he helped Kevin unpack the Jeep and change air filters, looking hopeful until I'd shake my head—*No, I haven't seen them. No, I haven't seen her.*

That night, Wesley brought out a plate full of buns and set it beside the grill. "Hey," he said to Kevin. "Why do you bring us here instead of Lodi? I mean, that's where you live, right?"

I moved to end of the railing. If this was Wesley's warm-up before he asked Kevin the *big* why, I didn't want to be close enough for Kevin to think I cared too.

Kevin plunked a steaming hot dog into a bun. "The guiding is a big part of it. That and the fact my two-bedroom is cramped for a pair of growing kids. Come on." He tightened the knob on the propane tank under the grill. "Let's eat."

We settled around the wobbly patio table. His two-bedroom couldn't have been any smaller than the one we were living in with Mom. Maybe the allure of Truckee was that the lake and the ski lodge were better babysitters than he'd ever want to be.

Wesley, his face to the sun, squinted at Kevin and asked, "You ever do any boating anywhere else? Like north of Lodi?"

North of Lodi was Gridley. Us.

"Sometimes." Kevin heaped an ungodly amount of sauerkraut from the jar. "When I don't feel like driving all the way here. Lake Orville usually."

"Up ninety-nine," Wesley said, careful to not look at me.

Kevin's hot dog snapped between his teeth as he nodded.

Driving 99 to Lake Orville meant passing right through our town. Never once stopping, calling. Wesley was finally going to ask. *Why now? Why after all this time?* I braced for it.

"Could you—um, pass the relish?" he said.

Maybe it was just the blinding sunlight, but his eyes looked wet.

After we'd finished eating, I carried my plate inside. I reached under the kitchen sink for the dish soap and there was a piece of paper taped to the inside cabinet door.

12 a.m. You know the place. Bring a flashlight. Not some reading-in-bed, batteries-not-replaced-for-a-year thing. And not your phone. Something with oomph.

A sudden rush. I was sure my feet rose off the floor and my hair floated into the clouds.

Someone snatched the note from my hand. "Hey!" I said.

But it was Wesley, his eyes scanning the page again and again. He must have read it three times, as if he were drinking down those four words: *You know the place.*

Lowering the paper, he said, "Do we really know the place?"

I took the note back from him.

I thought of all the places we'd been—the heights of the Honeyridge and Zion Ledge, the cold depths of the ice cave, the dusty creaking boathouse. I tried to think like Grace, but I didn't know how to do that—create magical places that didn't just exist in stories.

We left Kevin snoring in the recliner with the TV on, passed out in front of the coffee table scattered with twenty-year-old photos he'd found in the attic. Wesley had seen a Maglite in the woodshed, so he'd taken Kevin's keys for the padlock.

The woodshed door opened, and tied around the Maglite was another note: *If you didn't know the place before, you do now.*

Under his breath, Wesley said, "How the hell?"

Beneath the Maglite was a plastic key card with the Honey-ridge logo.

We didn't bother with the flashlight because the moon shining on the asphalt road lit the way, the dry summer air warm on my skin.

In the parking lot, I noticed a picture stapled to a utility pole—a sly smile I remembered, and the word *Missing* above the photo. Candace wasn't missing, though. She was *found*. She was out there, I imagined, living it up in a bustling city that was electric after dark, or some romantic seaside town. The Candace I saw was sunshine mixed with a little bit of hurricane.

"Come on," Wesley said. The key made a clicking sound inside the door. "Hurry before someone sees."

We pounded up the Honeyridge stairs but slowed halfway, panting, remembering the agony of this climb. At the top, light shone through the space below the door. Hand tight around the handle, Wesley inches behind me, I opened it, breathed in the warm night.

Rand stood up from where he was leaning against an air vent.

He'd sprung up since spring, at least two inches. His jaw had hardened a bit, less boy-like, more grown-up. Still, his nose barely reached my chin. His mouth was the same—serious, then a smile; blink and you'd miss it.

I didn't want to miss anything.

"If you're interested in reuniting with the second-most dynamic member of the Grace-Rand duo," he said, walking over, "you're about to be thrilled to bits."

Wesley angled himself in front of me. He fist-bumped Rand the way he'd greet his friends from home. I hung back.

"So where's Grace?" Wesley asked.

"Good question." Rand moved past him to reach me. His lips slipped into a smile again. "Welcome to summer."

I was living the moment I'd been waiting for over the past three months. "I didn't know if you'd be here," I said. "I—"

"Same," he said, still smiling.

"And look—we're all here," Wesley said impatiently, "except where the hell is Grace?"

"There's a note." Rand flashed a small paper. "Well, not a note. More of a map."

We jogged past the Honeyridge, the closed restaurant where we'd ordered bread bowls in the spring, and trailed down a winding path into the forest. With the Maglite cutting a line through the darkest section of the resort, we found ourselves at the base of the ski lifts with the map leaving us nowhere else to go.

"We could've read the map wrong," I said.

Back when we'd still had cell service, Wesley had jotted down some notes about the actual distance. "No, this is the place," he said.

The dry summer ground spread out beneath our feet as we searched the hillside.

"We may have miscalculated," Rand said.

Wesley stared at his notes.

Rand took the paper from him. "This is your handwriting?"

Wesley's grin could light the night. "It's *lovely*," he said. "Miss

Beckinsale told me in third grade. You trying to make something out of it, man?"

"Not at all," Rand said. "Your pretty penmanship makes me love you all the more."

Up, up, up, I looked to the top of the closest ski lift seat. "There." I pointed.

With the flashlight in his mouth, Wesley climbed onto the swaying seat. He shone the light on the brown paper bag taped to the back of the seat, then snatched it and hopped down.

Rand read the note over Wesley's shoulder. *"And now you fly."*

Wesley looked around. "What the actual fuck?"

As he said it, light from the overhead ski towers fell over us, bright and complete. My eyes burned. I blinked hard. A slow rumble traveled through the ski lift and the machine roared to life, the chairs jerking into sudden motion.

"Now we fly?" I yelled up to the sky. "Really, Grace?" I turned toward the peak of the mountain, hoping she'd hear me—she couldn't be far.

"This is lunacy," my brother shouted, laughing.

The first chair sailed past us and Rand and I looked at each other. His jaw was tense and his feet firmly planted.

The memory of that day at Zion Ledge rushed up.

My gaze darted between the lifts and the top of the hill. That's where Grace's surprise had to be waiting. I couldn't ask him to do this, and I also couldn't leave him behind.

"Our chariot awaits," he said.

"What? *No.* You—"

"Let's go," he said.

"You don't have to."

His hand slipped into mine, warm. "I want to."

Then it was the three of us running between lifts, into the path of the next one.

My hand in Rand's, the chair tapped the back of my legs. We fell into the seat together, and off we rode over the hills. I looked back as my howling brother hopped into the chair behind.

The air felt warm against my cheeks and catching my hair, the metal of the lift cool against the backs of my bare legs. Below us, the dark ground moved with the shapes of trees and the ski-run-beaten ground.

Rand reached up to pull the safety bar close against our laps. "Grace's next adventure better be on the ground." He shifted in the seat as the chair rose higher, hands clasping the bar, chin up, eyes closed. "When I decided to do this, the lift was much closer to earth."

The rapid rise and fall of his chest made me nervous. I scooted closer and squeezed his arm. "What do they say? Don't look down?" I forced a smile.

"Not funny."

My eyes scanned the treetops below. "My alternative was, there are worse ways to die."

He swallowed. "Better choice the first time."

I thought of Grace up on the hill, watching, enjoying. "Why does she do this to you?"

"She thinks she's helping. And she enjoys it." He smiled, winking one eye open to look at me, then closing it again, his smile faltering. "Bending us—the universe—to her will."

A prickling feeling rippled over me. I loved Grace, these nights, but I didn't love this. "She can only do this to you if you let her, though."

"Mm." Rand touched his tongue to his top lip. "The problem at hand is . . . I'm not ready to stop letting her." Rand's eyes stayed closed. "The thing about not looking down, it works. Maybe it's that Nietzsche thing," he added. "Maybe *down* is the abyss. You gaze long enough into the abyss and the abyss will gaze back into you. Grace loves Nietzsche."

I couldn't imagine Grace spending much time buried in books. "And Nietzsche was . . . ?"

Rand snorted. "One catastrophically fucked-up dude."

"And his relationship to the abyss . . . ?"

Rand looked sad for a second, and then he smiled. "What if everything but right here, right now, is the abyss." He shifted closer to me. I could feel the warmth of his leg against mine.

"Nora"—Rand's eyes went wide—"it's going to run out." He clenched his hands around the safety bar. "We're going to have to jump."

My voice came out a little strangled. "But you knew that when you got on."

He said, "I think I knew that from the moment I met Grace."

Before I could reply, there she was, feet planted, hair a halo around her head, lit by the bright lights at the top of the mountain.

Rand exhaled and said to himself, "What are you trying to do to me, Grace?"

"She's never going to tell us how she pulled this off!" Wesley called from the seat behind.

I looked back. He was grinning and shaking his head.

The end of the line started to run out, and as much as I wanted to know what Grace had waiting, I wanted to stay with Rand, suspended here.

He shifted in the seat and accidentally rocked the cage forward. He squeezed his eyes shut again. "How do we do this? How does this thing come up?"

Brushing his hands away, I slowly lifted the bar.

Grace was growing larger as the lift rushed to meet her. Hands cupped around her smiling mouth, she shouted, "Jump!"

We didn't have snowboards or skis to gently glide us to the ground as I imagined you were supposed to do. We didn't have snow to cushion the fall.

Between my dangling feet, the ground was still far away. We had to reach that little flat peak at the top.

"Five," I said to Rand. "Four."

Rand shook his head.

"Three," I said. "Two."

I jumped a little early and my feet smacked down. Rand hit behind me, lost his balance. I felt his arms catch me around the middle. I spun, fell. We hit the ground, absorbing the shock together. The three-quarters moon above was a giant white orb in a light gray sky, and Rand was blinking up at it with his mouth half-open.

"It's over," I said.

He craned his neck to look at me. "If you think that, you don't know Grace."

We lay there until Grace's face appeared over us. Her copper hair was shorter, barely skimming her chin. I leaped up and flung my arms around her, remembering that the last time I'd seen her, I'd left her alone at the edge of the dock.

"Enough," she said, smiling before dodging me.

Rand stood with his hands on his hips. He'd walked far back from the view.

"No hug?" Grace asked.

"You're going to be my undoing," he said.

"What? Oh shit"—Grace glanced behind us—"Move!"

Wesley was coming in fast. Rand grabbed my hand and we leaped out of the way.

But Wesley didn't jump. He was messing with the safety bar— he hadn't raised it fast enough. The lift darted back around, faced down the mountain now, carrying Wesley with it.

"Shit," Wesley said, laughing, his head craned around to see us. "Shit."

We laughed too—Rand and me. Grace, though, she had her teeth pressed deep into her bottom lip.

When Wesley was about fifteen feet away, far past us and heading back down the hill, the lift shut off. Darkness landed on us hard as bricks.

"It's okay," I said. "He can ride the lift back around. Just start it up again."

Grace rested the tips of her nails between her teeth. "No, he can't. Neil, the um—the guy I paid to start up the lift, he was only supposed to keep it going until you reached the top. If he turned it off, he's gone."

"Call him," Rand said.

Grace lifted her phone. "No reception up here."

"I think I could jump?" Wesley said, looking down between his feet.

The drop-off was extreme. At least twenty feet of air separated Wesley from the ground, and this wasn't the soft, snow-powdered hillside of winter. This was dry summer soil.

"Don't," Rand said. "You'll break an ankle at best. It's too far."

I turned to Grace. "So you're telling me my brother's stranded all night?"

The lift made a gasping, wailing creak behind me.

"Holy bastards!" Rand said. "Don't!"

A breath stopped halfway down my throat as I looked up to see Wesley dangling by his hands, swinging from the cord that held the lifts.

I'd seen my brother try to climb a gym rope, only to get halfway to the top and rug burn his palms on the way down. That was in middle school. I hope he'd gotten better at it.

"Wesley, hurry!" Grace yelled at the exact moment I called, "Take your time!"

Hand over hand, Wesley inched closer to us. He grinned when he was halfway.

Then his hand slipped.

Rand was the one who yelled out. Grace was silent.

My brother dangled, swinging by one free hand while the other grasped at empty air. I didn't think the fall could kill him, but I worried I was wrong. I imagined what it'd be like to wake up Kevin, to try to explain this, to place that call to Mom. To be alone.

With a grunt, Wesley thrust his other hand up and regained his grip. He smiled again—at Grace—but with less bravado this time. The closer he got, I could see his veins popped up under the skin on his forearms. Face bright red.

Finally, his feet touched down on the hill beside us. Rand reached up awkwardly to throw an arm around his shoulders.

Eyes never leaving Grace's, Wesley wiped his forehead with his shirt and grinned. "We would have been here sooner if not for your shitty, not-to-scale map."

Grace kissed him on the cheek. "Welcome."

"Welcome?" I said. "Welcome? You could have killed him, Grace. You—"

"Nora, stop." Her hands closed over my shoulders, squeezed. "It's over now. He's okay. We're all okay. Just enjoy . . . this."

"Enjoy what?"

Grace tilted her face to the sky and I noticed her hair was peppered with something white. A cold little sting wetted my cheek. I turned around. Snow was floating down around us.

Wesley squinted up. The white flakes started to come fast, raining down. "Is that, like, a snow machine?"

Rand gave Grace a sideways glance. "Doesn't the resort store this equipment in summer?"

Grace smiled and shrugged. "They do."

The machine would have taken something heavy to move it, especially all the way to the top of the mountain. No way she moved it on her own. But Rand didn't ask. Maybe making a big deal about the magic destroyed the magic.

White flakes billowed toward the leafy trees, the spikey pines that surrounded us, landing between delicate blades of green grass and then melting into nothing.

"Snow in summer," Grace said. "It can happen."

Wesley dropped to sitting. Rand stood with his arms crossed, his eyes intense.

I'd never seen anything like it. I'd never even seen *real* snow falling.

"Maybe it's snowing where Candace is." Grace bumped my shoulder, her words only for us. "Maybe she's in . . . Alaska. Her hair full of flurries, wearing a pair of snow boots, tromping through knee-deep drifts in a fast-falling summer blizzard. Maybe she feels like this."

It was the first time I'd heard Candace's name since the break before. The way Grace said it, her voice shaking a little, I didn't understand.

Grace spread her arms into the air. I lifted mine too, catching snowflakes on my tongue.

"Candace should probably trade her snow boots for snowshoes," I said. "She wouldn't be knee-deep if she had proper Alaskan attire."

Grace laughed, and the sky became crimson around an egg-yolk-orange sun that rose over the faraway horizon, and I thought about this new scene, this story, that Grace had created for us. Maybe we were her inventions, ready and willing to bend to her will. We just didn't know there was only so far to bend till we'd break.

CHAPTER 10

SUMMER

Even three hours away, Mom's illness held us hostage. She'd called my phone three times while we'd been at the lake that afternoon and twice more while I'd been in the shower. Now that she had me, she wouldn't let me go.

"I wouldn't have gotten dressed and driven all the way down there if it hadn't been filled," she said. "The pharmacist said the computer flubbed up—like that's an excuse."

"But it'll be ready tonight, right?" I said, pacing the small bedroom.

Wesley slipped a piece of paper into my hand. A squiggly, confusing, hand-drawn map with a note in the bottom corner: *Swimsuits required! Unless skinny-dipping is your game (spoiler alert: Sometimes it's mine).*

Wesley actually tapped his flip-flop on the floor as he eyeballed me.

"You want to say hi to Wesley?" I asked into the phone.

He mouthed *No.*

"Here he is." I tossed the phone to him, then went to the bathroom to put on my swimsuit, pulled my shorts and T-shirt over it, jogged down the stairs, and stepped out onto the front porch, leaning forward into the railing. I shouldn't have pushed Mom off on Wesley. And I didn't want her to feel like she couldn't call. But my life at home—I didn't want to make room for it here.

Something rustled beside me—Kevin with the newspaper.

"You two want to check out the lodge tonight?" He folded the paper in half and set it on the bench beside him. "My night tour group canceled. I'm gonna meet some friends in the bar there. You and your brother could come."

A lot of fun that would be, hanging out at the Honeyridge while Kevin got drunk.

"Not tonight," I said. "We're meeting some friends—" I couldn't say we would be at the Honeyridge too. "On the dock. To see the stars."

Kevin smiled in the direction of the water, making the lines around his blue eyes deepen. "Watch out for the lake monster."

I turned to him. "What?"

"I'm just messing with you," he said. "Every lake's got a monster, right? Stories get passed around." Again his eyes crinkled, remembering. "Shit that kept me up at night."

"Who told the stories?"

"My dad—your grandpa. He thought it was funny, but then he'd get mad at me later when I was too scared to jump off the dock. Your grandma'd be like, well, that's what you get for telling him those stories." Kevin chuckled. "But then one time, I swear I saw something."

"No you didn't. You *just* said it's not real."

He shrugged. "It was a foggy day across the lake, where the whole thing looks kind of steamy, like a bowl of soup. Something came up out of the water, high. Then higher. Too big to be a fish. Then it dove back down under the surface. My dad believed me. My mom did not. Called it just another tale for a gullible tourist."

Whatever adventure Grace had planned involved a swimsuit, so I couldn't imagine it not involving us submerged in Donner Lake.

"There's a story every so often. Someone gets a picture of the beast rising from the water." He shrugged. "Or they just got their thumb in the shot. Either way, it's a headline."

I relaxed a little. "So you *don't* believe."

Kevin moved to my side, propped his elbows on the railing, looking thoughtful. "There's a lot of things out there we don't understand. Not just under the water."

"I wish I'd known this place when I was little," I said before I could remember not to. Known *him* even. But I shook the thought away.

Wesley came shuffling out then, and handed me back my phone. "I'm done. Let's go."

"Nora," Kevin said as I pushed off from the railing. "Me too."

I wasn't sure I believed him. I told myself not to look at him as we walked away, but I couldn't stop myself from stealing a glance over my shoulder.

Kevin, his mouth twisted into a sad smile, lifted a hand as I looked away.

Wesley was already splashing like a sea lion when Grace reappeared from behind the lifeguard stand with a stack of crisp hotel towels.

I hadn't remembered that Candace and her girlfriend had been swimming until Grace produced a key to the for-guests-only, closed-down-for-the-night Honeyridge pool.

Grace wore a caramel-colored sweater that hung past her shorts, all the way to her knees. The fabric was woven throughout with tiny white beads. Even girls I knew back home whose parents drove them to school in white, freshly washed cars didn't have anything so luxurious.

She peeled it off, revealing her swimsuit, a mismatched set of high-waisted red-and-white polka dot bottoms with a plain black bandeau. I imagined her picking it out at the mall, shunning pieces that matched. She dove under, popping up in the very middle of the pool, legs kicking.

Wesley bobbed in the deep end, tucked under the diving board. He reached up and grabbed on to the sides, suspending his chest above the water.

Hair slick and wet, Grace treaded in the deep end beside him. "How long could you do that?" she said. "Hours?"

"Nah, not hours." He dragged himself closer to her as she started floating away. "My arms would give out."

She draped her own arms over Wesley's freckled shoulders. They were staring at each other like they were the only two people in the pool, at the Honeyridge, in Donner, on Earth.

My toes dipped under the surface, making the water ripple.

Grace smiled from beyond Wesley's shoulder, and pushed off. "Nora! Meet me in the middle."

I took a step back and jumped in.

Sinking down, down, down, I felt the water envelop me like a cool glove.

These chlorinated waters were the last Candace swam in before she abandoned the crush of the world she knew to embrace the wide-open. As my feet touched the gritty bottom, I hoped they could be the same for me.

I popped up beside Grace just as Rand came padding out of the men's locker room wearing coral swim trunks with a bright yellow pineapple pattern. The waistband hung low on his hips and the fabric bagged when he walked. He strutted along as if it were a perfect fit.

Wesley let go of the diving board and swam out to the middle. "Dude, were you planning on growing when you bought that?"

"It was a gift, thank you very much," Rand said.

Grace shrugged. "I overestimated." She'd bought it for him— of course. "High dive!"

Smiling, Rand held up his middle finger. I still didn't know what to make of Grace's obsession with pushing Rand's fear of heights, and Rand's willingness to let her.

He dove into the pool, a perfect graceful arc that barely rippled the surface of the water, then butterflied across the surface and came up for air at my side.

"Show-off," Wesley called.

"It's true," I said, nudging him with my hand. Grace snorted and swam back to Wesley.

Rand slicked his wet hair back, grinned bright, then looked away. "I'm all right. My parents have a heated pool, so I swim all year."

"And you dive?"

Rand flicked his eyes toward the deep end, toward Grace, then back to me. "Off a standard regulation diving board. No high dives for me."

"Why do you let her do this to you?" I asked quietly.

He sighed, paddling closer. "You don't know what it was like before I met her. This heights thing, I don't know if I can beat it, but she makes me believe I can."

I floated out a little bit. "You're different," I said, "than you were in the spring. I mean, you're yourself, just more you than you were."

He laughed, a single bright sound. "Spring is cold. It takes me an extra season to thoroughly thaw."

I swam to the side of the pool and held on to the ledge. "You don't like the cold?"

"The cold—I suppose it reminds me of where I grew up. England."

I stretched my arms out so my legs floated up. "You didn't like England?"

"No, I did. London, I mean—art and theater. I just—I wasn't the happiest kid there."

Grace, gliding on her back, kicked lazily over to us. "Where do you think Candace is, Nora? In a pool like this? Or maybe bigger."

"Hm?" I said, turning to her. "Oh. I don't know. Maybe, yeah. Or one of those infinity pools where the water runs off into the ocean . . . This was the last place she was. That night."

Grace flipped over and sunk partway below the surface, circling me, slow-moving.

"What?" Wesley asked, from across the water.

"She and her girlfriend were wearing their swimsuits under their clothes," I said.

Wesley torpedoed to Grace's side. "You think this was her tipping point?" He smiled. "Are we blowing this place at midnight too?"

Rand didn't say anything, but Grace's eyes went brighter. "Maybe. The night is too young to make any life-changing decisions. Yet." One tug of my hand, and Grace pulled me into deeper water. "What do you think she did that night, Nora? Knowing this was her last night in Donner, her last Honeyridge swim?" Water whirlpooled around us as we spun. "Launched herself down to the bottom of the deep end, looked up through chlorine-red eyes at the lights, wondering how the world would look streaking by an airplane window?" Grace kicked fast under the surface, getting breathless. "Maybe she went into the bathroom here at the Honeyridge, dragged on clothes over her wet suit—because if she took the time to change, she knew she'd lose her nerve. She was still scared to go, frustrated she had to. On her way out the door, she stared one last time in the full-length mirror, then kicked it hard. She was out and headed for the parking lot before she noticed the crack she'd left."

I smiled. "And within the hour she was long gone."

"Um, guys?" Rand said.

The door that led from the hotel out to the pool had opened.

Rand and I slid away from the edge, low in the water and treading quietly.

Grace swam to the steps and stood up, water falling off her as she planted her hands on her hips. She smiled. "This is a private party, Neil."

Wesley climbed out of the pool and walked to the far end, toweling his face with a fresh Honeyridge towel.

I craned my neck to see past Grace. It was the blond boy who'd let us all in the back of the Honeyridge last spring. He wore a white dress shirt with navy pants and a pair of shiny reddish brown shoes that matched his belt.

"So, what's the deal?" Neil asked. "Now that the Honeyridge's resident breaker-and-enterer is gone, she passed the torch to you?"

Grace had already said she didn't know Candace.

She flicked her eyes back to me, almost as if she was watching for a reaction.

I treaded slower, just enough to keep my chin above water.

Neil gave Grace the up-down. "Nice suit."

"You like?" she asked, stepping back into the water.

A helpless feeling washed over me. My fingers bit into the edge of the pool, legs kicking beneath the surface. I wanted him to leave.

Neil crouched low at the pool's edge. "I could get you a more permanent key, if you want to swim here more often."

Grace moved closer to him, arms dragging through the water. "And what would that cost? Fifty?"

He watched her with his breath held. "A hundred and fifty," he finally said.

She tipped her chin down. "Sixty it is."

I smiled. She was playing him, playing him to buy us this night. "Cannonball!" Wesley yelled.

He took a running leap and threw a wall of water over us, the deck, and Neil.

Neil stood fast, white shirt soaked and dripping. "What the actual fuck, man?" He wiped his face on the back of his arm and stared at Wesley.

"I yelled cannonball." Wesley shrugged from the middle of the pool. "That's kind of a universal warning. Sorry you didn't back up, bro."

Throwing drops of water, Neil said, "You did that the fuck on purpose."

"Maybe," Wesley said, swimming close to Neil.

I looked between them, Wesley and Neil. Rand was still beside me, stoic but watching closely. Grace had her lips pursed in a way I couldn't read.

Grace, treading water, sighed. "If you didn't want to get wet, Neil, you shouldn't have come to the pool."

Stealing Wesley's towel, Neil said, "Pool time's up. All of you need to clear out."

Neil's words lingered as Grace and I went to the locker room to change. He could ruin things for us in a more permanent way. We were trespassing, except it hadn't felt like that until the minute we were caught. If he told, our summer could be over before it'd barely begun, and I'd spent too many months wanting this to lose it so easily. And that thing he'd said—passing the torch.

"Grace," I said, toweling off my hair, "what did Neil mean? About someone breaking into the Honeyridge? Was he talking about Candace?"

She laughed. "How would I know?" She plunked her bag onto the bathroom counter, narrowed her eyes at me in the mirror. "You're far away. Too far. Where are you, Nora?"

"What if he tells someone?"

"Neil? He won't bother us." She tucked her towel around her waist and removed a comb from her bag, looking thoughtful. "A girl used to come here," she said, "every winter, spring, and summer—two years before you and your brother showed up. You remind me of her."

"Yeah?"

Staring into the mirror, Grace combed through her hair. "She spent the summer locked in her cabin, trying out every cleansing mask they sold at the drugstore, looking at all the stupid social updates from people back home, making her own. She couldn't forget who she was. Even when she went outside"—Grace pulled her hair back into a bun—"she didn't feel the sun on her face or the wind in her hair. She couldn't let go of what they'd said. She lost a whole summer like that."

Maybe this was that first season—before Rand. I wanted to ask her what people had said—was she inviting me to?—but all I managed was: "Where is she now? This girl." And I shivered, cold after our swim.

Grace didn't answer, just worked her arms free from her sweater. "Take this."

She pressed it into my hands. The fabric felt soft—expensively soft. "Oh—no, that's okay."

"You're cold," she said, "and I'm hot anyway—all my scheming has me overheated."

I slipped my arms into the fabric, wondering if being a good friend meant keeping quiet or pushing her to reveal more. "I'll wash it after. Or . . ." It was probably dry-clean only. "I'll have it cleaned." I'd come up with the money.

Grace flicked a hand through the air and shook her head. "Keep it."

I couldn't imagine why she'd give me something like that. Maybe the money didn't matter. I wondered if I'd think about money all that much if I was someone who had it.

Grace kept me balanced on a precipice. I felt like I got her, but I wasn't entirely sure.

She carried her bag into one of the stalls. "Don't be like her, Nora. Be bold. Create something real for yourself." I could hear the smile in her voice. "Be like Candace."

I came out of my own stall before Grace did. In the tall mirror by the door, I looked at myself, swallowed up in Grace's oversized sweater.

I leaned closer, looked up.

There, running like a vein through the bathroom mirror, was a hairline crack all the way through.

CHAPTER 11

SUMMER

The steaming-hot driveway burned my bare feet when I went looking for Wesley. That morning I'd found his bed an empty tangle of sheets. He had to be with Grace.

I'd told him about the mirror, Grace's story. He'd held his knuckles to his mouth for a second, then relaxed into a smile and told me not to worry about it—that crack could have been from anything. But there was something else. An intensity in his eyes, like he was afraid I'd do something to ruin our summer.

I hadn't asked Grace more about it. But through two weeks of lazy, sunburned days, the four of us perched on the dock, sticky hands from sno-cone syrup, heads bent, plotting how to make each day of summer top the last, the questions sat between us.

Out on the driveway, there was no Wesley. Only Kevin under the beating-down sun, spinning the lever on the ski boat and dropping the trailer onto the Jeep's hitch. He straightened up when he saw me, squinted, and the two lines creasing his forehead were familiar. He didn't look like Wesley—his expression was something I'd seen in my own mirror.

Kevin took a drink from his water and wiped his mouth. "You ski?"

"No, I've never even seen snow," I said. At least not real snow.

"No, *water*ski." He hopped up into the boat and tossed me an obnoxiously green life vest. "Try it on."

Wesley came out of the garage then, carrying an ice chest, flip-flops slapping the blacktop. I pulled the vest on. It just fit. Only the bottom buckle was broken.

"I got a deal because of that," Kevin said. "It's a perfect fit. Hey, uh—" He held up his phone, as if he'd heard this was a ritual dads were supposed to do. "Lemme get a picture."

Wesley wrapped an arm around me. I smiled and stood tall as the camera clicked.

Kevin began untangling a massive knot of neon-colored rope. "You'll love it, Nora." He nodded to the space behind me. "Bring your friends too."

I didn't understand until Grace emerged like a phantom from the other side of the Jeep, wearing a giant pair of leopard-print sunglasses. "Ciao. We were just in the neighborhood."

By the motor, raking his eyes over me as if my vest were the most curious atrocity he'd ever beheld, was Rand. "You look smashing," he said. "And very neon."

Wesley and I traded a look. So far, we'd kept Kevin and our friends separate, and I liked it that way.

"I don't go in the lake, but we'd enjoy seeing Nora and Wesley ski," Grace said. "Wouldn't we, Rand? I bet you'd be a natural. You ski, don't you, Rand?"

Rand tipped his sunglasses down the bridge of his nose. "I'm more a spectator."

Grace clapped her hands together. "Then let's spectate."

"You've got this!" Kevin yelled. He spun his hands on the wheel. The boat circled me where I bobbed, my life vest around my ears, in the middle of Donner Lake.

The smell of gasoline from the motor, the pond taste of the water, the sound of Kevin braying encouragements—this wasn't supposed to be summer.

Another loop of the boat and the rope floated close enough for me to lurch and grab it.

"Ready?" Kevin shouted.

The slippery handle tugged out of my hands. "I lost it!" I called.

"You couldn't get me in that lake for anything." Grace rested her chin on her hands at the edge of the boat as she talked to me. "Imagine your legs just kicking away beneath the surface, keeping you afloat. Just bobbing along. Until . . . something shimmies along your knee."

I swear I felt something slick brush past me. "Please don't say *shimmy*!"

Wesley laughed, sliding into the seat at Grace's side. "How about *slither*?"

Rand held the little orange flag high above his head. His role was simple: Hold the flag in the air whenever I was in the water instead of being towed behind the boat. It was so other boaters wouldn't run me over. He'd been holding the flag a long time.

"You're doing great, Nora," he said. "Don't let them get to you."

The motor started up, which meant Kevin was ready to go again. Another turn of the boat, and I finally had the handle. "Say *hit it* when you're ready," Kevin said.

Trying to hold my skis together, tips above the water, I yelled, "Okay, hit it!"

Four or five seconds of dragging and drinking a wall of water, and I let go.

The boat made a wide arc and U-turned back to my side. Kevin, one hand on the wheel, one arm resting on the side, asked, "One more time?"

I shook my head. I realized I'd wanted to be good at this for him, and that surprised me. And it pissed me off. And made me sad. Hand over hand, I paddled to the boat and leaned my life jacket into the ladder to catch my breath. I couldn't pull my Jell-O limbs back into the boat.

I reached out a hand for Kevin's help, but he turned away and I felt the sting of it like a slap, until I heard him say, "I should have taught you this seven years ago."

I swallowed down the burn at the back of my throat, grabbed higher on the ladder, and hoisted myself up, skinning my knee as Rand tried to help me into the boat.

He gave me a thumbs-up as I collapsed on the seat beside him. "A for effort."

"Five glittering stars." Grace nodded, staring down into the murky waters. "I wouldn't have even tried."

Wesley tossed me a bottle of water from the ice chest. But I'd already drunk enough of Donner Lake to worry I'd ingested a brain-eating amoeba.

"Rand," Grace said. "What would Nietzsche say about letting this boat drag him around all day?"

Wesley groaned. "Not this again. This bullshit's like being back in school."

"You're awfully critical of our philosopher, Wesley," Grace said. "Maybe you'd like to delight us with one of your own personal theories?"

"I don't have time for personal theories, Grace."

"Fair enough," she said, leaning forward, an idea sparking in her eyes. "How about just why?"

"What do you mean, *just why*?"

"Why keep going? What makes you go—when you're busy, tired? Why?"

"I don't know." Wesley sounded irritated. "I just—I guess I just remind myself that I'm only as good as, you know, how well I take care of who I love, and what I love."

Grace squint-smiled up at him.

"That's not a bad philosophy," Rand said.

Wesley's face went just a little pink. I couldn't help but smile.

Kevin held a hand up to shield the sun. "Maybe Wesley wants to give it a try?"

In the boat's rearview mirror, Kevin smiled at the reflection of Wesley cutting back and forth across the wake. He was a natural, which made me happy, for Kevin's sake.

My thighs prickled as they dried. "Maybe I could do this if I could slim my legs down," I said.

Grace's hair whipped around as she faced me. "That has nothing to do with anything. Maybe you're just not good at skiing. Maybe you're a hiking diva."

Maybe.

Or maybe it wasn't just that Kevin wasn't any good at being a dad. Maybe it was that I wasn't good at being his kid. For just a moment, I wished both of those things weren't true.

I unhooked the top hook on my life vest. The broken bottom hook had slipped free. Rand was leaning over the back seats, cheering Wesley on. But Grace had her eyes on me.

"Candace couldn't waterski either," she offered. "She'd get out there and try and try but end up just drinking the lake. That's one of about a thousand reasons why she left. She belonged somewhere more befitting her skills. Like flying. I bet she's hang-gliding in the Swiss Alps right now." Grace looked at me, one eyebrow cocked, waiting.

But I didn't take up the story. "Could she really not waterski?"

Grace laughed. "I told you—I didn't know her."

"What about that thing you said at the pool? Candace hitting the mirror in the bathroom, leaving a crack. I saw it."

Grace's eyes flashed and then her expression went flat. "It's a *story*, Nora. Damn, you're totally breaking my fourth wall. That crack's been there forever."

Wesley let go of the rope, and like that, I'd lost Grace's attention. We were thrown to the left as Kevin U-turned. He pulled up beside Wesley and cut the motor.

"More power next time." Wesley pushed his floating skis to the boat. "Still too much drag." Wesley looked up at Rand. "Did you get some good pictures, man?"

Rand held up Wesley's phone. "Your Instagram following will be delighted."

I remembered what Rand told me, that all of Grace's social media had disappeared.

"Wait," Kevin said, sliding a ski back to Wesley. "It looks like you're ready to slalom."

"Slalom?" Wesley asked.

"One ski," Kevin said.

"I want to follow your accounts, Grace." I sat back against the seat cushions, sipped my water. "I'm sure they don't disappoint."

"You'd just be bored," she said. "Everything lately has been from summer. Why would you want to see pictures of all these things you've actually lived? I don't think so."

It took Wesley three tries. Then the ski was like an extension of his body. He crossed the wake again and again, graceful, sure, catching air each time he came off the white-tipped crest.

We took a break and ate the sandwiches from the ice chest. I found myself wishing Wesley could have made them more special somehow. Slices of cheddar and turkey weren't the fare Grace was accustomed to, I was sure. But she ate hers as if it were a steaming pot of mussels on the roof of The Honeyridge on a starlit night.

Then Kevin took off his sunglasses and turned to me. "You want to give it another go, Nora? I mean, you don't have to."

My legs shook a little as I stood. It maybe wasn't the best idea. But I'd heard what he said earlier. And I saw how he'd looked at Wesley. "Sure, okay. One more time."

The life vest was as wet and cold as Donner Lake itself. I hooked the top snap. Shivered.

"Um," Rand said, pointing at the loose snap. "You're undone."

"Just one is broken," Kevin said. "No big."

"You sure?" Rand asked.

I hopped off the back of the boat into the cold water before Kevin could respond. With one hand, Rand held the flag high in the air, and with the other, he sent the skis floating my way.

Another loop of the boat, and I got a good grip on the handle and a decent sense of balance. "Hit it!"

All afternoon, the boat had dragged me around while I drank the lake. This time, the engine roared and my skis planed smoothly across the water. I felt myself lift up. Gliding, sailing, I realized I was doing it. My wet hair slapped against the back of my neck, tangled and loose. I didn't care. I was skiing.

Navigating between other boats, Kevin glided ours into a little cove. Rand kept looking over his shoulder at Kevin, then back at me. He had the flag poised, waiting. Grace nodded, leaning forward. Wesley kept trying to get her attention, but her eyes were on me.

My ski skipped under me before I could blink. I went down. But down wasn't down anymore and felt more like up. There was a thud. And then nothing.

My head in Rand's lap.

The rest of me sprawled out across the bottom of the boat.

The clouds sailing above.

"She's awake," Wesley yelled.

Kevin jumped into the driver's seat, hit the throttle, and sent the boat barreling across the lake so fast, I could feel the front end lift out of the water.

My lips parted, and Rand said, "You're okay. We'll be at the shore in a minute."

When I next opened my eyes, the paramedics were over me. But I was still swimming under Donner—drowning in it, the cabin, the boat, the Honeyridge pool.

"Back up, kid," someone said. "Kid, back up before you make us back you up."

Rand—I think he took it as a compliment that they saw him as some kind of obstacle.

With penlights in my eyes and a stethoscope on my chest, they said things I didn't catch.

"We don't have health insurance," Wesley blurted. And with that, everything pulled into sharp, excruciating focus.

Kevin looked at him, surprised.

I tried to sit up, see if Grace and Rand were still close enough to hear this, but someone's hands weighed me down. I worried they'd call Mom, get her stressed, bring on another bout of her headaches.

"Is she allergic to any medications?" a paramedic asked someone.

"No," Kevin said.

"Yes," I said, but my voice was thick, too quiet to rise above the noise of the parking lot, the chatter of tourists, my frantic friends and brother.

Wesley's voice boomed above the chaos, "Codeine! Nora's allergic to codeine."

Someone shook me gently and I blinked open my eyes again, feeling weirdly calm except for the pounding in my head. Wesley was seat-belting me into the back of the Jeep, and Rand was sitting beside me holding my hand.

"What happened?" I asked.

Wesley sighed. "You must have hit a reed or something just right. You flew up above the lake and hit the water hard enough to knock your life jacket loose."

"I didn't see anything sticking up," Grace said from the open door, where she stood sipping a bottle of water.

"The broken buckle didn't help," Rand said. "But we think your forehead struck the ski."

The Jeep lurched, and I realized Kevin was at the back, attaching the boat to the hitch.

"The scariest part," Wesley said, "was we couldn't find you. Kevin cut the motor when we saw one of your broken skis."

Rand rubbed his thumb along the back of my hand. "It was intense. I felt like I was on the top of Zion Ledge, about to go over. We looked around, and up ahead, in a patch of reeds, was your life jacket." Rand shuddered. "You weren't inside it."

"I—" My lungs hurt when I tried to speak. "I was under?"

Wesley nodded.

"So someone pulled me out?" I looked to Rand—he was the best swimmer.

"It wasn't me," he said.

Wesley flicked his eyes outside, where I could hear Grace directing Kevin as he guided the boat onto the tail hitch.

I sat up higher. "Grace?"

Wesley nodded. I craned my neck to see her out the back window.

"Hey, hey," Rand said. "You have to take it easy."

"She dove in headfirst," Wesley said. "And when she came up, she had you."

"It took all of us—well, the two of us and your dad—to drag you back into the boat." Rand brushed his fingers across my temple. "Your forehead has a goose egg. Wicked shade of purple."

I licked my lips and looked around. "Water?" I whispered.

"I'll find some," Rand said, opening the car door and climbing out.

"They think you have a mild concussion," Wesley said. "We have to take you home. Watch you."

Outside, I could hear Rand and Grace talking. "That's kind of an important thing to forget," Rand said to her. "Codeine?"

Wesley looked over his shoulder, then got out, thunking the door shut behind him. Vaguely, I heard him say, "We all only just met a few months ago. He didn't know."

"A few months?" Rand asked. "Isn't he your dad?"

I felt my limbs shrivel, draw in on themselves, making me small—but not small enough to disappear. I hated that we didn't have health insurance, that Kevin didn't know about my allergy.

Most of all, I hated that Grace and Rand were hearing all of this.

"You shouldn't have let her get in with that broken vest," Rand said, now facing Kevin.

Kevin, walking around the side of the Jeep, looked defeated. I liked him a little more for it. But I knew this wasn't really his fault. I was the one who chose to do it. To try. I'd said I wouldn't try with Kevin. But then I saw the way he'd looked at Wesley.

Grace poked her head inside the Jeep. I thought she'd say something about Kevin, but instead she said, "Don't think of it as a goose egg. It's a unicorn horn."

I sighed. "Grace. Thank you."

She removed her sunglasses. Eyes puffy and ringed in melted mascara, she forced a small smile. "I couldn't lose you. Not like that. I'm not sure the person I want to be exists without all of you."

My lips parted, and I stared at her. Grace had always seemed like the exact picture of who she wanted to be. I thought I understood her—at least sometimes. But maybe I didn't.

How could I if I didn't know who she was without us? Back home? I wasn't sure I really wanted to know.

Outside, I could hear Wesley speaking low. It dragged me out of my trance.

"Your mom," Grace said. "He said he needed to call her."

Hearing about my accident wouldn't be good for her. I tried to sit up. "He shouldn't—"

The weight of Grace's hand on my shoulder anchored me to my seat.

"What, Nora?" she asked, her voice soft.

Words pooled in the back of my throat, thicker than the lake water I'd inhaled that still burned inside my sinuses. I wanted to tell her about Mom. But what if everything came flooding out

121

then? The money trouble, the move, the dad who was dead, then alive. The truth was that the person I wanted to be didn't have a sick mom. It was easier that way. And I hadn't realized it could be till I'd gotten here.

"Nothing," I said. "Never mind."

Kevin appeared in the open Jeep door, blocking out the high sun behind him. As Grace moved away, Kevin leaned in. His red, weary eyes tugged his face down. "I'm sorry, kid."

His hand was out, bracing himself against the door. Without thinking, I covered it with my own.

My dad and I weren't fine yet, but maybe we would be.

CHAPTER 12

SUMMER

My prescription was five days of laying low. That meant five Rand-less and Grace-less summer nights when the last half of our vacation was dwindling toward fall.

One afternoon after the accident, I woke up to the weight of Wesley sitting on the edge of my bed. Blinking at the light streaming in, I rolled over. "What's going on?"

"I was just, um, I was with Grace." Head bent, he knitted his fingers together. "She went home, but she didn't stay home. I saw her leave again. So . . . I followed her."

I sat up fast. "Why? Wesley, that's so creepy."

"I know. I—" He shook his head.

"Where did she go?"

"Um, the Honeyridge. She was talking to that guy, the one from the pool. She gave him some money. I don't know for what. I know—it was—it felt wrong, spying on her."

He was right about that. Still, I wanted to know more. "And?"

"She saw me."

"Is she mad?"

He shook his head. "I asked her what she was doing, with that guy. She said he, like, gets her things. Like letting her in the back door that spring. Things for all of us. I told her she shouldn't do it anymore. It's not because I'm jealous—okay, it's not *just* because of that—but I don't like her doing it. I just don't trust him."

"What did she say?"

"She laughed at first, but then she hugged me. Told me not to worry. She said she had other means to get things here. Knew other people."

"She's just manipulating him. You know Grace. Always in control." But I wasn't so sure.

He looked at me. "Do you think she'll stop?"

I sighed. "We don't know that she's really ever lied to us."

Wesley took a deep breath that puffed out his chest, then exhaled. "I want to believe her."

I scooted over to sit on the bed beside him. I knew what he meant—the way Grace could make you feel bigger, more alive.

"Nora, she told me I could get a baseball scholarship. I mean, *college*. She said if I made varsity as a freshman, then I had to be amazing." He rubbed his face. "I didn't tell her the truth."

"You don't have to tell her everything," I said quietly. "I mean if you don't want to."

"I feel like a dick. I'm over here questioning her. Her honesty. I'm the one who lied."

"Wesley," I said. I didn't want him telling Grace our secrets, the mess of our real life. "It's okay."

"Really?"

I leaned my head onto his shoulder. "It'll be fine." I hoped I was right.

After Wesley went to his room to Zoom with some friends back home, I took out my phone and did another search for Grace. If she'd been posting pictures all summer, I wanted to see them, us. I wanted to see this world she'd created and the world where she actually lived.

But I didn't find her.

For all the things Grace didn't know about us, there was more we didn't know about her.

My second day of confinement, I'd fallen asleep on the couch when I woke to find Kevin tucking a blanket under my chin. The gesture reminded me of something Mom used to do, something I didn't realize I'd missed.

"Sorry," he said, straightening up and shoving his hands into his pockets. "I didn't mean to wake you. Just thought you might be chilly."

"It's okay." I blinked my eyes wider, focusing on the muted TV I'd left on. "I slept long enough."

Kevin turned the fan off and sat beside me. "I like this show too."

"Yeah." I scooted over to give him more room.

He smiled. "Yeah."

The distance between us felt a little smaller, if only until the credits rolled.

Wesley asked Kevin to take him waterskiing again, so that sweltering afternoon they'd parked me in my bedroom with an oscillating fan and an ice pack for my forehead that made me layer on Grace's sweater even though it was summer.

My phone rang like it had been ringing all day. Mom again. But my head hurt too bad to take on any of her suffering too. I felt horrible about it, guilty.

Someone banged on the front door, and dizzily, I padded down the stairs to open it.

The sun glinted off Rand's shiny MacBook Air as he held it high. "Days of the finest streaming that Netflix offers, ours for the taking."

"I'm—" I looked over my shoulder at our disheveled, decrepit cabin. "I'm supposed to take it easy. Rest. Ice my unicorn horn."

"I'm game." He eyed the soggy ice pack swinging from my hand. "I'm also adept at freezing water and turning it into ice. I can even make soup, which will go perfectly with my surprise." Reaching into his pocket, he retrieved a crinkly packet of oyster crackers.

"When Tyler hits the car with the baseball bat, and the alarm doesn't go off," I said. "That's when we should have known."

Rand and I were on our stomachs across my bed, the laptop propped up on a couple of books, the movie credits to *Fight Club* rolling across the screen.

"You got that the first time?" Rand popped up on his knees, excited, then settled back. "I saw this at least five times before I picked up on that."

I turned away from the screen, looked at him. "Maybe some of what we have here is all in our minds. Do you think Grace is always honest with us?"

Rand startled, then relaxed. "Where's that coming from?"

"I'm just wondering . . . The stories. Where do they begin and end?"

He sighed. "Sometimes if you tell yourself a story long enough, it's not just a story. And maybe that's a good thing. Maybe it makes you a better person."

"I'm not following."

He gave me a little self-conscious smile. "Okay, so the first summer I met Grace, I was lonely and sad. Grace, she was quiet back then. Maybe even kind of paranoid. I remember, it was like she was always looking over her shoulder. But she insisted on basically being my best friend. We sat by the lake, we skipped rocks, we hiked. She was cagey about her home life, and school. And these pictures I saw of her online, fabulous and confident as she looked over her shoulder, pouty lips and the brim of an oversized hat shading her eyes, these posts with clever little captions and bits of advice—they didn't match up. Then Grace came back that winter. And it was like the Grace from those pictures had come to life. That's when the adventures started. But it was like she wanted some other version of *me* to spring to life too."

"What happened to her between summer and winter?"

"I—I don't think I should tell you that."

I looked at him, and there must have been a question on my face.

"It's just . . . maybe there should be some mystery here. To this world Grace has created. She's worked hard at it," he said. "And she'd tell you if she wanted to."

I pulled back. "But I'm asking you because I'm worried about her."

Rand inched closer, tilted my face to meet his eyes. "Are you? Really?"

I started to tell him yes. But when I thought about the crack in the mirror, the way she'd upped the ante on our adventures, I realized I was more curious than anything.

"Look, I've thought I was worried about her before too," he said. "But that feeling passes. Grace is fine mostly. This thing we all have going here, it's a delicate balance."

"So I shouldn't ask questions?"

"It's tricky. Sometimes I feel like there's all of us and then there's each of us with Grace. She'll scare you at times. But she'll also tell you things that maybe you shouldn't tell me. Or Wesley. I just don't want to ruin something. This. Us."

"Okay." I sighed. "These other versions of you . . . can we talk about those?"

"She just—she made me start telling myself I wasn't shy and awkward. I didn't like it at first, actually. But Grace—Grace kind of saved me. I don't know—" He blushed, looked away. "Maybe I'm still a little shy, awkward, but I'm also here with you. And that's—something."

"It is *something*." I smiled and let my socked feet brush his. "But what happens if Grace goes too far?"

The laptop screen went dark and he said, "Like how? *Wesley, I want you to hit me. As hard as you can.*" He cackled, a laugh that flashed his white incisors.

My smile made my temple ache, and I touched it.

"Nora. If you're ever really worried about Grace, let's promise to tell each other, okay? Deal?" His focus shifted. He said, "It should have been me who jumped in after you."

"What? No, you—"

"I'm a better swimmer than Grace. I just . . ."

"You panicked. I'm sure Wesley did too."

Rand rolled onto his side to face me. He was inches away. "If you'd really gotten hurt—"

Everything went still then. Time seemed to slow. I moved closer.

But Rand didn't close the distance. "What did you do between spring break and summer?" he said. "I never asked."

I sat up quickly and took a breath, looking at the ceiling. "I—um, first, I ran a three-minute mile, then I spent two weeks in total mindful meditation, and then I learned German and Japanese. And Mandarin just for kicks."

The old mattress springs creaked as Rand leaned closer and brushed my hair away from my bruise. "I . . . I took a placement test for math. I don't know how I did."

I pressed my fingers to the line between his eyebrows. "But really you solved an unsolvable proof. Now you're skipping high school altogether. Heading to MIT?"

He lifted up on his elbow and propped his head in his hand. "My parents want me to take Algebra II, but I'm afraid I'll get placed in geometry. They've been fighting a lot. Sometimes I think it would be better if I didn't get into Algebra II. Then they could focus on worrying about me and not each other. But at the same time, I just want to be left alone."

I'd thought we were playing the game. Coming up with my own real answers—those truths stung. I wasn't sure I wanted that.

"Rand . . . I . . ."

He blinked hard. "Don't tell Grace I said any of that."

"Why?"

"She'd—" He smiled. "She'd kill me for being so boring." He cleared his throat, ran his fingers over the laptop's track pad. "What next? There's *Groundhog Day* if you want more Nietzsche-esque fare? Or if you're just in the mood for bendy mindfuck-ery . . . *Pulp Fiction*."

As the movie began, I realized this was the first time Rand and me felt like a real possibility. But as Rand's smile traveled from the laptop screen to me, I wondered what he wanted. What I wanted. Stretched out in my bed, our socked feet brushing together, this was the most normal day we'd shared.

We must have fallen asleep, because I woke to Wesley standing over me.

"It's time to go home, man," he said to Rand. Rand, bleary-eyed, sat up.

I opened my mouth to tell my brother to back off. Until I noticed his hand. Knuckles white, his fist tight around his phone.

CHAPTER 13

SUMMER

Oncoming headlights shone through the trees and made patterns on my sweater—Grace's sweater—as Wesley drove the Jeep down the dark mountain road. We rounded the corner, drove past the DONNER CITY LIMITS sign. "They took her to Enloe Medical Center."

I sank deeper into my seat. It was a good hospital, just far away. "It's going to take a lot longer to get all the way to Chico."

The steering wheel creaked as Wesley gripped it tighter. "Kevin won't care we took the Jeep, okay?"

"How do you know that?" I tugged at the seat belt. "You never even asked him why he wants us now."

"How 'bout I don't care what Kevin thinks." He squinted at the headlights. "And I asked him, okay? He said he was too selfish to be a dad back then and now he wants to try."

"Selfishness is a luxury," I said. "We've never had that."

I expected Wesley to argue, to tell me, *We do here,* but instead he said, "I know."

Wesley burst through the hospital doors ahead of me. Minutes felt like hours. We showed our IDs, checked in with security at the main doors, found the room where they'd admitted Mom—all as if we were swimming underwater.

We pushed in, but the bed was empty except for some wrinkled sheets.

The floor gave under me, and I caught Wesley's arm.

"Wesley," I said.

When he'd gotten the call, they'd said she was complaining of extreme pain.

A doctor came in then, combing his fingers through a chart. "You're Kate's children?"

"Is she okay?" I said.

"Let's take a seat." The doctor motioned to three light blue chairs lining the wall.

I sat slowly. The last time I'd talked to Mom, I'd blown her off.

Wesley grabbed the hair at the back of his head. "You have to tell us if she's not okay."

The doctor pulled a chair out for him. Wesley collapsed into it, and the doctor sat down opposite, resting his elbows on his knees.

"Your mother first complained about back pain and requested an injection of Demerol." The doctor shifted, his white coat shushing against the armrests. "When that didn't happen quickly, she said she had a headache. Your mother—has she ever been treated for an opioid addiction?"

"Of course not," I said.

Wesley, his mouth held in a solemn line, only shook his head.

The doctor's voice went quieter. "She's the one who called the ambulance and said she was in pain. She wanted to be admitted for treatment, to receive prescription painkillers. Has she shown any symptoms of a problem with medication? Slurred speech, small pupils, sweating . . ."

"Her speech is slurred because of the meds she has to take," I said. "And the sweating—it comes with her migraines, when she's not feeling well."

The doctor sighed, and I felt a sudden, hot rush. A hundred of Mom's too-sick moments swam up to meet me. Orange pill bottles. Office visits. Twenty-dollar bills passing into the hands of pharmacists.

A quiet place inside me grew louder and louder.

I'd been so impossibly stupid.

Tears sliced down my cheeks and collected at my jawline. I wiped them away.

Wesley cut his eyes to me. Once. Then again.

And all the air sucked out of my lungs.

He knew.

Wesley knew, and I didn't.

I hadn't figured it out.

And he hadn't told me.

The doctor reached across Wesley and squeezed my shoulder, pulling me back into the room.

"We're going to keep her for a few days," he said. "We need to do a mental health evaluation. Unfortunately, she won't be able to see guests."

Cold tingles ran up my arms, and I wrapped Grace's useless sweater tighter around me.

Wesley's hands choked up on the steering wheel as the Jeep careened back toward Donner in the darkness.

A part of me did know she was too reliant on the pills. "But the headaches?" I asked.

"Migraines are a symptom of withdrawal," he said. "Maybe she had them a long time ago. Probably still has them. Now she just craves more meds than the docs will prescribe. It throws her into withdrawals all the time. I'm—I'm sorry. I know we need to do something . . ."

"What are we going to do?" I asked. "You want CPS involved? They'll separate us."

"What about Kevin?"

"We—" I looked at my brother. "Can we count on him?"

His breaths turned ragged, but he stayed silent. It was all the answer I needed. Finally, he said, "What are we gonna tell them?"

"Who?"

"Grace." He cleared his throat. "And Rand. He probably knows something's up."

The seat belt cut into my neck as I faced him. "Are you joking? That's really what you're thinking about right now. What about the fact that we have no *insurance*?"

Wesley gripped the gearshift. "It's just . . . what will they think if we tell them?"

All this time, I'd been afraid of Grace and Rand learning where we came from, who we really were, the circumstances of our lives, how we'd even *gotten* here. It had felt overwhelming. But now I wondered what it'd be like to share this little bit of truth. To not carry it on our own.

"That's what you care about the most?" I asked. "What about Mom?"

"Of course I care about Mom. It's just—" Wesley's voice cracked. "What will they think of us?"

I sat back in my seat, not angry anymore, just achy. "Wesley," I whispered.

All the stress and strain of our lives was something the two of us had shared, even if we'd dealt differently. But Wesley, the truth he'd known about Mom for—I didn't even know how long—the weight of that. It had been something he'd carried alone.

Kevin jumped up from the couch when we walked through the door at nearly five o'clock in the morning.

Wesley had been the one to call and tell him we'd taken the Jeep and were heading back. I didn't know what to expect from him.

"Is Kate okay?" He lowered back down to the couch, rubbing his fists into his eyes.

I thought he'd be furious.

Wesley, slow with exhaustion, nodded. "She'll be okay. She—"

Our mother wasn't sick. Not the way I'd thought.

And I didn't know how to be here—Donner or anywhere at all in the world—if Kevin thought she'd been a bad mom. She wasn't perfect, but at least she'd been there. She'd wanted us.

"They think it's just a bacterial infection," I said. He couldn't

135

know the truth. "They're going to give her a few days of antibiotics and then she'll be fine."

Wesley looked over his shoulder at me. Then he turned to Kevin and said, "With an IV. So they get it right into her bloodstream, you know?"

Kevin nodded. "That's great news. Kate's strong." He cringed. "She'll pull through."

It was a small thing, but I appreciated it from him.

I moved up the stairs as if I were still underwater, taking long slow steps that felt like they'd never carry me to my bed. Everything I thought I'd known about my mom and our life . . .

I didn't know how to go to sleep, and I definitely didn't know how to wake up into this new world. As the light streaked in across my flowered sheets, I finally fell asleep knowing that, for now, Wesley and I would have to hold this secret between the two of us.

CHAPTER 14

SUMMER

Three days after we'd driven back to Donner, I came down the cabin stairs to find Wesley standing in the kitchen, surrounded by the contents of the fridge—bread and mayonnaise, cheese and tomatoes, pickles and mustard—but watching them as if they were going to assemble themselves into a sandwich on their own.

He cleared his throat when he saw me and started throwing cheese onto bread as if dealing a deck of cards.

"Feeding an army?" I pulled a glass from the cupboard.

His knuckles pressed into the counter as if he needed its support to stay upright. "Dad and I are going out on the boat."

My hand paused reaching into the fridge. "*Dad*?"

"You're good with calling Mom *Mom*. How much of a mom has she been?"

I took a step back. Since the hospital, I couldn't stop wondering if there'd every really been headaches, if Mom could recover—really recover—if all along I'd been helping or hurting her by bringing her more meds when she asked for them, for not seeing what had been there all along. Every time I thought I'd hit the bottom, a trapdoor would open and send me tumbling down again.

The mental health hold was officially up now. Mom had been released. They weren't going to put her in rehab, even though Wesley and I knew they should. The doctor said addiction was only a suspicion.

We wanted to come clean to him, but if we couldn't afford insurance, we definitely couldn't afford rehab. I still had no idea how we'd pay the hospital bills, and Wesley kept dodging the conversation.

"I'm sorry," Wesley said. "I am."

I didn't know if he meant he was sorry about Mom's addiction or sorry he'd never told me.

Wesley opened his mouth to say something else, then closed it, shaking his head. He smacked some turkey on top of the cheese.

"Why didn't you ever say anything?"

He didn't answer.

"Did you think I wouldn't believe you?"

"No." Wesley tried to tear a piece of lettuce, but it shredded between his fingers. "I— It's not like telling you would have done any good. It's not like we could afford rehab. Playing nurse to her at least made you feel like you were doing something, right? And—" He sighed. "I'm the big brother. Our dad was 'dead.'" He made air quotes. "I'm supposed to protect you from what might hurt you, right? How was I supposed to tell you the problem was the meds?"

"You don't have to be sorry." I sighed. "I probably *wouldn't* have believed you."

"Nora." Wesley pressed his fingertips to his eyes. "I wanted to, like, protect you from it. When you were a kid, I used to take you to the park, on walks, to—anywhere, just to get you away."

He was only a kid himself, just two years older than me. "It's okay, Wesley. Really—"

"Then later I just, I don't know, left you there with her. Making money to pay bills is something, you know? But it kept me from being there, from knowing you—"

"You know me now," I said, my own firmness surprising me. "We know each other."

"Time is a flat circle," Rand announced, and Wesley chucked an empty water bottle at his head. The late-summer sun came up over Donner Lake.

We'd borrowed a telescope from Rand's house and camped out all night for the mid-August meteor shower that had rained through the sky.

Grace, buried in Wesley's sweatshirt and arms, elbowed him, then clapped her hands delightedly at Rand. "Explain this theory, my love."

"It's the eternal return," Rand said, reaching for the bottle. "Everything that's happened will happen again." He launched it back at Wesley, who dodged it, laughing.

"Bullshit," he said.

Rand shrugged. "It's a theory. There's infinite time, right? But a finite number of events. So given enough time, all events will recur over and over again. Infinitely."

"Like this summer?" Grace asked.

Wesley wrapped his arms tighter around Grace, rested his chin in the crook of her neck. "I hope so."

"Me too," Rand said.

Grace craned her neck to look back at Wesley. "Will you think about summer when you're working all day?" She shimmied her back against him, settling in closer. "Or are you too busy to day-dream, being the manager?"

Manager?

I looked at Wesley, and he cast his eyes to the ground.

He swallowed. "I'll think about summer."

Later, as the boys packed up the telescope, Grace plopped down beside me. "Two more weeks," she said. "Until home."

Remembering what Rand told me about Grace, the way she'd changed, I decided to be bold. "Who are you going to be, Grace? Back home?"

Her eyes snapped to me, then slowly softened as her lips curved into a smile. "Who are *you* going to be, Nora?"

A worrier, a caregiver, a freshman, maybe hungry, the child of a mother with an addiction I never even knew about. But I couldn't say it.

Paper crinkled, something in her hands. I peered into her lap at a hand-drawn map of Donner—our homes, the lake, the Honeyridge, the ski lifts, the ice cave, the boathouse. All the places we'd been. The places Grace loved. The labels were handwritten too—all of them in Wesley's lovely cursive.

140

Smiling down at it, Grace said, "This one's to scale."

"Wesley made this for you?" I asked, feeling a brightness inside me.

"He's something, your brother." Her teeth came over her bottom lip, but then her eyes went brighter, greener. "I think he's the best story I've ever made up."

I felt my brows draw together, and I looked away.

Whatever existed between them—I wanted it to be real.

I didn't want Wesley to be another character in one of Grace's tales.

As Grace and I stood in the sno-cone line, waiting for our giant cups of frozen sugariness, my skin soaked in every last bit of sunlight. I had less than seven days left before I'd be facing home, and truths about Mom I'd rather keep denying.

Rand's parents had won two tickets for the Truckee Railroad Museum. Wesley'd been wanting to see it since he'd watched a documentary—or junk science, as Rand called it—about a conspiracy theory involving the Truckee Donner Railroad Society. Grace hated history and I wanted some time with just Grace, so it was only us in line.

"I only have a five," Grace said, flipping through her wallet.

She'd always had plenty before—Grace was rich. "Don't worry," I said. "I've got this." I had barely enough.

Something brushed the back of my knee. I turned around and there was Neil, skimming a bag of Doritos against Grace's legs.

She switched her purse to the other shoulder and shook her head. "If this is your attempt at flirting, Neil, you're failing to impress either of us."

"I haven't seen you around the Honeyridge," he said, looking at Grace, the straw from his drink against his mouth. "It's kind of breaking my heart."

"I didn't know you had one," Grace said.

Neil laughed, and turned to me. "Grace is rude, never introducing us. I'm Neil."

"Nora," I said, extending my hand.

His handshake was firm, like he'd just made a lucrative deal with the chairman of the board. But it was weird touching him, having him speak to me.

The couple in front of us took their glistening, already-melting cones. Our turn to order.

"Hey, Grace," Neil said. "See you tonight. Don't be short this time."

My heart thudded against my ribs.

Grace tensed, then wiggled her fingers in a wave. "I have plenty of cash. Don't you worry."

I didn't turn around. Just kept my eyes on the sno-cone menu. "How much do you owe him? And for what?"

"Enough," she said. "Don't worry. I'll get it."

Neil's shadow lingered on the warm asphalt a few seconds before drifting away.

CHAPTER 15

SUMMER

On the last night of summer, we raced across the night-damp lawn that connected the Honeyridge to a smaller hotel called the Sheldrake. Blades of sprinkler-wet grass cut against my ankles. My feet slid in the cold slip of my flip-flops. I thought about Neil pressuring Grace for money to buy us another adventure. Then I thought about Grace, suddenly broke for no apparent reason. I wondered what had happened, and how far she'd go to turn it around.

"Hurry up!" Grace yelled as she bounded to the top of the hillside on the eastern end of the Honeyridge. She planted her hands on her hips. "We're going to miss the previews!"

I looked back to see Rand walking the lawn as if he were out for a summer stroll.

"It's a movie?" Wesley panted, slowing—we'd already spent the night chasing a map just to finally find Grace. "We're going to a movie? After all this, a *movie*?"

I was glad for that—glad our night didn't involve something that required favors or deals. But up until now, our evening events had been free of charge.

"Wesley," I said, low. "We didn't— We don't have money." I wondered if that would give away his lie—a manager had to make a decent living.

"Admission is free," Grace said over her shoulder, and I cringed—she'd heard. "The movies are on the green above the Sheldrake. Every third Friday during the summer."

Rand stopped walking. "Aren't those screenings strictly for the hotel's guests?"

"I don't believe in exclusionary policies," Grace said. "Any objections?"

We jumped the metal fence.

Borrowed Honeyridge towels under our butts, the four of us perched ourselves on the eastern side of the Sheldrake with three bags of microwave popcorn that Grace pulled from her tote. I kicked off my flip-flops.

The movie was some summer blockbuster about aliens, playing on a big projector screen that overlooked the lake. Grace watched intently. "This is better than a theater," she said as she fisted some popcorn. "The wide-open outdoors! Ours and only ours."

"Except for the fifty resort guests down there." Wesley gestured down the hill, then slapped at his arm. "And the mosquitos."

"Don't be such a baby," Grace said.

Rand tossed him a bottle of bug spray. "I told the rest of you to use this."

"Excuse me for being allergic," Wesley said.

The last week had come too fast. It reached up out of the depths of August and latched on to us. Summer meant saying goodbye. It meant facing high school and trying to make new friends—knowing I'd never meet anyone like Rand and Grace. It meant taking care of Mom.

"Rand, tell me," Grace said. "What have you done since spring?"

"Let's see." Rand tapped his finger against his chin. "Taught myself German, trekked the Inca trail, and lost my virginity . . . twice."

Grace threw her head back laughing.

I glanced at the place where Rand's pant leg touched my ankle. He looked away.

Wesley filled the air with a white cloud of poison large enough to exterminate anything within an hour of Truckee. "I'll swell up like a balloon by midnight, just you wait."

Grace kissed him on the cheek. "Wouldn't want to damage your delicate skin."

The humans soon realized the aliens had a weak spot, and they were rallying. Just as the lead character was storming Area 51 for the technology to dismantle the spacecraft, I glanced to my friends.

Rand scratched his neck as he watched with disbelief. Wesley, biting a knuckle as he stared at the screen, held his knees to his chest.

"Where's Grace?" I asked.

Rand shrugged and so did Wesley. They were used to her ghosting in the middle of the action. Maybe I should have been by now too.

Gunfire erupted on the screen and Wesley jumped an inch off the grass. Rand, eyes narrowed, shook his head to himself. Down by the water of the Honeyridge, far at the end of the dock by the boathouse, I spotted Grace.

"Hey, I'll be back." I pressed my water into Rand's hand. "Too many of these. I'm going to find a bathroom."

I took the towel I'd been sitting on and wrapped it around my shoulders, then followed the lit trail down to the water's edge, my bare feet enjoying the feel of the ground.

Grace looked small as she sat on the end of the dock.

"You gave up on the movie so soon?"

She blinked twice when she looked over her shoulder and saw me there. "I was rooting for the aliens," she said. "It was starting to look like things had gone south for them."

"That's an interesting perspective," I said. "They only wanted a clean planet to raise their young. If they'd waited any longer, with us and all our plastics and pollution, Earth would have been beyond saving."

Grace's lips curved into a smile. "You get me."

Crickets chirped in the brush. I sat down beside her on the dock and took a breath. Then another. Now that we were so close to saying goodbye, I couldn't wait any longer.

"Grace, how much do you tell us that's not . . . strictly true?"

Her attention snapped to me. She studied my face a moment. "What do you mean *not strictly true*?"

I stayed quiet. I wasn't going to define it for her.

"I thought you liked my stories," she said at last.

"I do," I said. "The stories. But there are other things—Sometimes I don't know what's real and what's not."

"Candace," she said.

I shrugged and looked at her, waiting. Candace, Neil, whatever had her crying on the dock last spring.

"Why is that so important to you anyway? Would you feel better if I told you I saw her around, summer after summer, being miserable with stupid boys when she knew she wasn't into boys? Would you feel better if I told you I watched her from afar, fighting with parents who tried to force her to be someone she wasn't? That she wasn't chasing something beautiful but running from something ugly?"

I blinked, wondering what parts of this were real—if any of them were. Maybe I really didn't want to know. I cleared my throat. "But you—you lied to Wesley too."

Her eyebrows shot up. "About what?"

"You told him you'd stop paying Neil for things."

Grace sighed. "I didn't say I'd stop. Not exactly. Neil gets me things, yes. I don't think I've ever made a secret of that. And I told Wesley I'd stop because I knew it bothered him."

"But Wesley thought you did," I said.

"Semantics," she said. "What I do gives us swims in the Honeyridge pool and snow machines and secret boathouse hideaways and nights spent on hotel rooftops under the stars. I don't want our summers to be sitting around streaming the same five shows with our parents watching us from the other room. I deserve better and so do you."

I didn't know what I deserved exactly. But I thought back to the boat that day. That wasn't what I wanted these vacations to be either.

"You don't have the money," I said.

Grace winked. "You don't know what I have and what I don't."

"But you and Wesley—if you can't be honest, are you two even real?"

"Wesley and I—" Grace's breath shuddered. "We're like some romantic movie that you never want to end, you know?" She was quiet for a little, so I was too. "Maybe Wesley and I are just too perfect for real life."

I didn't begrudge Wesley and Grace having something here that was separate from life at home. But I didn't know how they could be real if they weren't actually real.

I swallowed. "What about me and you? Are we too perfect? Like, if I were a new girl at your school, would you even be my friend?"

Grace's eyes shined and she blinked fast. "Nora, if you were new at my school, you wouldn't want to be mine."

"What do you mean? There's no world where that could be true."

"What would you say"—she leaned toward me—"if I told you there was a world where I'm not me?"

"Okay, tell me about that place," I said. "Tell me what happened back home. Before."

Grace laughed a little, her eyes turning fierce. "Nora, if you were new at my school, I'd make every ordinary moment an adventure, and I'd protect you from anyone—any*thing*—that could hurt you."

"You couldn't do that. Even if you wanted to." Grace couldn't have stopped Wesley ignoring me, or bills piling up, or Mom's addiction, or Kevin's . . . whatever Kevin's deal was.

"Yes, I could," she said, squeezing my hand. "I'd put myself between all those terrible things and you. I'd never let them through."

Maybe home wouldn't make me feel small if I could just tell Grace about Mom and the money problems and Kevin and Wesley. Maybe if I could just tell her . . .

Or maybe once Grace knew everything, that truth would hang like a shadow over every season to come. Maybe she'd be afraid to be so fabulous in front of me, knowing my reality was anything but. Maybe she'd feel sorry for me. I couldn't bear that.

"Don't go home and forget, Nora."

"Forget what?" I asked, looking at her.

"Who we were out here. Who we were in the dark." Grace smiled, then looked over her shoulder at the faraway movie screen. "We should head back." She took off her leather sandals and handed them to me.

"What are you doing? Carry your own shoes." I nudged her and tried to laugh.

"Take them."

"No," I said. "You have to walk just as far as I do."

"My feet are tougher." She pushed the sandals into my hands. "The boys will be angry, won't they? Us sneaking off without them. They hate to be excluded," she said. "Wesley's so pouty when he doesn't get his way, like a little boy."

I didn't think Rand and Wesley minded much that we'd stepped away. Grace was either lying to herself or lying to me.

Wesley had a Twizzler hanging out of his mouth when we got back. "When the aliens decide to come down here again, do you think they'll really want to blow us up?"

"*When*," Rand said. "Did you really say *when*? And *again*?"

Wesley bit off his Twizzler and pointed the stub at Rand. "Hey, I don't know who you think built the pyramids, but aliens is a good enough answer for me." Wesley waited for Rand to take the bait, but Rand just rolled his eyes.

"Grace, what do *you* think?" Wesley asked.

Grace folded her legs under her. "I try not to think that far into the past or future."

"Because neither the future nor past exists," Rand said. "Right, Grace?"

"Really?" Wesley snapped his head toward Grace, then Rand. "You both think that?"

"Of course." By the way Rand's lips twitched, I knew it wasn't exactly true. "Philosophical presentism. The past and the future—events and entities—how do we know they exist? How do we know that anything exists except what we can reach out and touch?"

Wesley's eyes narrowed. "So, like, you don't think the breakfast I ate this morning was real? You think the last day of school didn't happen?"

Rand crossed his arms over his chest. "Prove it did."

Wesley chuckled. "What bullshit. What total crap. You mean

to tell me you believe that? What am I supposed to do, stick my finger down my throat and produce an Eggo—"

"Now, now, boys, if anyone regurgitates anything, that will surely ruin this present moment we're enjoying."

Wesley had started playing with his cell phone. Grace ripped it out of his hand and said with a grin, "Sacrilege, darling. You should leave this at home. That's how they get you. The government, I mean. That's why I never carry mine."

"While you've got that, type in your number, okay?"

"Yeah, right." Grace slid it across the beach towel. "I thought we'd settled all that the first night we met."

I looked up. "Wait—really? We're not going to even talk until Christmas?"

Rand watched me. But he broke his stare, busied himself tearing apart blades of grass.

"You agreed, Nora." Grace faced the screen, pulling her knees against her chest and wrapping her arms around them. "We all did."

It hadn't sounded so depressing when we'd all agreed back in the spring. Back then it hadn't even sounded real. Now I couldn't imagine so many months without them.

Wesley threw an arm around Grace's shoulders, pulled her close. "It's a good idea. When we come back here, it'll be like—like the first night on the rooftop."

But I didn't know what I'd do without Rand saying exactly the right thing at exactly the right moment, without Grace's eyes wild and bright, and without Wesley walking around loose and carefree.

"We're all okay, right?" Grace asked. "We have to be okay before we go."

I picked up the sweater Grace had given to me, still so smooth against my skin. "I'm going for a walk," I said, setting her sandals next to her and grabbing my flip-flops.

I didn't know what to think. Maybe it *was* better this way. Wesley could have told her any number of untrue things. And as much as I loved Grace—and even though she lied to him too—I didn't know how she'd react to his truths.

Grace would make the most interesting, most sophisticated hypocrite.

As I made my way across the cool grass, I heard the gentle pound of someone's footsteps behind me. Expecting Grace, I turned. But it was Rand.

"You okay?" he asked.

I let my hands fall to my sides. "Is this what you want? Three, almost four months of not talking to each other, not even once?"

Rand shook his head. "I—I don't even know. I don't know what I want. I don't like the idea of being home in Walnut Creek—getting up every day, breakfast, swimming, barely hanging out with my friends, running track, studying, going home, pretending I can't hear the shouting through the walls. Repeat. All that without any of you."

"Walls are too thin, aren't they?"

"Impossibly thin." Rand's smile lit the dark. "But we did agree. I mean, it was informal, but Grace—she holds on to things like that." He nodded at the lawn. "Come on. Let's walk. Just around the hotel. Just to walk." He smiled. "Come on. I need to get back in shape for track."

"Do you—do you like—track?" I asked as we walked, wondering if some sport or hobby could be the thing to save me too.

"Um. Not particularly."

I turned to him. "Why do you do it then?"

He snorted and shrugged. "Why do I do anything?"

"Answer your own question."

"Why does *anyone* do anything? To prove our lives matter? That we're not all just random mistakes?"

"No one could ever think you were a mistake."

Rand was quiet. Everything was quiet except the crickets and the lake's waters lapping against the shore. Finally, he said, "My dad could."

My breath hitched.

Rand cut his eyes behind him to the sidewalk, crossed the lawn. Stunned, I followed a beat later. He raised his chin in the direction of the Sheldrake and the movie. "She won't back down."

He was trying to change the subject, so I didn't ask about his dad.

The gravity of what we'd agreed to sank deeper into me. We could have this, our foursome, only by placing months of distance and silence between us.

He moved close. "Would you rather have a little of something amazing or nothing at all?"

"I just want something amazing enough . . . enough to make the rest of it bearable."

Rand let out a long breath and inched closer. "I've been wanting to ask you something. You don't have to answer. That night Wesley woke us up—I watched you, and I saw you take off in the SUV. Where did you go?"

"Stalking me?" I looked away, trying to sound light. "That's halfway creepy."

"You don't have to answer."

I turned and met his eyes.

"My mom got put in the hospital."

He looked surprised. "Is she okay? Was she sick?"

"Super sick," I said. "She's addicted to—she has an addiction to opioids."

Rand blanched, then his surprise melted into something like sadness.

"I've never said that out loud," I said. "To anyone."

"I'm glad you said it to me."

As we came up on the other side of the Sheldrake, I searched the green.

The grass where Grace and Wesley had been was empty except for a couple of damp towels rumpling in the wind. "They're gone."

"Where do you think they went?"

I sighed. "Maybe the bathroom or the boathouse. Or hitchhiking to Reno to get married."

"Let's try the boathouse first," he said. "They won't get married without witnesses."

We moved down to the water and I pressed my ear against the wooden door. It felt splintery against my cheek. I didn't hear any sound from within.

I opened the boathouse door. Soft, sleepy breathing echoed through the air. I walked toward the paddleboat where Wesley's head was tipped back. My foot caught something. A tangle of clothes. Wesley's jeans and Grace's teal lace bralette.

I backed away, but Rand's voice broke through the silence. "Hey, you two, wake up," he said.

Wesley and Grace both came to fast. Wesley grabbed for his pants, but Grace—wearing Wesley's hoodie zipped over her—only yawned.

Turning quickly, I moved out the door.

I heard Wesley say to Grace and Rand, "This is weird."

Rand came out just behind me. "Let's—"

"Forget this ever happened?" I said.

Rand shrugged. "I was going to say run away and start new lives. It's the only way to never face them again." Then he just laughed.

It was all so weird. I started laughing too, so hard I hiccupped.

Something popped in the distance; then above us, the black sky exploded with fireworks.

"The Honeyridge." Rand watched another bright trail shoot high above the movie screen. "They have a big party at the end of August, special discounts to entice people to take one more vacation before back to reality. They shoot off fireworks every night."

"They're beautiful." Only, my voice sounded sad.

He looked over his shoulder in the direction of the boathouse, then he took my hand. "If this is it till winter, we're obligated to make it amazing."

Fireworks were radiant across the sky, and I turned to look up at them.

Rand moved behind me and looped his hands around my waist. My skin carried the tingle of a slight sunburn, and summer—hot but dry—still filled my lungs. As I gripped the wooden railing, I leaned to the left so he could see around me. His chin, warm and faintly rough, almost level with mine when we faced each other, touched my bare shoulder.

I craned my neck around to see him, read him for any hint he wasn't serious, didn't really mean this. But he was looking at me. There was a dizzying pull, and our lips brushed. "Is this okay?" he asked. I nodded and I let mine slide against his again.

We kissed—my first kiss—until my mouth felt swollen and my body loose.

All sights and sounds faded into the background.

We pulled apart, our foreheads touching, our mouths curving into grins. But even with my lips still full and tingling, my throat began to ache. Because like everything else we had, this kiss could only exist here.

WINTER: NOW

CHAPTER 16

The snow flew faster. I stared out the cabin's front picture window, watching the deck disappear under solid white. I'd managed to get the pilot light going, so at least the vents pumped in some musty warmth.

Behind me crouched a pile of brown boxes half-filled with everything I'd searched through so far—drawers filled with swimwear stiff with sunscreen from summers before, a T-shirt I'd once borrowed from Grace, a brochure for the Truckee Railroad Museum, a star-shaped rock from the shores of the lake. Some token from some faraway memory had to hold a clue to what had happened, some missing link that would connect me back to Grace.

I had to find her. It had been me, after all, who'd last seen her.

The news reports had grown dire, like Rand had warned. I'd switched to local channels for anchors used to living through a little winter storm. But even their voices were tense, urging everyone to stay in place.

My phone rang. Kevin on the caller ID. I checked out the window—Wesley was still chopping wood—before I picked up. "Hey."

"Got a problem, kid," Kevin said. "Cal Trans closed the road back in. It looks like I'm stuck in Reno. Maybe for the night."

The line crackled, and I switched my phone to the other ear. "Are you sure? All night?"

"The good news is that it's cold enough my Costco haul won't thaw." He tried to laugh. "I got those bagels you like."

I remembered the woodshed. "While you're waiting it out, is a hardware store nearby?"

"Uh, yeah. Why? What do you—"

The phone went dead. I checked for bars. No service.

We were going to be alone for the night. Just Wesley and me with nothing and everything to say. The weight of that settled over me as thick as the snow falling outside. He must be freezing out there.

I swung open the door. "Wesley! Get inside," I yelled, then shut it fast.

He took his time coming in—hacking one last log, his cheeks red against the white.

Finally, the back door opened and he shrugged off his snow-heaped coat. "I was trying to finish up with the wood—but it's green and sappy anyway. We're fucked if the power goes out."

"We're already fucked," I said. "Kevin's stranded in Reno."

He balled his coat and hurled it at a heap of boxes, then sighed. "We'll be okay."

"Maybe." I lowered the volume on the TV. "The storm's supposed to blow through tonight. If Cal Trans gets the road cleared early, he could be home before dark."

It was a possibility, but storms like this could settle in for days, or the sky could fall for only one night and block even the most certain of paths.

Wesley plopped down on the couch and kicked his snowy boots up on the coffee table. He closed his eyes. "If all goes to hell, you still have my permission to eat me."

From the rack by the door, I took down my snow coat and zipped it to my chin. "Getting some firewood. Maybe some of it's not too green."

Wesley, slumped on the couch, kicked his feet through old photos on the coffee table.

"While I'm gone"—I nodded toward the kitchen—"heat up some soup?"

I looped a scarf around my neck and paused at the new security panel by the door. Wesley's jacket on the coatrack had blocked it from view.

"Oh, Dad installed that before you came back," Wesley said. "He didn't like the idea of you being here after— He wanted to have more protection."

I opened the door to a vortex of snow. There was so much Wesley still didn't get.

A security panel wouldn't protect us from whatever happened to Grace.

The soup Wesley warmed bubbled in a pot by the time I finished bringing in wood. I ate on the couch with the bowl balanced between my knees. My cell sat silently on the table.

Wesley checked his and said, "Cell tower must have blown out in the storm." He stood at the front window, shoveling spoonfuls into his mouth as the falling white sealed us in. It felt heavy even through the glass that separated us from it. I remembered the weight of all that snow on my shoulders, felt the cold down my throat the night we searched for her.

I coughed on my soup and Wesley looked over at me.

"So what did that jackass want?" he asked.

The air on the back of my neck felt colder. "Why the hostility?" I said. "You and Rand had been so very friendly once upon a time."

"I said I was sorry for that," he said. "The way that dude looked at us, in front of his parents and those cops—it was like we didn't even count." He paused. "What do you think he'd have done if Grace had been in the room, huh?"

"If Grace had been in that room, *we* wouldn't have been in that room."

"She would have been so pissed. Grace, she—" Wesley gripped his soup bowl. "Did you know they sold theirs?"

"Their what? Who?"

"Grace's parents. The Lombardis. I walked up there after Kevin took off. I looked in the windows. Other people live there now. It's painted a different color—blue. Grace hated blue."

I closed my eyes at the thought of Grace's parents. I'd never even spoken to them, only saw them in the distance, watched them as if they were characters on a screen. Whoever they really were, I'd never know the truth. They'd been spun into story, myth, fantasy.

I eyed the boxes crowding the room. Our own cabin, even needing a remodel, would go for almost two hundred thousand—more than enough to pay off bills and help Wesley and me get on our feet.

"What do you think theirs sold for—the Lombardis'?" I asked.

Wesley kicked one of the boxes, caving it in on the side. "Can we get some of these out of here? I don't need the constant reminder you're ruining the only good thing we ever had. And turn the TV off. I don't want to hear how bad it's gonna be. Knowing won't make a difference."

I picked up the box. Nothing had been broken. "You can't be mad at me about this. Kevin said it too—he can guide anywhere. We don't need the cabin. It could pay for college or—"

Wesley chuckled. "College."

"Or whatever. Give you a deposit on an apartment. Or something. And the one good thing we ever had? Whatever that was, Grace took it with her when she left last spring."

Two hard pounds shook the cabin door. I threw my gaze to Wesley. Nobody could have made it to our door. The road had to be impassable by now.

Snow stung my cheeks when I opened it. I squinted against the blinding white. Rand grasped the doorframe. A trail of blood ran from his hairline down to his chin.

WINTER: YEAR ONE

CHAPTER 17

Donner in winter was a place where people died, so many people over the last two hundred years. But as I drove the snowmobile higher and higher up the night-dark mountainside that first winter, I'd never felt the blood rush so hot through my veins.

Powdery snow kicked up and caught in my hair. Real snow— softer than the artificial flurry last summer. I'd never driven anything before, not even a bike, but I flew past the NO TRESPASSING sign like I'd done this a hundred million times.

Behind me, Rand's arms tightened around my waist, his long legs on either side of mine.

Grace zoomed close on Rand's other snowmobile—his family's. "All the way to the top!" she shouted over the growl of the engines.

Wesley, riding behind her, whooped into the night. I'd last heard that sound from him after the final football game of the fall. Him riding off in the bed of a truck, his arm around a girl.

Moonlight and headlights twinkled off the freshly fallen snow, diamonds across an icy white sea. The last few months at home, I'd been trying hard to ignore all the signs of Mom's addiction. Mostly failing. All I had was my unfinished story, my character still bound up in the box. But now, traveling up the mountain, I'd never felt this free.

We reached the top, Rand and I the first to dismount. I turned to him, legs still shaking.

Each break, I arrived with the image of Rand from the break before. And each time, I was surprised by all his subtle and not-so-subtle transformations. Now, this close, I had to look up to meet his eyes. In the ten months since we'd first met, he'd stopped looking like the kid in the Honeyridge parking lot. Though his quick smile was the same. And his tan from summer had faded to a golden glow that looked to me like liquid sunshine against all the snow.

But in the glare of the snowmobile's headlights, his eyes were tired in a way I hadn't seen before. He closed them now and leaned in, kissing my smile, his own lips curving under mine.

The summer was four months gone, and it had started to feel like a sun-soaked dream. Donner was a different kind of lovely in winter, shrouded and cold and white.

Grace tossed up a spray of snow as she thrust her machine into park.

"Not bad," Wesley said, getting off and knocking Rand on the shoulder.

Rand offered a wry smile. "What a little parental guilt can buy." He motioned to an abandoned firepit stuffed with fresh kindling. "Looks like we're over here."

I wondered how early Grace had gotten here to set it up. I looked in the direction of the lodge, hoping this escapade hadn't involved Neil.

Grace pulled a bottle of lighter fluid out of her bag and doused the wood.

One lit match thrown in and the heat on my face was enough to make me step back.

"Sorry," Grace said, then lower, "Too much."

Logs had been dragged around the firepit. Rand sat on the far one. I'd been to my first bonfire this past fall back home. Bailey and Sasha, girls from my PE class, had invited me. We were friends because we were always the three to take the longest to run a mile and we ended up lagging and panting and sweating together. Sasha had rolled her eyes and giggled when Bailey caught a marshmallow on fire, some kind of inside joke I didn't understand. But I'd fake-laughed with them as Bailey licked sticky s'mores off her chipped fingernail polish.

"You put too much kindling in, or someone else?" Wesley asked.

Grace took the one spot next to Rand, leaving the other log for my brother and me. "Careful," she said, "you'll kill the mystery."

Rand worked the zipper on his jacket up and down as he stared into the flames. Grace leaned into him and put her head on his shoulder. Wesley straightened up, watching.

"Me, of course," she said. "I put in too much kindling. Too much lighter fluid too."

Wesley groaned and shook his head to himself.

I'd never admitted to Wesley what I knew about Neil. I wanted

Grace to be whoever she wanted to be, and I wanted that for Wesley too. I didn't like the idea of Neil having a place in our adventures, being paid for them, but I knew Grace could afford it. And I trusted she had a handle on things.

Her eyes darted, settled on me.

"How was it?" I asked, before she could say anything. "Being back home?"

Grace blinked, then straightened her back. "Does it matter?" Then she smiled, stretched her arms. "We're here now. Being the people we really are."

"Are we?" I said.

Rand looked up at me, quick.

Grace's lips parted. "What does that mean?"

The question had been in my head, then out of my mouth before I could think.

"Never mind," I said. I felt my brother shift uncomfortably beside me.

"Are you wanting to say something, Nora?" Grace asked.

I unfastened and refastened the Velcro strap on my mitten. "I just— Even if we're the people here we want to be, we're still— I mean, people still get hurt. We still get hurt."

Grace leaned forward, eyes suddenly bright in the firelight. "Did someone tell you? Did someone tell you something about me?"

"No. Grace, no." My cheeks were hot. "No. I was— It was—"

She leaned closer, narrowing the distance between us. "Nora, I—" Then she sat up straight. Smiled. "Of course, you're not the kind who gets hurt. You were voted most popular."

"What? Oh." I looked down. "Yeah. And homecoming queen."

Grace sat back with a half smile and twinkling eyes.

"And I'm class president," Wesley said.

Rand shook his head, then shrugged. "I'm the tallest guy in my grade."

But I couldn't shake the crushing sense of sadness that had settled over me. I felt like I'd lost a chance.

Grace sniffed the air. "Is something burning? Something . . . plastic?"

Wesley jerked his boots back from the flames. "Damn it. I melted the treads off!"

Rand laughed—Grace too, her eyeteeth winking in the firelight.

Wesley inspected his boots. "They look kind of cool, though."

Everyone was silent for a beat. From this high, I could see the lake, a white expanse of quiet below.

"Have you ever seen this moon?" I heard Grace ask. She was staring straight up. It glowed huge and full, close enough to fall on us all in a giant smash of light.

"Why?" Wesley chuckled. "You gonna tell me that if there's no past, then I haven't seen *this* moon before?"

Grace laughed. "Well, now that you mention it . . ."

Rand smiled. And the image of Wesley with that girl in the truck—Lauren—floated into my thoughts.

Wesley had missed Grace—I could tell by the way he'd brightened when that alien movie came on TV one day in the fall. Going back home after a summer spent having something so big—it had dug a hole in me, deeper and deeper, till it was finally time to pack for winter break. Somehow with Lauren, Wesley had found a way to deal with that empty feeling.

Grace stood and held out her hand to him. "I was just thinking this moon could make a person forget about every other moon they'd seen before."

I watched and waited for him to resist—because maybe he should have—but his fingers hooked around hers easily. "Come on," she said. "We'll count the stars."

Wesley groaned, but I could tell he kind of loved it.

They moved far away from us under the cover of trees, where they definitely couldn't see much of the sky. Even though Grace and Wesley seemed to have a silent pact that they'd only be together here, I was glad she didn't know about Lauren.

Rand sat down on the log beside me. "Is it terrible I couldn't wait for them to leave?"

"Yes." I glanced to where they'd disappeared between the trees, then at Rand. "And no."

Wesley's and Grace's faraway laughter rippled through the cold air.

"Look how easy it is for them," he said. "To fall right back in where they were."

"Your nose is pink." I touched it with my mittened fingertip.

He pulled me close and buried his nose in my coat. I wrapped my arms tight around him, thinking about school and home. The bright spot had been crossing off days that stood between me and here.

"It *does* hurt," Rand said. "For the record."

"What?"

"To be surrounded by people, when nobody really knows the truth," he said, and he nudged me with his elbow. "Even for the tallest guy in the class."

I smiled for a second but kept my eyes on his, waiting for him to go on.

When he didn't, I looked up at the stars. "I don't know," I said. "It's just—when I'm in Gridley, even if I'm at school, I can't stop thinking about home. Not like I can when I'm here. Why is that?"

Rand looked at me, his face serious. "Because I'm such a debonair distraction."

"Yes," I said. "That's it."

He smiled.

"But I—I notice things now—like, Mom calling the pharmacy to check for updates on her prescription, hounding her doctor's office for a refill. This weird thing that happens—her eyes gain focus just after she swallows a pill, then they, like, slowly glaze over as she fades out. I worry about her all the time."

Rand was quiet, then sighed. "Don't blame yourself for not seeing the signs before."

"Wesley saw them," I said.

"It doesn't matter. When you're too close to something—someone—you can't always see what's right in front of you."

"But I shouldn't have said all that," I said. "Just now. To Grace. Even if part of me wanted to."

"Okay. Why?"

"Because it was"—I shrugged—"terrible. Especially when Grace is so—*Grace*."

"You don't think Grace has things she regrets? Things she's worried about?"

Grace made a soft sound from behind the wall of distant trees. They weren't even trying to hide that they were all over each other.

I wondered how far things had gone with Lauren. Not that I actually wanted to know.

I took a deep breath of mountain air that froze the back of my throat. "Hypothetically, if someone met someone back home"—I glanced behind me—"what would it mean for us here?"

Rand stared off to where Grace and Wesley had slipped behind the trees, and lowered his voice further. "Wesley? Really?"

"Yeah."

A few seconds later, feet crunched through the snow behind us, and Rand and I sat up a little straighter. Yellow leaves were stuck in Grace's hair. Wesley's lips were swollen.

As they moved closer, Rand whispered, "She doesn't want to know—she's been pretty clear about that."

Grace's snowmobile clipped in front of mine on the way back. Rand was driving this time, me behind him. The gold-ringed top of the Honeyridge sign, lit up, appeared over the tree line. Since summer, the *y* and the *g* had burned out.

We lurched as Rand hit the hand brake. Over the engine, he said, "Sorry. Grace is stopping."

We pulled in close behind. Now we could see over the brick half-wall that circled the property. Three police cars were parked in the valet circle, sirens off but lights flashing.

Grace swung a leg over the snowmobile and peered across the parking lot. The glass doors spun and two cops came out, leading a boy in handcuffs. His head low, he didn't need to look up for me to know it was Neil.

Wesley laughed. "Couldn't be happening to more of a dick."

Rand was quick to hop off and go to Grace's side. "What do you think happened?"

One of the cops lifted his chin, shone a flashlight over the low wall.

Grace slipped back onto the first snowmobile. "That's our cue."

As Rand drove us away, I kept my arms tight around his waist, my heartbeat pounding fast against his back.

CHAPTER 18

WINTER

On top of my comforter, I lay awake with my hand over my thudding heart. If the police had taken Neil, Grace could be next.

Downstairs, the sound of Kevin and Wesley's horror movie seeped through the kitchen walls while the world outside went white. An actor screamed and the vibration of the TV speakers shook the framed baseball collectibles on the walls.

This place wasn't designed for this—horror movies at home with Kevin. I already missed Grace and Rand.

My feet hit the carpet. I looked out the window toward Rand's cabin, down by the water's edge. Rand had finally pointed it out to me, though I couldn't quite see it from my vantage point. But I could imagine the aluminum roof, shiny and reflecting the winter moon. I'd never been inside, even though he'd been here—this room—with me.

Up the dark road, beyond the snow-frosted trees, high in Grace's window was a taped sign: *2 a.m.*

As Wesley and I jogged down the trail to meet them, he glanced at me once, smiled, looked away.

"What?"

"Nothing," he said. "It's just—you're, like, happy here. Giddy. You should do things like this more. At home."

My feet slowed. "What do you mean?"

"Stuff," he called back, still running. "With friends."

"I have friends," I said. "Rand and Grace."

Wesley glanced back, opened his mouth to say something, then shrugged and ran on.

Snow blew hard in our faces as we charged across the winter-white forest, an hour into our middle-of-the-night hike. We'd left Rand's snowmobiles when the trees became too thick, at least thirty minutes before. Now I could barely feel my cheeks.

We could freeze to death. With the Fahrenheit dropped into the teens, it wouldn't have taken much to do us in. A wrong turn, a twisted ankle.

"What are we doing out here?" I called to Grace, hugging my warmest coat tighter. "Are we almost there?"

"There's no there," Grace said.

Wesley's teeth chattered. "So we're just what? Donner Party cosplaying?"

A snowball exploded against the tree beside us. We jumped apart.

Grace tucked another fat snowball tight between her palms and sent it sailing through the air. "People *have* died in these woods."

The ball exploded against Wesley's coat. He brushed the snow off his chest. "That's supposed to make me feel good about being out here?"

Grace smiled up at my brother, and then bolted ahead. Her beige boots were dark from melted snow and salt from the road. I kept forgetting to breathe as I watched her, waiting for a glimpse of the Grace I saw at the top of the mountain.

Rand pulled his hat down low over his ears and blew a breath into gloved hands. "We need to go back."

Wesley skipped ahead of me, slipped his hand inside Grace's. They rounded the corner by a crooked tree. Her boots slipped and she started to go down. He caught her, twisted her into his arms, and she laughed as he lowered her down, letting their noses brush until her feet touched the snow.

Rand came up behind me, his arms bunching his jacket close to his body. "We could push them off the edge and everybody would think it was an accident."

"Nobody would even question us." The cold on my teeth hurt when I smiled.

Rand gently squeezed my frozen fingers. My hand felt smaller inside his than it had the summer before. "Come on," he said.

We made it to a winter-white clearing in the middle of the forest, where Grace and Wesley had already stopped.

"You two are disgustingly cute." Grace's white smile flashed as she nodded to my hand in Rand's. "Does it snow where you live?" With bare, ungloved hands, she piled a heap of snow onto the ground. We didn't help her—not me and not Rand. But Wesley got in there, mounding snow as if the snowperson they were building would someday save the world.

"No," I said. "Never."

Wesley, taller now and wider in a muscular way that lifting tires all day could do, leaned over and kissed Grace. I'd seen him kiss Lauren a couple times—he didn't kiss her like this.

"Is that why you didn't bring your truck?" she asked. "Because you don't have chains?"

"Yep," Wesley said, his nose bright red at the tip.

I squeezed my eyes shut. He was lying to her; she was lying to him.

"Did anyone ever hear anything about Neil?" I asked.

Grace searched for pebbles to use for the snowperson's smile. She didn't answer.

Rand sighed. "What happened, Grace? Why did they arrest him?"

"Fine. You guys remember that girl, Candace?" she asked.

Rand and I looked at each other.

Grace pressed two round stones deep—shiny gray snowperson eyes. "They think he might have been involved," she said.

I stepped forward, feet sinking into unpacked snow. "They think he took her? We know that's not true. We saw her get into the car. Saw and heard. She left because she wanted to."

"Exactly," Grace said. "And that's the kind of truth that comes out on its own."

So many truths still to come out. I hadn't been sure I believed Grace when she'd said she didn't know Candace. Now I knew for certain she'd been lying.

"Wait," Wesley said. "So if we don't tell what we know about this girl, this guy Neil could end up in jail over something he didn't do?"

"Grace." Rand shook his head, eyes weary. "Grace, come on. Enough is enough."

A sharp look passed between them.

Grace sighed. "There's no reason to come forward. He's only a person of interest, and since he's innocent, there's not even the tiniest speck of evidence connecting him to her."

"We should have come forward that first night," I said.

The cold breeze picked up Grace's hair. She blinked through flying strands as she looked at me. "You know why we couldn't do that, Nora."

"No, I'm not sure I do anymore. Explain it to me," I said, and waited, finally, for the truth.

"I'm with Grace," Wesley said. "I mean, even if this does fuck up his winter a little, that guy is kind of a dick."

"Grace," I said. "How do you know all this anyway?"

"I have sources." Even Grace's teeth were chattering now. "Come on, Nora—think of Candace out there, staying out all night every night, living her life in bold neon colors. If we said something, they'd find her and drag her out of the sunlight, drag her back home."

Rand took Grace's hand, pulled her in the direction we'd come. "I hope she, at least, is someplace warm. It's too cold to be out here. Come on."

She shook him off. "Think of her passport collecting stamp after stamp. Think of it."

I wondered if this was the time to force Rand to talk to us, and to tell him the bad feeling I had about Neil, but he shook his head and disappeared through the wall of snowy pines, back the way we'd come.

Grace watched him, then faced my brother and me. "Just the three of us," she said. "And the cold." Her face cracked into an odd smile as she settled her attention on Wesley. "Are you still game to be the first we eat?"

Wesley didn't answer, just fell in step behind me.

Grace followed. "I guess we can't let him walk back alone."

CHAPTER 19

WINTER

Thursday, we'd followed hand-drawn maps—Grace had tucked them inside the books we were each reading—to icy West End Beach. Friday, we took snowmobiles across iced-over Donner Summit Bridge. On Saturday, Grace had wanted us to sleep out all night in the boathouse, but I'd gotten so cold, my lips were turning blue, and Rand insisted we all go home.

Now it was Sunday night, and with a screwdriver and a smirk, Grace broke into the projection area of a theater that showed classic movies. Our nights out in the cold had us relishing an adventure that didn't freeze us to the bone. Even if I didn't love breaking and entering.

The movie was *E.T.* I'd seen it a couple of times and so had Wesley and Rand, but Grace watched it with an intensity I'd never noticed in her, her eyes shiny with tears. In her determination to show us something wonderful, she'd managed to amaze herself. Wesley held Grace's hand, stroking his thumb over the back of her knuckles.

Past them was the empty place where Rand had been.

They didn't look away from the screen as I moved out of the projection room and down to the snowy sidewalk, where Rand's silhouette was shrinking into the distance.

I half ran, half jogged to catch up with him. "What's wrong?" I asked. He turned, and I tried to smile. "Don't worry. E.T. makes it home in the end."

Rand's lips twisted. "For a supposedly happy ending, it always makes me sad."

Home was supposed to be E.T.'s happy ending, but Rand was right—every time I watched it, that part rammed right through my heart. Going home meant leaving Elliot.

"That's not why you left, though," I said.

"I'm not even leaving. Just taking a walk. I—I shouldn't complain. I mean, it's just that I'm not looking forward to the car ride day after tomorrow."

Rand never revealed too much about himself, or the dark sadness that pressed down on him, especially in winter.

My feet stepped lightly toward him. "Maybe we need to make tonight even more amazing. What could we do?" I looked up toward the theater.

He laughed a little, a sad sound. "Oh God, let's not involve Grace." Shaking his head, he said, "She's making a huge mistake. Candace. This isn't something else she can finagle. I'm worried about her."

"What do you mean?" I asked. "Grace knows Candace. Doesn't she? Is—"

"Sorry." He rubbed his nose, sighed. "Let's let it go. It's time to head home again in a couple days. Forget about this, us. Until spring. God, that's never felt shittier."

"No, you're right, Rand. We made a mistake that first spring break, when we didn't tell. All the lies. It's— We have hard facts about Candace—about what happened that night."

"There are no facts," he said. "Only interpretations."

I didn't even ask.

His eyes narrowed, and he closed the gap between us. "Why did you say *all the lies?*"

I sighed. "It's just . . . Wesley. He's not a varsity baseball player. He didn't even make JV. He isn't the manager of the mechanic shop—he's barely a mechanic at all. The truck? If he had a truck, he couldn't even afford gas, let alone insurance. And Grace, she lies to him too."

Rand's eyebrows lifted. If it was surprise or confirmation, I couldn't tell.

"She—she's using Neil to get things. Paying him, I guess. Not that it was ever a secret. But last summer, she told Wesley she'd stopped. And she hasn't."

Rand squeezed his eyes shut.

"You knew all this?"

"Not exactly," he said. "But I'm not surprised. I've worried . . ."

"About what?"

"The four of us, how much can we share and also hold back. Do you—I don't even know how to feel about it. Do you think the lies make what we have here less real?"

"I—I don't know," I said. "Maybe." Then I met his eyes. "Do you lie too?"

He frowned. "No." He gestured to his watch. "Movie's over. It's time to go home."

Not just home for the night. Home until spring.

Grace and Wesley appeared on the sidewalk, walking under the streetlights, hyped up on theater candy swiped from the concession stand and humming the *E.T.* score.

Rand caught my hand, hard enough that my eyes went wide as they met his. Into my ear, he whispered, "Just because we said we wouldn't talk, doesn't mean we can't. Me and you."

"Wesley would tell her," I said.

"Then don't tell *him*," he said. "You and I are the only ones who have to know."

I thought about what it would be like to live without one hundred and seventy miles of separation. Traveling down telephone lines, through Internet waves, and bouncing around between satellites. We could have something that was only ours.

My blood pounded in my ears. I said, "Okay," and Rand's body relaxed.

Grace and Wesley raced ahead of us back to the snowmobiles, but Grace turned back halfway there. "Guys. *Guys.* I just realized— our next break is spring. The one-year anniversary of *us*." She flashed a smile, radiant. "Don't worry—I've got months to plan."

CHAPTER 20

WINTER

The messages had started out innocently enough.

One Friday night, just home from my new job, I had a DM from Rand pop up:

Am I breaking the laws of winter, spring, and summer if I tell you I love a woman in uniform?

He was talking about the pizzeria T-shirt and matching baseball cap I wore in the last picture I'd posted. That bright shiny feeling of spring, summer, and winter glowed through me. It outshone my embarrassment that he knew I worked at a pizza place.

My fingers fumbled to message back: *The laws of summer be damned.*

Two days later, Wesley and I were cleaning up dinner while Mom napped on the couch when my phone rang. *That name.* No caller ID had ever before been so beautiful.

"It's work," I said to Wesley, my fingers covering the screen. "Can you finish up?" He gave me a look, and I wondered if he somehow knew the truth. If he did, he went back to drying and let me go into my room and say "Hello?"

"Greetings from the real world." Rand's bright smile was in his voice. "Is this an okay time?"

"It's fine. Everything's fine. What—what's going on?"

"Something of the utmost importance . . . *Fight Club* is on. You've got me analyzing it in new ways. If we're all characters in the movie, Grace is definitely Tyler and Wesley is Marla."

I laughed. "Oh and he'd just *love* that comparison."

"But I've been trying to figure out—who are we?"

"Maybe you and I aren't in *Fight Club*. Maybe we're from, I don't know . . . *E.T.*"

"Well, I always did identify a lot with Elliot. Not just because we share the same name—his first, my last."

"Wait. Does that make me E.T.?"

"In the most charming way," he said. "Big beautiful eyes. A glowing ember-like finger."

I laughed.

"This is actually making being back home kind of okay," he said. "Talking to you."

I smiled into the phone. "Not so terrible being in the real world together, is it?"

We didn't hang up until the sun rose over the dry grass outside my bedroom window.

"I—I'm failing Algebra II," Rand said as I moved down the hallway to my bedroom that Friday night. "My parents—they're actually getting me a tutor."

The door shut behind me and I took a deep breath. "And you're delighted?"

"Thrilled. Relieved. At dinner, all they could talk about was me. All the philosophical texts in the world can't help me make sense of today."

I curled into my bed, hugged a pillow against my chest. "If Nietzsche can't provide the answer, we're doomed."

"If Nietzsche *is* our answer, we're doomed," he said.

"You know you're betraying your guru."

"Not mine." He paused. "I'd heard my dad say those things all of his life. He was searching, I think. Then a couple years ago, he stopped searching. I don't know why. But it was like he passed the torch to me. If he wasn't trying to process the world around him, then I guess I thought it was my job. And I'm more of an Aristotle guy."

My door slipped open, and there was Mom with her eyes squinting at the light from my lamp and her hand against her forehead. "Two pills just aren't cutting it," she said. "Do you know where that new bottle went?"

"Hang on," I said to Rand. From inside my backpack, I pulled out the fresh white paper bag from Walgreens and spun the bottle cap open. "I picked them up today." I'd been holding on to the prescription for a week. I doled out a single pill. "Try just one more for now."

"It's going to take more than that, Nora," she said before she dry-mouth swallowed.

"Just for now," I said.

As the door closed, I said into the phone, "That wasn't as bad as it sounded."

"Nora," Rand said.

"I know—I'm doing the best I can. I know I need to get her help. I just—I need to figure it out." We were silent a beat. I said, "Rand, if we let each other see the awful stuff, what if there isn't room for the rest? What if we crowd it all out with real life?"

He was quiet. Then he said, "Maybe we will. Crowd it out. But remember what you tried to tell Grace in the mountains? The hurt comes with us. So what's the point in ignoring it?"

Rand's texts seeped into my time back home. The little things got me through the day—what he ate for breakfast (usually an omelet he cooked himself); where he went to eat lunch at school (the library because he could be quiet without people thinking he was weird); what he thought about while his parents argued through dinner (the feel of Donner sunlight on his face). I had a twinge of guilt that we had something separate from Grace and Wesley. But I needed this.

As I pulled my hair back into a bun one night, my phone dinged. A text from Rand:

Truth or Dave?

I smiled.

Work had called and wanted me to come back in. Overtime. Time and a half meant more phone cards, more minutes I could buy to tide me over until spring.

Dave, I wrote back. *Definitely Dave. I assume he's your evil twin brother.*

Another ding. *Right. Totally meant Dave. It's a variation on the popular game. I invented it . . . basically now. You name a favorite*

Dave and explain why. If you can't, you're stuck with truth.

I laughed and a new text popped up. *Donner Party documentary at 9pm.*

I checked the time. The city bus was running in less than five minutes. I had to hurry. As I threw my uniform on, I texted back *K.* When I dropped into a too-warm seat on the bus, my phone started ringing. I picked up.

"You texted *K* instead of *OK*," Rand said. "What's going on?"

"Sorry to omit the all-important *O.* I got called into work and was in a rush."

"Okay, this won't take long, but I have something to tell you. I've—I've been thinking about what you said about the awful stuff."

"Yeah?"

"We don't have to let it fill us up. Not if we don't want to."

"I don't want to," I said. My grin was so big, the girl across from me was staring.

"Neither do I." As the bus squealed to a stop, he said, "I'll let you go. Remember, *two more weeks.*"

Two more weeks until spring vacation. Smiling into the phone, I said, "K."

My steps were light and quick as I walked the block to work. In front of the neon OPEN sign, my feet slowed. It would be our anniversary—the four of us. I didn't know what that meant exactly. Only that wherever home was for her, Grace would be plotting.

WINTER: NOW

CHAPTER 21

Rand gripped the doorframe, blood and snow matting his eyebrows.

I reached out. His skin was like ice. "Rand, what happened?"

"Crashed the snowmobile," he said through chattering teeth. "Lost control on some ice about three hundred yards from here. I—I passed out. I don't know how long."

"What the fuck's he doing back here?" Wesley asked from the kitchen. "You got some sack, man, walking in here after—" He saw the blood. "Shit. What happened?"

"Get inside." I grabbed a blanket off the back of the sofa and threw it around Rand's shoulders before I pushed him down onto the couch. He flinched as I pulled apart the gash on his forehead to check the depth of the wound. Blood rushed from it. "You need a couple stitches."

"It's not worth wasting an ambulance," Rand said. "Lots of accidents tonight. They likely couldn't get through to us anyway."

"Do we have anything here?" Wesley asked. "Gauze or something?"

"First aid kit's in the bathroom, under the sink," I said.

I filled a hot mug with soup from the stove, wishing we'd tried to build a fire with what little green wood we had. We'd been saving it in case the power went out and we lost the heater.

"Drink it." I mashed his icy hands around the steaming ceramic. "We—Kevin couldn't make it back with the groceries. It's slightly expired chicken noodle."

Rand shook as he pulled the mug to his mouth. "It's great. Worth getting botulism."

Wesley dropped to his knees beside the coffee table, spreading out the first aid kit and a container of rubbing alcohol. "When'd this happen?"

"Right after I left here." Rand held his mug as if it might jump away. "It was closer to walk back here than to go all the way to my parents' place on foot. They're away—Reno for the night." He looked to the darkening window. "I could try a little later maybe—"

"No," I said. "You couldn't get back there before dark. You've got a head injury and you're freezing. You'll stay here."

Rand eyed me as I cleaned and bandaged the wound. It was a look I'd enjoyed so many times before, but now it made me unsure.

"I'm very sorry, Nora," he said quietly.

I paused briefly. I didn't know what he meant. All the past that stood between us—what we did, what we didn't do, the night Grace disappeared, all the things he didn't say.

He had a lot to be sorry for. We all did.

"I meant—that I didn't mean to end up stranded on your door-step," he said. Then he reached over and squeezed my hand.

I uncurled his fingers from mine. Rand couldn't be trusted. And neither could Wesley.

"Don't be sorry," I said, standing. "Now we all get to catch up. Or maybe you two would like me to leave so you can really reconnect. You know how I love being kept in the dark."

Three of us together under one roof for the night. One of our foursome missing—still missing. For a second, I allowed myself to imagine Grace here, legs draped over the arm of Kevin's easy chair, like I cut her out of our summers, winters, and springs and pasted her into the scene.

With the boys around, I didn't know how to keep looking for answers. And I hadn't found a single one yet.

Lights flickered. A sparkling aura fell over the house for a few seconds. Then a black whoosh rushed through the room. The TV went dark, the hum of the fridge and the lights cut out, and we were standing in evening grayness. There was only the sound of our breaths.

"Power's out," Rand said.

Wesley hadn't moved from the couch. "Thanks, Captain Obvious."

"Cover the windows," I told them. "And the gaps under the doors. We should trap as much heat as we can."

Wesley rose from the couch, his rangy limbs loose in his too-big coat. "It'll be back on soon."

"It might not be," I said. "We don't know."

Within ten minutes we'd used up the few blankets and towels we could easily grab. Still, there were windows uncovered and drafts coming in.

"What do we do?" Rand asked.

My gaze shot up. "There's some old bedding and towels in the attic." I hadn't tackled cleaning out the attic. Not yet. "Hang on."

I went upstairs and used a broom to trigger the latch on the pull-down stairs outside the bathroom. The attic steps creaked under my feet. I felt the weight of someone climbing behind me.

Rand was halfway up. "I'm coming with you."

"There's no reason."

That didn't stop him.

In the darkness, I grabbed a flashlight from the spot on the floor where we always kept one. A circle of light lit up the far side of the attic. Board games were stacked waist high as I scooted my feet over the plywood. Old plastic baby dolls covered in bits of marker and owned by second cousins I'd never met and trucks missing wheels were piled into open cardboard boxes.

I'd always assumed they were toys from when Kevin was a kid. But I'd never asked.

Rand's breaths warmed the air behind me, and I felt his hand on my shoulder. A sense of calm radiated from his palm and down my back. Still, I inched away. "Easy, Professor."

A pained sound escaped his throat. "I wish you wouldn't call me that." The weariness of the last year was fully apparent in the way his shoulders fell then. "Where are the blankets?"

"The far side, I think. Follow me." My flashlight drifted over them. "Careful."

Rand opened the drawer of an old dresser as he passed by.

"Not in there," I said. "This way."

"Was Grace ever here? In the attic?"

I looked up, then away. The thought had occurred to me too. But I didn't want to get my own hopes up. "Not that I'm aware. But with Grace, you never know."

I pulled some old bedding from a box and piled it into Rand's arms. As I did, his eyes caught mine. "Don't you wonder?" he asked. "Aren't you ever back home and you're trying to focus on an algebra problem, or you're making a pizza at work, or you're supposed to be enjoying the book you're reading, and your mind just, I don't know—wanders?"

I sighed as I dug through a second box. "Of course I do."

"Because when I'm back home," he went on, "I may be planted in a desk at school or in my car or whatever, but I can't stop wondering what could have happened to Grace."

"Don't talk like that," I whispered.

"Nora." He raised his hand to my shoulder, hesitated. I didn't move. "May I?" he asked.

"Yes," I said, because I wanted to. In that moment, I wanted just a little of what we used to have.

I felt the familiar weight of his hand, the jerk of my pulse against his thumb, his blood against mine. His hand slid lower until it sat right over my heart. I pressed my hand over his. I'd missed how it felt to touch him, to have him touch me.

"You knew her as well as I did," he said.

I huffed. "Did I?"

"Oh, come on. Tell me you can't let go of her that easily. Tell me you can't make your brain turn off and stop wondering."

I can't, I wanted to scream. My fingers closed around his hand, and I pulled him away from me. "The trouble with that is that I *didn't* know Grace. Just like we didn't really know each other— you and me. None of us did, because we didn't let us."

I sat on an old trunk. "Wherever Grace is," I said, "it's some- where she wanted to be. Like Candace. You and Wesley didn't hear the way she was talking that night."

"Like Candace," he said. "Really?"

My guilt had been filling me slowly; now it felt ready to burst. I'd fed Grace's obsession with telling stories about Candace. I'd enjoyed it too much.

"Grace is out there now," I said. "Floating through the world and hopefully keeping herself distracted and busy and curious enough to be happy."

Rand, his arms still loaded with blankets, lowered down beside me. "How do you feel about that?"

"I feel like my time to help Grace was seasons ago." I'd give anything to go back to the day I found her crying on the dock. "But I didn't know how to help her. You made sure of that."

Rand recoiled. "I said I was sorry, Nora. In texts and DMs and voicemails. I would have sent a carrier pigeon if I thought it would do any good."

I ripped the blankets out of his arms and headed toward the stairs.

"I talked to the Lombardis," he said.

"What?" I spun to face him. "When?"

"See, you do care," he said. "I drove to Henderson."

I blinked. "Henderson?"

"Where Grace was from. Henderson, Nevada. I told them I was Grace's friend and that I wanted to know what was happening with the investigation. I don't think they believed me at first—when I said I was her friend. I didn't know things about her that I should have known."

"Huge surprise," I said.

"They talked to me anyway. Maybe they believed me, maybe they didn't. Either way, they were desperate for answers."

"What were they like—the Lombardis?"

"Separated. The divorce will be final in the fall, or that's what Mr. Lombardi hopes. Later, they met me at a coffee shop—together. They thought since I was Grace's friend that maybe I'd heard from her. Missing girls usually reach out to someone eventually."

"Well, we know Candace did," I said.

"Nora, um, if Grace has contacted you, do you hate me too much to tell me?"

"No, and she hasn't—" And then all at once I got it. Rand thought I didn't care about where Grace went because I already *knew*.

I sighed. "Anyway, if she was going to seek anyone out, we both know it would be you. And I hate that."

His shoulders fell. "I know."

"No you don't."

My tears started to fall.

"I know you, Nora. You can tell me I don't, but saying it won't make it true." He tipped his head back, then looked at me. "We fucked up a million times when we kept quiet about Candace. We can't do it again—this time it's Grace who's gone."

I turned away. "I've been looking," I said. "Out of all of us, I was the one who should have found something. I was the last to see her that day."

Rand pulled away, searching my eyes as he blinked. "No"—he shook his head—"you weren't. I was."

SPRING: YEAR TWO

CHAPTER 22

Stepping tentatively onto the rooftop of the Honeyridge that first night back, I gripped my jacket tighter and peered into the darkness. The hotel's sign was dark. And the overcast sky above washed out the stars and the moon. Only the lights from faraway houses speckled the black.

I hadn't expected Grace to lead us here, not after everything that had happened with Neil over the winter. He'd made bail—I read it online—but that was all I knew. For the first time, I didn't want an adventure. I just wanted to be with my friends and know they were safe.

Rand stayed close to the door, giving me knowing sideways smiles. My pulse raced. I wasn't just worried about Grace's anniversary surprise. With the secrets Rand and I shared, it felt like a dozen tiny truths were threatening to burst out of me.

Wesley and I walked out a few steps. Bright lights shot on. I blinked and shaded my eyes.

Grace slowly came into focus wearing a pointed party hat and blowing a kazoo. Around her was a spread of oysters and clams—and this time, Skittles and a bottle of red wine. She tossed a handful of confetti into the air and clapped her hands. "Happy anniversary."

My heartbeat slowed.

Laughing, Wesley stormed forward and lifted Grace into a twirl.

"That sweater," Grace said to me as her feet touched down. "It never looked like that on me." She hugged me. "I'm glad it's yours."

"Are you sure you don't want it back?" I asked. "It's cold up here."

She laughed. "I'm immune to the cold. Immortal."

"Brava, Grace," Rand said, still hanging back. "We are anything but underwhelmed."

"Excellent," Grace said, but she gave me a wink I didn't know how to interpret. "Eat up."

After we'd eaten everything but the Skittles, Grace sat on the rooftop ledge, her back to the sky, looking down at Wesley and me, and Rand a few feet beyond. "Truth or dare, Wesley," she said. "And don't be boring."

"Truth," Wesley said.

Grace straightened up. "If you could make a map to anywhere, where would it take you?"

Wesley smiled to himself, then got up and unzipped her jacket, only an inch. His finger brushed a crisscross pattern over her heart. "X marks the spot."

Grace's cheeks glowed pink. Looking away, she said, "Good answer."

She poured more wine into Wesley's cup, but he held out his hand. "Not too much. I have to be up early tomorrow. Fishing."

"Ugh. Nora, you're lucky Rand doesn't fish." She swung her feet and let the heels of her flats bounce against the wall of the ledge. Wesley climbed up next to her, letting his shoes slip off. "Okay, Rand," she said, "you go. Ask anyone."

"Okay," Rand said. "Wesley, truth or Dave?"

I cringed. Rand clamped a hand over his mouth.

"Dave?" Wesley asked. "Who's Dave?"

Grace pushed her hair out of her eyes and looked between Rand and me. "It's almost like Nora already knows."

"It's just a game I made up," Rand said. "Told Nora about it, when was that—like last summer? You either tell the truth or answer with your favorite person named Dave."

"Your favorite Dave?" Wesley asked. "I don't even know a Dave."

"Make one up," Grace said. "An amazing Dave."

"Or a celebrity would work," Rand said dryly.

"David Tennant," Wesley said, the last of his wine sloshing out of his cup. "Because he wanted to be an actor just so he could be Doctor Who. And then he fucking did it."

"He goes by David, not Dave," I said, taking a handful of Skittles from Grace.

Rand lifted his chin toward Wesley and said, "It counts. It definitely counts."

"Of course it counts," Wesley said. "The Tenth Doctor is the jam." He stood and moved to the ice chest, but his foot made a squishing sound.

He stopped, looked down at his shoe, then took another slippery step.

"What the hell?" he said. "Is my sock, like, wet?"

Grace threw her head back, laughing. "I may have—" Holding her stomach, she leaned forward, barely able to speak through her laughter. "I may have spilled my drink."

"In my shoe?" Wesley asked, limping as he started to laugh. "Really, Grace?"

I bent over, gripped by silent giggles. Rand whooped. The four of us were everything we'd always been. Maybe it'd all be okay.

Red wine did the boys in early. They napped together on the picnic blanket while Grace and I sat on the rooftop ledge eating Skittles. I stared down into the parking lot, remembering that first night, that first spring.

"Did Neil get you a key again?" I asked. "What did that cost?"

"Why are you always trying to spoil the mystery, Nora?"

"How is he?"

She rolled her eyes. "He'll be almost off the hook in no time. Like I said he'd be, right?"

"Really?"

"Remember that first night on the Honeyridge?" she said. "He killed the security cameras. Not for Candace—for us."

I looked at Grace. "What are you talking about exactly?"

Grace shrugged. "Some investigator with a hard-on for Candace's case thinks it looks questionable."

"Grace," I said. "Does he have some kind of, I don't know, defense?"

"Of course he does. He's telling them the hotel periodically turns off the cameras for maintenance. It was a coincidence it happened the same night. His dad owns the Honeyridge. He'll cover for him."

"But what if the cops see through that?" I asked. "People lie for their kids all the time. Any good investigator will know that. What if this comes back to us? To you?"

"You're so imaginative, Nora. I love that about you." Grace took a sip of her water, looking over at the boys, sleeping. "They're adorable like that," she said. "Like toddlers after a good story-time." She passed me the bottle of water. "I hope Wesley isn't boring this spring, always fishing. Always where we're not."

"Hm . . . Do you ever think about him when you're home?"

Maybe I was high on red dye number forty, but I suddenly, desperately wanted to tell her what had happened between winter and now. I wanted her to know that Rand and I had jokes and our own nights that stretched into mornings and how we were us because she'd asked me to follow her up that hill a year ago.

"Why?" Grace laughed. "Does Wesley think about me? He shouldn't."

Maybe Wesley did or maybe he didn't. Lauren was never too far from him when we were at school, and sometimes they went out on weekends. He never had her over, though.

But I hadn't invited anyone over to our house either.

"I don't pretend to know what Wesley thinks about," I said. "Do you miss him? When you're home?"

"Never," she said. "Wesley is for here. Not there."

"What about home makes him so unfit?"

She looked at me. "Wesley isn't the one who's unfit for home. Home is unfit for him."

With the sky lightening, we started to clean up our mess, until I caught Wesley blinking into the distance. "What the hell is that?"

I looked over my shoulder, trying to figure out what he was staring at. Something bright and colorful was lodged in the *o* of the Honeyridge sign.

"That," Grace said, "is Rand's gift."

Rand's eyes went wide before he flashed a bright smile. "You fucking keep it, Grace."

"That's going to make your life very difficult," she said. "Your cell phone is in that bag."

"Oh, come on!" he said, his palms slapping the rooftop.

I didn't know when she'd taken his phone—we'd all drifted off to sleep at one point, but this was too far.

"Grace." I turned to look at her. "What's going on? That's just plain mean."

Grace stepped back as if I'd slapped her. "No, it's not. If you think that, you don't get it at all. Last year when we were up here, Rand didn't get anywhere near the edge. Now he's closer than ever. It's called exposure therapy. I googled it. He does this and he can conquer his fear for good."

"Do you have insurance on the phone?" Wesley asked.

Rand shook his head. "No, and even if I did, eventually the Honeyridge is going to have to rid their *o* of a gift bag and find my phone. My parents will love hearing me explain."

Wesley glanced over at him. "It's okay, man. I got it."

"Really?" Grace stuck out her lower lip. "So much for exposure therapy."

As Wesley threw a leg over the edge, I thought of Grace out there placing the bag while we slept. Whatever Grace had done to get it in there had been dangerous.

"Thanks," Rand said, looking uncomfortable. "Thank you, Wesley."

"Don't mention it," Wesley said, climbing toward the giant *H*.

His fingers hooked the bag. Then I heard a crunch. A snap.

Wesley yelled out, dropped.

I ran to the edge. One arm hooked around the *H,* Wesley dangled below. I stretched for his hand but couldn't reach. On my other side, Grace flailed her arms out. "Wesley!" Her hands dragged through the air. "Oh my god!"

Someone pulled at my shoulder from behind.

"Let me." Rand squeezed in, reaching his long arms down. Behind him, Grace was saying, "I'm sorry, I'm sorry," over and over.

He fisted the shoulder of Wesley's jacket—got him high enough that I could grab him too. Together we pulled Wesley back over. They collapsed on the rooftop, and I looked down, down, down at the bag, exploded on the asphalt below.

Grace bent low beside the boys. She cradled Wesley's head, whispered something. Her attention turned to Rand and she put her hand on his knee.

Knocking it away, Rand stood and walked to the rooftop door. "You've gone too fucking far, Grace."

"It wasn't supposed to happen like that," she said.

Cheeks red and eyes wild, he said, "Of course it wasn't, but it did! You can't make me conquer this. You can't fix me any more than you can fix yourself."

Rand left through the door, and I went to follow him, then doubled back to where Wesley sat, rubbing his shoulder.

"Are you okay?"

"I don't know. When I caught myself I—" Gritting his teeth, he groaned. "I might have dislocated it."

"I'm taking him to an urgent care," I said to Grace, before I looked around. "Clean up."

Eyes brimming, Grace said, "Okay."

I got him up and helped move him down the stairs, but he stopped. "I'm not mad at Grace." He looked at me. "You shouldn't be either."

I huffed a dry laugh. "Let's go."

I thought back to that first night again, one year ago almost to the day, when we first talked about the Donner Party, joked about who we'd eat first.

"Well, the choice is easy," Grace had said. *"Wesley has* already *volunteered."*

I thought of Wesley dangling from the ski lift. Now this. In a way, Wesley had been first. I wondered which of us would be next.

Late that afternoon, I knocked on Rand's door, stood back, smoothed my T-shirt.

Rand, eyes tired, answered the door.

"Sorry I didn't check on you sooner," I said. "Wesley dislocated his shoulder. We've been at urgent care."

"I'm sorry. I didn't know—"

"It wasn't *your* fault," I said.

Something clanged behind him, and he glanced over his shoulder before he stepped out onto the porch. "Come on. Let's walk."

We moved along the trail, and Rand was quieter than usual. As we reached the edge of the lake, he pulled something out of his pocket. His phone—or more like the pieces that remained.

"Oh shit," I said.

"It's—it's not a big deal," he said. "It's not like Wesley's shoulder. Besides, I get to come up with a good story to tell at the AT&T store back home."

I tried to smile. "Have you, um, seen Grace?" I knew she had to feel guilty—and rightfully so—but that didn't mean I wanted her to suffer.

He gave a somber nod. "We're—almost okay. I told her I need some space. I told my family I want to drive back tomorrow, not Friday."

"Tomorrow?" My throat seized up. I wouldn't see him until summer.

He cringed. "She's sorry. Of course she is. I just need some time. I think the more desperate she feels, the more she pulls this stuff."

"The more desperate? Like nearly killing my brother?"

"She wasn't trying to kill him. She was trying to kill me—well, the old me, is what she'd say. The one who was—is—afraid." He sighed. "Maybe she's still trying to kill the old Grace too."

"The old Grace," I said.

"Look, I want to respect her wishes—her privacy. But I also don't want you to hate her."

"I don't *hate* her." The sound of our steps turned hollow—we were on the dock. "I just—I don't understand."

Rand took a deep breath. "Grace, she was living a pretty impressive online life when I met her. But I think that was the only place her life was impressive. From what I know, she was tormented a lot at school. Online—I think that was her way of escaping. Kids found out and something happened. That's when she took down all her accounts. That was the summer when she came back here and sort of . . . *became* the girl she'd been online."

"And who is Grace back home now?"

Rand shrugged.

I looked over the lake. "If you see her again, tell her I'm not mad, okay?"

"You're not going to see her yourself?"

"With you gone, it's not like I want to be the third wheel."

Rand shifted, not meeting my eyes. "It . . . may be a while before you and I talk again."

I folded my arms even though it wasn't cold. "What does that mean?"

"Nora." He shuffled his feet. "When we get home, maybe we shouldn't keep this up. Constant contact."

The dock felt like it was giving way under me. *"Rand."*

"It's not you. But you know that—you should know that. Right now, I just need some time away from this place and these stupid . . . adventures, or whatever they are."

The ache in my throat built to a burn. "And me?"

He rubbed his hands down his face. "The four of us. And anyway, maybe it would be good for you too."

"Look at me and tell me what that means."

He exhaled, long and slow. "We've talked enough that I know you don't have—I mean, maybe if I'm not taking up all your time, it'll be easier to make friends at home."

"I have friends," I said, my anger forcing its way into my voice. "Sasha and Bailey invite me to things."

Rand's shoulders sunk. "Nora, that's not—I mean, is it like things are here with Grace and me, and Wesley?"

"That's not fair," I said, grabbing his arm. "Home is home and it's never going to be like it is here."

He took my hands into his. "But do you laugh with them? Do they call you? Do you call them? Do you all love the same movie or song? Do you really *talk*?"

Each question was a brick placed on my chest.

He squeezed his eyes shut. "Nora. My god. Sorry. I just—I worry I'm holding you back. Us—it's supposed to, I don't know, enrich our at-home life. I'm afraid it's replacing yours."

Maybe I was the one holding him back. "It's okay," I said, swallowing hard. "You're right. We won't text. We won't call. We'll go back to—how it was."

He grit his teeth. "I don't love it either. But I think we should try it."

"Yeah, we'll try," I said, pulling away. "It's only a few months."

We walked back to Kevin's cabin with me trying to stay a few steps ahead. I didn't want to talk. At the same time, I didn't want these words to be our last until summer.

"Hey, um." Rand took my hand as we closed in on Kevin's cabin. "I'll see you."

Our fingers slipped apart as I leaned back. He reached over, squeezed my thumb inside his palm, coaxing me back.

"I'm sorry," he said. "Nora, I—"

"I know," I said. "Me too."

I pulled him in, and a brush of our lips turned deeper, hungrier, a kiss that would have to last three cold, lonely months. Then my hand was empty except for his warmth, still radiating inside my palm.

CHAPTER 23

SPRING

Back home, Mom moved us into another duplex with Sheet-rock walls. "There's a yard," she'd said, as if that made it an upgrade from the apartment. She failed to mention the single bedroom, the dead grass, and the neighbors next door who revved their car engines till three a.m.

Without Rand's texts and calls, I took his advice and started hanging out with Sasha and Bailey. They were obsessed with an older boy who worked at Guide's Mechanic shop, and they'd sit on a picnic table across the street at Riley Park and watch him work after school.

While we ate Froyos, I wished we had secrets to share. Inside jokes. I missed Grace and Rand and the last days of the break that should have been ours. Not weighed down inside the cabin, wishing already for a summer to undo something that maybe couldn't be undone.

* * *

A boy named Chase moved to Gridley a couple weeks before prom.

"How do you make this thing work," he said into the air in chem lab as he shook his Bunsen burner.

I made it light up and stepped back to work on my own project.

"You want a partner?" he asked, pushing his sandy brown hair off his forehead and quirking his head to the side. "Or do you like being alone?" I enjoyed the slight tease in his voice, the way he searched my expression for a reaction.

I was fine on my own, but still I told him, "I'll work with you."

As we handed in our conclusions, he said, "I really can't believe you don't have a boyfriend."

His eyes were blue, reflecting the glowing flame. I liked the way he looked at me, I liked feeling known in my real-life world.

A couple days later, I was standing by my locker, watching Wesley hold the door for his girlfriend, when Chase came up behind me.

"Hey," he said. "Hey, you want to go to prom or something?"

I'd never gone to a school dance or barely even a football game—those were on Fridays and Saturdays, the busiest days at work. I needed the tips. A surplus to cover electric and rent, for when Mom couldn't make it into the department store where she worked or the day we dreaded the most—when her boss finally had enough.

Wesley, moving through the hallway, was half smiling as he held Lauren's hand. Maybe I needed to be a little more him and a little less me.

Maybe a life couldn't be lived in only a few weeks of summers, winters, and springs.

"Sure," I said to Chase.

We weren't supposed to be in the parking lot after first period had started, but Chase had a song he wanted me to hear.

Skipping class felt elicit—not quite like riding shut-down ski lifts on a summer night or breaking into the Honeyridge pool, but a small taste of that.

Besides, there wasn't much else to do in town. We'd gone bowling with Sasha and Bailey and a couple other guys, but I couldn't relax surrounded by so many people I didn't know.

Now Chase tapped the volume until I felt the car speakers vibrate against my leg.

"It's kind of a long intro," he said, voice loud over the music. "Give it a minute and it'll really take off."

"It's pretty," I said, then realized that wasn't what a guy like him wanted to hear.

My phone lit up on the dash.

"It's probably my mom," I said to Chase as I reached for it.

Dave Grohl of the Foo Fighters broke his leg onstage once. And finished the show!

Officially the best Dave, I texted back, my whole body lit up, tingling.

A breathless second later: *Is there such a thing as too much space? Because it feels like there is. You feel a world away.*

I exhaled as I typed. *No. A galaxy.*

"Nora," Chase said. "*Nor-uh.* You're not even listening to the song."

I set my phone screen-down in my lap. "Sorry."

I wasn't sorry at all.

The day of prom, after I'd wasted a paycheck on a beautiful blush-colored gown and told Wesley we could live on ramen for a while, Chase called me. He said he had a family emergency and needed to go out of town.

Wesley was outside wrestling with the lawn mower that wouldn't start—the landlord said if we didn't clean up the front yard by the end of the weekend, we were out. Mom was banging around the kitchen, searching for a bottle, any bottle, that would rattle with the sound of her pills.

It was all too much, and I slipped out the back door and walked to the fence. There were loose boards at the bottom. I scraped up my leg getting through them. On the other side, where nothing existed except a green weedy field, I let myself cry.

My phone vibrated against my hip, and I answered without looking—it could have been Chase saying everything was fine and he could go. "Hello?" I said, probably a little wobbly.

"Are you okay?" Rand's voice.

I took a deep breath and wiped at my cheeks. "Just getting some fresh air."

"You're crying. What happened? Is it your mom?"

I told him everything, and the line was quiet for a long time. He asked, "So this douche-canoe, Chase, you want me to kick his ass for you?"

I laughed at the image of him trying.

He paused. "I wasn't joking."

"It wouldn't make anything better."

A beat later, he said, "Let me take you to the dance."

I rolled my eyes. "Oh, yeah, great idea."

Rand in my high school, mingling with kids who wore athletic shoes with their prom tuxes, swapping philosophies—he'd be so out of place, they'd think he was from a movie.

"Nah, I'll love it," Rand said. "I'll drive up from Walnut Creek. I'll spike the punch and everything. The whole shebang."

I laughed. "You'll be crowned king and I'll be queen."

"Precisely," he said. "We'll have loyal subjects."

We talked until I heard Wesley rolling the lawn mower into the garage, motioning me in for dinner. "See you soon," I said, barely believing it, wondering if it was real.

That evening, after the sun went down but the sky was still gray, I answered the door wearing jeans and a white crewneck sweater. There was Rand.

He stood on my porch in a burgundy velvet tuxedo with satin lapels. The sleeves were too short and he looked like a pimp from the seventies.

I could barely form words, but I managed, "Nice monkey suit."

He grabbed on to the lapels and did a turn. "Well, thank you. I arrived in this fine town without remembering I lacked proper formal wear. Thankfully, the thrift store down the street from your house had this baby for the bargain price of twelve dollars. What do you think?"

I felt my eyes fill. "It's so versatile," I said. "Day to night in the blink of an eye."

A TV turned on behind me and Rand glanced into the house.

A look passed between us, and we both understood that I wouldn't invite him inside, and he wouldn't ask.

Wesley came out of the bathroom with his arm still in a sling and fiddling with his cummerbund. "How the fuck am I supposed to buckle this thing?" His shoes squeaked against the tile as he stopped too fast and noticed Rand there. On our porch. In Gridley.

"You're a splendid-looking penguin," Rand said.

"You too, bro. You're a splendid-looking . . ." He ran his eyes over Rand's head-to-toe burgundy. "Well, you're something, all right." Wesley shot me a wide-eyed look, then straightened up. "You shouldn't be here."

"Nora was in need of a date," Rand said. "I was happy to oblige."

Wesley huffed. "Well, should I call Grace then and make it an even foursome?"

"I think you've already got a date," Rand said.

Wesley's attention snapped to me—accusing—then went back to Rand. "It's not just that. It's us, the three of us here without her. What will she do when she finds out?"

"She won't. You won't tell her," I said.

"So, we're supposed to what?" he asked. "The three of us go to prom together and then sit around making up stories about walking on the moon and shit. Without Grace?"

"You have your secrets too," I said.

His face contorted. "Lauren? That's not the same at all. Grace doesn't *want* to know."

"She isn't going to want to know about this, either," I said.

"What? You want me to just pretend this didn't happen?"

"Why not? I'm going to pretend Lauren isn't happening."

Rand slid between us, his hand on Wesley's chest. "Nora, just go change. We'll wait."

"But—"

"I got this," Rand said.

Before the front door shut, I heard Rand say, "Look, I know you love her, but there are things about Grace you don't understand . . ." They moved off, their voices fading.

When I came outside again, Wesley looked at Rand. Then me. Then Rand again and motioned to his arm sling. "For the record, Lauren thinks I did this mountain biking."

The velvet of Rand's tuxedo sleeve was soft against my skin as we walked up the steps to the dance. All the way from the school parking lot into the gym, my feet didn't touch the ground. They sailed over the asphalt.

As we stood in line outside to take our photos, Rand leaned forward and said to Lauren, "I have to apologize to you for ruining your pictures, Lauren. This guy is a maniac on a mountain bike, but I led him down the wrong trail."

Smiling her shockingly white smile, Lauren laughed and squeezed Wesley's arm. "The sling will give our pictures character."

"A little pizzazz," Rand said. "I knew I liked you."

Wesley glanced over his shoulder. "You look really pretty, Nora. Enjoy yourself."

He hadn't said he'd keep it from Grace, but I knew he would.

I wondered what Rand had told him.

Rand rubbed one of his lapels. "Your peach dress is going to look amazing with this burgundy. Maybe it's not the most natural combination, but I think we're about to start a trend. And you look just . . . wow."

Lauren turned back to me and whispered, "I like your friend."

She looked a little bit like Cinderella on Wesley's arm, hair in an updo that made her neck look longer, and dressed in an ice-blue gown. She was the type of girl who had Audrey Hepburn quotes on the walls of her room and who smiled at everyone she passed in the hall. Some people said she was too nice for Wesley. But those people only knew one Wesley.

As he and Lauren took their pictures, I asked Rand, "What do you think of Lauren?"

He blinked enough times that I could tell he knew what I was really asking. "She's sunshine," he said. "She's no Grace."

Then we walked into the dance, and the weight of reality crushed me into the floor. Chase was there with Sasha. She crossed her arms, a challenge. A gathering flock of stares turned my way, everyone waiting for something to happen.

"That's Chase," I said. "With my friend. Everyone knows. Everyone's looking at us."

In a distant way, I wondered if I'd done this to myself. Too dreamy, too distracted, too anxious to leave them all and get back to Donner.

"That's not it," Rand whispered. "They're looking at me, I promise. It's this fine tux."

I took his hand and led him toward the stage. I couldn't look at him. It wasn't what happened—Chase throwing me over for Sasha—it was that Rand knew. I felt sick.

The metal stairs clanked under my high heels as we climbed to the stage and disappeared behind the curtain. My hand shook inside of his, but he squeezed back until my fingers stilled.

The music and the rumble of footsteps below were faint. He blew into his palms as if it were fifty degrees instead of eighty.

"They were all so envious of us," he said. "You can tell. And the music isn't so loud back here. It would be annoying. Out there."

I took a breath. I was here. He was here. We were now.

"I may never go home," he said. "What would you think if I ran away?"

I didn't answer. His words made me think of Candace. I was almost the same age she was when she took off. I didn't know how I'd make it if I were on my own.

"Rand, do you think we did the right thing, not telling anyone about Candace running away?"

"I—I don't know."

"I've been thinking . . . she couldn't have had a lot of choices. She was underage. If she'd been caught, maybe she could have gotten some kind of help. Therapy. A different living situation."

"I didn't think of that," he said.

I sighed. "Neither did I."

The song changed to something slow, and I slipped my arms over his shoulders. He pulled me closer and started to sway. "This place," he whispered. "It's the first place that's just been ours. Is it the same?"

I looked around the stage, all set up for a queen and a king. "It's better," I said. "*Because* it's just ours."

"I'm sorry, Nora," he said, "for pushing you away."

Even though I could barely hear the music, I touched my cheek to his, my chin grazing one of his soft velvet lapels. "What did you tell Wesley? About Grace."

"You heard some of it," he said, rubbing a hand over the back of his neck. "Just that Grace couldn't take knowing this—that she had a lot going on. I explained it would be kinder to keep it quiet."

"What's a lot?" I said. "Tell me."

He pulled me closer. "Nora. I trust you, but so does Grace. She'll tell you when she's ready."

"That's admirable." I paused. "And I get it—I'd want you to do the same for me." They had a special thing that I'd never know how to decipher. "I've never been jealous of you and Grace. It's not that. I mean, maybe you didn't expect me to be, but I want you to know I'm not."

"Good." Rand's hands spread across my back as we danced. "There's nothing to be jealous of. On your part, at least. Not on mine."

"What?"

"I would have hated it if that Chase guy took you to this dance. This was supposed to be us."

I took his face in my hands, pulled his gaze to mine, and asked, "You think anyone's jealous of us, Rand—me and you?"

He smiled that smile that lasted a second, then drifted away. "Everyone, Nora."

WINTER: NOW

CHAPTER 24

The storm pounded against the cabin's windows. I went upstairs to my old room to find something warmer and fumbled through the closet, able to hear the whistle of the wind.

I bundled myself into several layers, pushing hangers aside.

There, staring back at me, was Grace's sweater.

That last night—last winter when she'd gone missing—I'd packed for home thinking I'd never come back. I'd left Grace's sweater in the closet at Donner. I'd wanted as much distance from the idea of her as I could get.

Now, over my long-sleeved tee, I slipped my arms into the fabric.

We all faced forward and didn't speak—me on the center cushion, Wesley on my right and Rand on my left. It should have felt warmer on the couch, our backs against the only wall that wasn't an exterior wall and the power only two hours gone.

My eyes kept darting to Rand. The air felt heavy. Which one

of us had really seen Grace last? What had she done after that? I wished Wesley were gone so we could piece it all together.

I noticed Wesley staring at my sleeve, Grace's sweater.

"Grace was happy enough, right?" he asked suddenly.

Rand leaned forward to stare around me—to Wesley. "I think Grace was infinitely happier before Lauren came into her world."

"Shut the fuck up," Wesley said, rubbing his arms to stay warm. "I just hope there was something special about that last night the four of us were together. I know, fat chance with everything we said. I don't like the idea of her thinking . . . I mean, at the end."

"What do you mean, *the end*?" Rand asked.

"Wesley thinks she's dead," I said.

Rand wrinkled his nose. "Grace isn't dead."

Wesley pointed to the window, the direction of the lake. "Do you know how many tourists come through this area every weekend? Grace was alone most of that night. Running around and trying to make it special for us. Anyone could have done anything."

"You sound like the police that night," he said.

An icy emptiness crept through me that didn't have a thing to do with the temperature.

"It's time to break into the firewood," I said.

With three sticks of green wood and kindling loaded onto the fireplace grate, I lit newspaper beneath them. Tendrils of gray smoke drifted into the living room, and I coughed.

"It'll be better once the fire takes off." Wesley held his coat over his mouth. "Then the heat will rise and force the smoke up the chimney."

Outside, the wind threw snow against our walls, piled it onto trees. Before we'd tacked blankets over the windows, I'd seen branches bent with so much snow, I worried the trees would topple.

At last, a glow rose up from the white flesh of a log, and a spray of flames began to lick the air. We had a small fire.

Wesley burrowed his hands deep in the pockets of his coat and kicked his feet up on the coffee table. "When you two braved the attic, you couldn't have carried down a board game?"

Waving away the smoky air, I settled onto the couch again. "We've got some cards around here somewhere. The kitchen drawers or maybe Kevin's room."

"Poker sounds a hell of a lot better than listening to the walls creak. And the conversation." Wesley shoved aside the quilt he'd pulled over himself. "I'll see what I can find."

Once the rattling of the kitchen started up, Rand said, "You weren't the last to see her. I can promise you that."

"Then explain it."

"It's not that easy, Nora. But I'm sure." He flinched and rubbed the back of his neck. "That last night on the rooftop, after we followed Grace's map—did you, um— Do you remember where you found your map?"

I cleared my throat. "It's been almost a year, Rand."

I remembered that night the way you remember a dream, unsure if I really experienced all the strange and horrible things, or if my waking mind filled in the blanks.

What remained crystalline was an image of Wesley with a bottle of Captain Morgan in his hand as he stared out at a night that seemed darker and darker with the total absence of Grace.

"Nora," Rand said, like he was trying to wake me up with a whisper. "Where was your map?"

"I don't know," I said, but I remembered how it was just taped to my front door in a hurry. "Does it matter? Considering everything else that happened that night. What you said when your parents were watching, and the cops—you pretended you didn't even know us. Like you were ashamed. If Grace had been there, you probably would have pretended you didn't know her either."

Rand tapped his foot on the carpet, shaking the couch. "It wasn't about me being ashamed. I didn't believe Grace was really gone, and when she came back, my parents wouldn't be so keen on me hanging out with the three of you. Not after getting dragged out of bed by the police. That's why I pretended I didn't know you."

Those months after I was home, there were messages, missed calls. I'd been warming a little to the thought of talking to him when they'd just stopped. "Why didn't you tell me this?"

The whites of Rand's eyes had turned red from burning the green wood. "I should have tried harder with you. I just got so obsessed with why Grace never came back."

"That's what you've been doing, all this time—looking for Grace?"

I should have known. While Wesley did everything to block Grace from our lives and minds, of course Rand would have been looking. Of course Rand would have done anything to make sense of the Grace-shaped hole she'd left.

Rand looked over my head, toward the kitchen where Wesley was still clanging around in cabinets and slamming shut drawers.

"She wouldn't have ever left, if it hadn't been for him."

"Rand. You can't blame him," I said.

Wesley's words had shimmied under her skin, but that wasn't why Grace had left.

"Did she ever write you or Wesley letters?" he asked.

My gaze snapped to him.

"Not in the mail," he said. "Letters for you to find back home."

"Never."

"She wrote them to me. The notes, the maps—you know how Grace could get into every one of our places. Picking locks and finding open windows to slide through." He smiled to himself. "She loved being a phantom. But the letters, I'd find one in my packed bags every time I made it home to Walnut Creek."

Gloom washed over me. I wished she'd done the same for me—gave me a little bit to help me make sense of her. "What did they say?"

"Different things. The longest letters she left in winter. When my seasonal affective disorder was the worst."

"You've never named what it was."

"You've never asked," he said. I don't think he meant to make me feel guilty. Remembering, getting more animated, he said, "Sometimes she filled the letter with suggestions of things I should do. Some of them I'd never do—like rob a bank. Sometimes she'd tell me to skip school and ride the train into San Francisco. That letter even came with a map of the city, things to do. I actually did that, followed that map all the way to Nob Hill." Rand wore a small faraway smile. "I'd hoped you got the letters too."

"I wish I had," I said. "If Kevin had found something, he would have saved it for me."

"How are things with your dad?" he asked. "That night, I saw you two talking."

"Things are great," I said.

"Nora," he breathed. "Don't."

"They're different," I said. "Closer to fine."

Some gaps couldn't be bridged no matter how far Kevin stretched. Or maybe it was me, my fingers never quite able to reach. I wished we could close the distance.

A crackling pushed those thoughts away. I tried to sit up, but a loud whoosh pushed me back down.

My arms stung. Glass and falling snow scattered. I grabbed Rand and hurled both of us into the narrow hallway. Wesley buckled in on himself, head between his knees as we slid in beside him, against the safety of the solid wall separating the kitchen from the stairway.

I closed my eyes to the specks raining down, and only opened them when I could feel nothing but the icy wind against my cheeks. A tree had fallen through the front window.

SUMMER: YEAR TWO

CHAPTER 25

The first official night of summer, we went out for ice cream downtown. Everyone was hungry for something cold and seasonal. It wasn't an adventure that started with a clue or a map, but it didn't need to be. Nobody dared mention the rooftop accident the spring before, or the strange, unsettling distance between us the rest of that break.

Licking the top of a double ice-cream cone, Grace skipped ahead to catch Wesley.

Rand and I walked down the sidewalk hand in hand, his thumb skipping softly between my knuckles. Since prom, he'd visited twice, took me to a movie, played basketball with Wesley.

With my stomach full of cold deliciousness, I shivered. Rand helped me into his jacket.

Our mouths met easily now, lips that had sought each other so many times before. There was no clanking of teeth or noses crashing together as we kissed, just galaxies exploding and stars raining down over me like fireworks.

With his forehead against mine, Rand smiled. "That is actually a delight."

"This is the place I saw on *Ghost Hunters*!" Wesley said with his mouth full. "Why haven't we gone here?" Wesley was under a streetlamp, staring up at the sign for the Old Jail Museum as he ate his banana split.

"You'd want to go there? Really?" Grace asked. "Okay, we'll get tickets."

"Tickets," I said. "Really?" Tickets meant we wouldn't be breaking in, that maybe Grace was through with the over-the-top adventures.

"Well, they'll be the very best kind. First class," she said. "Nora." Her faux confidence softened, and she was all warmth when her arms circled me and she whispered, "It wasn't summer until right fucking now."

It wasn't an apology for the spring before, but I took it.

"Rand!" Wesley yelled. "Hey, give me a boost. I want to see inside."

While Rand tried to lift Wesley toward the window, the two of them arguing about how to do it, Grace stayed back by me.

"Come on, we'll be the lookouts," she said after a while, pulling me across the street with her. "They're like a bickering couple. Don't get jealous. I won't let Wesley steal Rand away."

"Not worried," I laughed. But alone with Grace, I felt all the truth in me threatening to burst out. I couldn't stop myself from saying, "Sometimes I think about Rand when I'm back home." I glanced at her. "What would it be like if we could do something wild together, like—I don't even know—go to prom or something?"

"Ha. What would you do? Dress him up in a tuxedo with a bow tie? Would he get you a corsage? You'd do your hair up in a pile of curls?"

She wasn't making fun of me. She just thought it was another story. So I pretended it was too. "Don't forget the diamond tiara I'd wear. No pile of curls is complete without that."

But it stung, that I couldn't even edge up to the truth without her making a joke. That I wouldn't want her to know it *was* the truth.

"You know you could tell me," she started to say, and it occurred to me that she knew our secrets already, and all the oxygen sucked out of the air, "if you actually wanted a tiara. I wouldn't judge you."

"Hm," I said, recovering. "Of course I don't, though."

Grace gave me a disbelieving look. I wondered what I'd said to give myself away.

The boys came laughing across the street, Wesley rubbing his shoulder.

"You practically dropped me," he said to Rand.

"Well, when I told you to get down, you should have actually gotten down," Rand said.

Grace stopped in front of a store window display. "That," she whispered. "That is perfect."

Her finger tapped the glass. On the other side was a silver necklace with a crescent moon, the shadow of a full moon behind it.

"Like one of our moons," Wesley said low as his fingers caught with hers.

I noticed Rand's eyes squinting at the sidewalk ahead. Grace had moved on, her feet planted wide now, unmoving in front of an electronics store.

On a huge curved TV screen that faced outward, there was Candace's picture. Beneath it, a caption: *Missing Girl Returns Home.*

The wheels that propelled our seasons fell off.

I looked down the street, to the turn at the end that led to the Honeyridge, imagining the parking lot where we'd watched Candace take off. I turned back. Taking jagged sips of air, Grace reached out to touch the window glass. The TV didn't put sound out to the sidewalk, so we could only read the captions. The sub-title said, *Teen to be reunited with mother.* Seeing the news wash over Grace, I didn't know how to feel. She was wide-eyed but totally still, a grenade about to go off.

She so obviously knew Candace.

I wondered if she'd dragged her along on adventures just like ours.

More than anything, I wondered what had gone wrong.

Rand spread his hand across Grace's back. "It's over," he said. "Come on, it's over."

Wesley scraped his spoon deep into his banana split and said, "Looks like Vineyard Vines is really off the hook now."

Grace snapped around to face him.

I squeezed my eyes shut. That was the wrong thing to say.

Our stories—they'd meant so much to me the year before. I

worried now that they'd meant even more to Grace. Too much. Whatever Candace was to her, I knew now there was more to it than I'd even imagined. I just didn't know what.

"This is a good thing for her, right?" I ventured, my voice soft. "She's going home. She's probably had every adventure by now and just wants to be home."

"We have to go." Grace tossed her uneaten ice cream into the trash. "We're going home."

CHAPTER 26

SUMMER

Grace's sun-warmed note clung to my bedroom door when I woke up. I was alone upstairs, still rubbing my eyes when I saw it stuck there with a Hello Kitty sticker.

Room 1201.

That was all it said, but it was in Grace's disturbingly bad writing, scribbled on a white cocktail napkin with an *HL* monogram—the Honeyridge Lodge.

An uneasiness sank into me. Two days had dragged by since Candace's resurfacing. I'd googled the news, but all I'd found was a quick clip of her reunion with her mom.

All Wesley would say was how he'd made a mistake that night with Grace and he had to win her back.

I hadn't seen Rand or Grace once. And now that she wanted to see me, I didn't know what to expect.

I walked down the stairs, smoothing my bed head, and noticed

Kevin sipping coffee on the couch. "I'm going out," I said over the noise of the morning news. "Can I take the Jeep?"

"Uh, sure," Kevin said. "I forgot you had a permit now. I guess that's mostly legal." I smiled at that. He knew I was supposed to have a licensed driver with me. "But, um, Nora, could you hold up?"

"Yeah . . ."

"Wesley and I went fishing early. He stayed out." Kevin took off his baseball hat and scooted to the edge of the couch. "I've been wanting to talk to you without him around."

"Why?" With each break that crept up, the distance between us only slightly narrowed. I wanted more, but for each movie we laughed through, there was always a memory, some hesitation, that set us back. There was a lot less space between him and Wesley.

He molded the bill of his baseball cap with his hand. "I already talked to Wesley, and he said no. But you need to have a say in the matter too."

I swallowed, sat on the chair across from him, the coffee table between us.

"This cabin, it's not really mine, not that it ever felt like mine anyway. Hanging up my baseball stuff didn't change that this place was always your grandparents'. I wish you'd known them. You and my mom were a lot alike. Before she died a few years back, she wanted me to know you. Your brother. Maybe that's why she left this place to the two of you."

I looked at him quickly.

It was ours?

I stared up at the wall. The wood panels peeling away suddenly looked lustrous.

It couldn't have been worth much, not as far as property goes. Whatever it was worth, seventy thousand or two hundred thousand, it was more money than we and Mom had ever had, more than I could even imagine.

The cabin was mine.

"As soon as Wesley turns eighteen, it's yours to do with what you want." He ran a hand over his face. "Whoa, does time fly or what?" Then he looked at me closely. "There's enough in trust to cover the property taxes and insurance if you two want to keep the cabin in the family. Or you could sell it, cash out. Your half of the sale would go into trust until your eighteenth birthday. It would cover whatever you and Wesley wanted it to cover. Education, an apartment, whatever."

That money, it could change everything for us, for our mom. Proper rehab. Better doctors. Bills paid off. And at the very least, a cash backup—savings.

The thought occurred to me that Kevin told Wesley first and not me. "You said Wesley didn't want to sell it?"

Kevin sighed. "He didn't."

"Why didn't you just tell us both on Wesley's birthday? Why tell him and not me?"

"Nora, come on. He's older. He—I thought he could make a mature decision."

"So you *want* us to sell it?"

"I've, uh, never done much for you and Wesley. I know that. Every day, I feel like kicking the shit out of myself for it. This cabin, it could be a new start for both of you."

"We can't." I stood up, took a backward step toward the door. "Not if Wesley said no."

But this wasn't really about Wesley. I wouldn't have made the other choice either.

Our friends. Our seasons. We'd lose it all if we lost the cabin. I couldn't imagine that.

Kevin stood too now, his arm stretching out to wrap around my shoulders, but I dodged him. "Wait," I said. "Your mom did this so you would get to know us?"

His eyes crinkled at the corners. "She was pretty pissed off at me for being a selfish kid and leaving you and Wesley behind."

Those words pinged around my rib cage. He knew it but didn't understand what he'd really done to us.

"That's the only reason, then? You never would have known us, except you had to."

"I don't know about that."

And right there—the biggest setback of all. All the ways I'd softened toward him, had *wanted* to soften toward him, vanished. A hardness formed around me, and I wished I could take back the waterskiing and the conversations on the deck and every question I'd ever asked.

"Well," I said, watching him refuse to look at me. "I do."

I crept the Jeep's tires up the twisted hills, away from the water, parking it on the far side of Honeyridge. I'd never entered before without at least one of my friends.

Neil, sitting behind the desk, lifted his chin as I pushed through the spinning glass doors. I'd never really spoken to him, just lurked behind Grace while she made her deals and trades.

I raised a hand and moved toward the elevator banks. The Honeyridge hadn't cleaned the carpets in a while, I noticed. Or maybe they just needed to be replaced.

A DO NOT DISTURB sign hung on the gold doorknob of 1201, so I knocked softly.

Housekeeping moved down the hallway with a pushcart full of toilet paper and miniature shampoos. A part of me worried they'd say something, but the one employee I could see had her back to me and she was busy running a vacuum.

The door slipped open.

"Took you long enough, sleepyhead," Grace said, and tugged me into the room.

Her catlike smile was the same as before, hair perfectly on-purpose messy, her body wrapped in a stark white, fluffy terry cloth bathrobe. This version of Grace she'd created, I wondered if she really had replaced who she was before.

"Waking up before noon is a slap in the face to the god of summer," I said, carefully taking in my surroundings. "Is this the penthouse?"

"Nope," Grace said. "That's one floor up. A different elevator even."

"What'd you do? Rent this room?" I hoped a joke could hide my wariness. "What are we doing, hooking?"

"It's *sex work*, Nora. And ha. As if anyone could afford us."

A gush of cold air rushed over me as I stepped under an air

vent. Goose bumps unfurled over my bare arms, and I rubbed my hands over them. "Why is it freezing in here?"

"Because it can be," Grace said. "I turned the air down to sixty. Here." She threw me one of the terry cloth robes. "Put this on." While I slipped into the fluffiness, she said, "Help yourself to the mini bar and don't bore me by going for the alcohol."

"What else in the mini bar is remotely worthwhile? Six-dollar M&M's?" I settled on a nine-dollar container of Jeni's ice cream, complete with a plastic spoon. "Breakfast of champions." Spoon still pressed to my tongue, I said, "Okay, what did you do, really?"

Grace dropped onto a king-size bed that was a tangle of sheets. "Well, the former inhabitants of the room have vacated the premises. We are taking advantage of the fact that they didn't expect an early departure and are paid up till two p.m."

This was somebody else's room.

I set down the ice cream on the nightstand, stood, and yanked the robe's belt free. "Don't you think this is going a little far?"

"Nora, relax." Grace reached around me to tie the robe again. "They're already gone." She went to the window, looked down at the forest below. "Wesley left your place early this morning . . ."

"He went fishing with Kevin."

"I was kind of hoping he'd spend more time with us."

"Are you two—are you okay now?" I asked. "After the other night?"

"Of course we are. He's extra sweet when he begs."

Usually, I could tell myself Grace was selflessly pushing us past our fears, but this—the hotel room, the robes, the minibar—felt different.

"And you?" I asked, facing her. "You're okay? I—I knew you loved the Candace stories. But . . . were they more than stories, Grace?"

"I just—" Her eyes turned sad. "I knew someone like Candace once. She was the kind of person who'd do anything to protect someone else. But then she left."

Grace shook her head, as if clearing away a fog. Then she smiled, and lifted her chin to the window, the lake below. "I hope Wesley won't be spending the entire summer on that boat."

"I hope not too," I said, disappointed she changed the subject. "I mean, I don't begrudge him a normal functioning parent-child relationship."

"Don't you want one for yourself?"

"I—I don't know." I took a breath after I said that.

Grace focused on me, and my embarrassment flooded my cheeks.

She saw, but she looked away and bunched some pillows against the headboard behind her. "He likes being with your dad. When he comes back smelling like the lake, with the shape of his sunglasses sunburned on his cheeks, have you noticed? He's smiley, funny. It makes me love him even more, like that's possible."

"You love Wesley?"

"Nora, really, how could I not love Wesley?"

She frowned, looked genuinely concerned. "You don't think I hurt him, do you?"

I thought of the rooftop last spring, his shoulder. "He's resilient."

She cocked her head to the side, then smirked and barefooted it to the bathroom.

Eating my ice cream and buried in my robe, I heard Grace yell, "Cha-ching!"

She came out holding a silky royal-blue dress against her body. She draped the hanger behind her neck and looked at herself in the full-length mirror. "It's my size too, I think."

"Where was it?" I asked.

"Bottom of the closet. It must have fallen down while they were packing their things. You know what they say—finders keepers."

"You don't think the woman will come back for it?"

"If she does, what does it matter?

"So it's like garage hopping? . . . Only legal."

Grace's eyebrows inched upward. "Garage hopping?"

"You know, where you go around and break into a bunch of garages to take beer and stuff out of people's fridges."

She turned to me. "You never cease to surprise me."

"I didn't say I'd done it," I replied. But that didn't matter to Grace.

"This dress." Grace held the fabric up to the light and examined it. "It's really more your color. And your legs, they're the kind that should be shown off."

"What am going to do with it? I don't have anywhere to wear something like that."

The silk made the most luxurious sound as Grace let it catch the air and land in my arms.

"You'll find somewhere. Maybe I'll *make* somewhere."

I hoped that wasn't true.

With the quartz tiles under my feet, I draped the dress over my T-shirt and shorts. Grace's story about the room wasn't making sense. It would be just like her to buy the room and then pretend it was some kind of ill-gotten good. This dress, I'd never know if it was stolen, left behind, or something Grace had charged to one of her parents' credit cards.

That seemed to matter less and less, though, because this dress felt like sunshine against my skin. It clung to my thighs. I came out wearing it under the robe, a slice of royal blue peeking from the deep V. It was the only way to survive the a/c.

"The time between spring break and summer break," Grace said, her gaze on the forest far below, "it felt longer."

"It always feels long," I said quietly.

Grace tossed me a bag of Skittles and I joined her again at the window.

"What do you think?" she asked. "I wanted to show you a different piece of this place."

"It feels special," I said, looking around at the glittering light fixtures, the fluffy down duvet, and my new satin dress. "But I don't need all this."

"In light of the death of Candace's adventures, I thought I should up the ante a bit."

I tipped my head to the side, unsure.

"Think about it, Nora. Candace was out there, living her very best life, and now she's not. *Some*one's got to live a big, beautiful life for her."

I sighed. "If Candace's life out there was so great, why did she come home?"

"Don't ruin the story," Grace said.

We'd been telling her story for so long, but I didn't know a single thing about the real Candace. "Maybe we shouldn't have made things up about her," I said. "She deserves something real."

"Sometimes stories are all we really have, Nora."

Grace shifted, then sighed. "I hate that every few months we all go our separate ways."

I felt sorry for Grace then. And a little bit for Wesley too. They didn't have late-night FaceTimes and mid-morning texts. I could still remember how the velvet of Rand's tux had felt against my cheek, and how my corsage had smelled like spring and fresh rain.

"Grace, don't you miss Wesley? When you're back home?"

"Never," she said. "I've told you: Wesley is for here. Not there."

I took her hand. I thought I understood. For all the money her family had, there was something about home she didn't want us to see. I could respect that.

"Then we'll go home," I said. "Like we always do. And we'll keep our closet doors shut every night, check under the bed before we get in. We'll plug in night-lights, and we'll never turn our backs on the dark."

Grace smiled, her face glowing under the chipped chandelier. "I like that."

CHAPTER 27

SUMMER

Just after sunset, the moon was a faint white spot in a quickly darkening sky. I moved onto the deck wondering how to put these vacations back to the way they were before.

At the other end, Wesley stood at the railing, facing away from me with his phone against his ear. "It wasn't even fair to you," he said. "I'm working too many damn jobs. There's never time." Over his shoulder, he noticed me. He faced the forest again, and said lower, "I'm sorry about it. I gotta go."

"I'm headed to Rand's," I said as he ended the call. "Who was that?"

"Just—" He sighed. "Lauren." He slipped the phone into his pocket. "I broke up with her."

"Why?" My feet made a hollow sound as I stepped across the deck. "For Grace?"

"For—" He laced his hands together behind his neck, stretched. "I don't know. It just never seemed right, her at home and Grace here. Made me feel like a jerk."

"If you think what you have here with Grace is sustainable . . ."

"Because we don't talk every day?"

"No—it's more than that," I said. "This isn't good for you. Maybe not for Grace either."

"Doesn't matter. It's the way things are—we're for here and for here only."

"But can't that be changed?"

"Apparently not." Wesley faced the road, Grace's parents' cabin. *That's the beauty of it,* she told me. *The freedom to love without consequences.* What consequences?

The trees that stood between us and the Lombardis' place wavered. Back and forth. Back and forth.

We all hiked to Zion Ledge the first full day of the calendar summer. It was balmy out, bright white clouds rolling over Truckee and thunder rumbling like diesel engines in the sky. Rain was headed our way, the kind that would drench us for only a few minutes before sunlight dried the drops from our skin.

I stopped hiking when we came to a break in the trees. The green and the weight of all those shadows gave way to an almost-aerial view of Donner Lake.

The lake was fuller this time of year, ink-blue water pushing at all the edges, right up to the bases of the evergreens covering many of the banks. The state lowered the lake's level every winter, at least eight or twelve feet. They did it to avoid flooding in Reno if the spring runoff got out of control. Ski boats sailed across the glassy waters, making white-peaked waves rise up out of the blue, and scarring the pristine surface.

We weren't too far from Zion Ledge now—I could tell by the bend in the road and the way the trees curved. Something else was unusual about this spot . . .

I felt someone squeeze my ankle. I screamed and leaped away. When I looked back, a hand was sticking out of the rocky mountainside.

Silver rings danced as Grace wiggled her fingers before she slipped through.

Our cave. Vines camouflaged the outside and some rocks had fallen, making it hard to see the depression in the side of the mountain.

Rand cupped his hands around his mouth and said into the hole, "It's too small, Grace. It's practically caved in." He twisted himself upright, faced me. "She'll come out eventually."

From inside, she called out, "Don't leave me in here all alone."

Wesley moved past Rand and angled himself inside.

"Wesley, come on," I said.

But he was the first to follow Grace because of course he was. He was always the first to follow Grace down whatever rabbit hole she chose to fall into.

Clinging to the mountain, I lowered myself into the dark. It was less than three feet high and only slightly wider than my hips. Once I was through, the ceiling grew a little with each step until I was standing fully upright.

Rand sighed and cleared the space next, but only by an inch.

My shoulder scraped the rock wall to my right. My left knee bumped a tree root that had twisted itself out of the dirt and into the air. I'd fit inside so easily the last time.

The lack of space forced us to huddle together in the one place where the cave ceiling didn't slope down. I felt like Alice in Wonderland, a too-tall girl in a too-small space. But the cave hadn't shrunk—we'd grown.

Grace flicked on a flashlight.

Wesley stood behind Grace with his arms draped over her shoulders. Looking halfway between annoyed and panicked, Rand had his back pressed against the wall and his shoulders hunched—he was too tall to stand fully upright now.

Grace looked between Rand and me. I realized Zion Ledge was never part of the plan—this was just another way for Grace to force us into an adventure.

Wesley looked at me. He knew it too.

Grace moved away from us, fingers skimming the cool slate walls. There wasn't far to go, but she kept as much distance from us as the cave allowed.

Then she gasped, which made me jump.

I stepped back to Rand's side.

"Our names," she said. "I forgot we added them."

Lit up by the beam of Grace's flashlight, low down on the wall, there were the names we'd carved that first spring.

"Rand," she whispered. "Didn't you say the body was mortal but the soul was immortal?"

"Uh, I might have." Rand shuffled his feet. "Some philosophers believe that. The immaterial soul."

"This is the closest we'll get to immortality," she said. "This cave. This wall. This place."

"You said you weren't going to do this shit anymore," Wesley said. "This isn't even fun. It's a stupid hole in the side of a mountain." He pushed past us. "I'm out."

I cringed.

Grace's shoulders slipped down after he was gone. Eyes shining, she looked around.

I wasn't very good at mustering faux excitement, but I said, "Hey look, the silver dollar's still here. We should take it—it's probably lucky and at least worth double now."

"I'll give you a dollar to put it back," she said.

Rand frowned at me. I set down the coin and took a step toward Grace—I didn't know what to say, but I wanted her to know we didn't need magic. I squeezed her hand.

A cold draft brushed by, and I shivered. "Maybe we should go to Zion Ledge." I hugged my goose-bump-covered arms. "I bet it's really something at sunset."

Grace blinked away the trance she'd talked herself into. "Yeah," she said. "Yeah."

As I angled myself toward the outside, I looked back at Grace. She was staring into the dark recess of the cave, glossy clear icicles glowing around her, tears streaming.

Rand waved me on.

Under the icicles, I looked back one more time.

Rand's chin was resting on top of Grace's head and his arms circled her tight.

"What did you do before break?" he asked.

She wiped under her eyes and smiled. "Ran a 4K, read three books a day, and walked on the moon."

* * *

The mountainside pass grew narrower the closer we got to Zion Ledge. It did the summer before too, and yet it was almost a surprise to glance down and see the tree-dotted drop-off.

I liked being up here, and I was glad I'd said yes, until I noticed Rand following my stare to the steep decline.

I slipped my hand into his. "Let's go down to the water," I said. "Alone."

His eyes brightened. He nodded as I took the lead.

Wesley and Grace were taking turns leaping off the lowest rocks while Rand and I watched them from the thin beach below. It wasn't the first time I'd ever seen Grace actually *in* Donner Lake, but it was still a shock.

Out in the distance, behind the small mouth that fed water into the still inlet, water-skiers raced by. But inside the cove, we were almost entirely obscured from view.

I lay on my stomach. Beside me, Rand had his face tilted up at the sky. His eyelashes were impossibly long and dark against his golden skin. As if he felt the weight of my stare, his eyes opened. "Truth or Dave?"

"Truth," I said for the very first time.

"Why don't you talk to Kevin about needing a little extra help? The state mandates at least a little bit of child support."

Kevin. I wish I'd never let myself soften toward him. "He doesn't really care about us," I said. "He never would have reached out unless he had to."

Rand looked at me questioningly, but before I could figure

out what to say, water splashed against the back of my thighs. Wesley rose from the lake and took off, slick-footed, running to the jump-off point again. They were close enough to hear.

"I've changed my mind," I said. "Dave Navarro because—"

"No."

I flipped onto my back and sighed up toward the blue. "Kevin doesn't have much of anything to give us."

Rand tipped his sunglasses down his nose and met my eyes. "He has a second home."

I looked back to the water. Grace and Wesley had swum far out. "Kevin just told me something. But I don't want Wesley to know I know."

Rand rolled onto his side, closer to me.

"The cabin, it's not Kevin's—it's ours. Our grandparents left it to me and Wesley."

His eyebrows shot up. "Oh."

"Kevin contacted us after our grandma died. The cabin was actually the only reason he did." I swallowed hard as Rand's thumb skimmed the back of my hand. "Wesley doesn't want to sell, though. It's old and run-down, but the land alone is worth something, isn't it?"

"This close to the lake?" he said. "Yeah. Hell yeah."

"What would you do? Try to convince Wesley?"

"I—I don't know." A sadness sunk into Rand's face. He wouldn't tell me to sell the cabin because then we'd all lose everything, even him.

Laughing in the distance, Grace and Wesley collapsed into a heap of beach towels and sunburned limbs.

"Okay, your turn." I touched Rand's nose and brightened my voice. "Truth or Dave?"

His lips slipped into a smile. "Truth."

"Are you two playing Truth or Dave?" Wesley called.

Grace's back shot up straight. "I'm in. But please, please, let's change the rules. Truth, Dave, or *dare*."

Rand tucked an arm around the damp swimsuit at my back and lowered his chin onto my bare shoulder. "Come on, Grace. Let's keep this easy, low-stakes."

"I'm down," Wesley said, wrapping an arm around Grace's shoulders. "But instead, the asker gets to choose whether it's truth, dare, or Dave."

Grace clapped her hands together, kissed him on the cheek. "I knew I could count on you."

"So Grace—truth," Wesley said. "Why can't I find you on any social apps—because I looked, okay? I'm not being a stalker or anything, but I definitely looked."

"Hey," Rand said. "It's not even your turn. It was Nora's."

"Question's been asked," Wesley said. "Grace, you have to answer."

Grace's water-speckled arm was pressed against Wesley's hairy one and she scooted away from him. "Sometimes something really big happens and it just changes you. You let go of childish things. Like social. So, there. Who's next?"

Wesley's sunglasses wobbled as he shook his head. "Not an answer."

244

Grace squirmed, her slippery sunscreened legs crossing and un-crossing. She squinted at Wesley. "It's—" She looked away. "Some-times, when you're really, really little, someone tells you something, and it becomes almost like a part of you. And even though there's a point where you don't believe it, you kind of still do. Until one day when you can't anymore. Like that your dad's happy that you were a girl. Or you're smart enough to be anything you want to be. Your dad is just friends with that pretty real-estate lady. Or your mom would much rather be at home with you than at work all day. Or your friends are your friends and they wouldn't hurt you."

"Grace," Rand said, reaching for her hand.

She moved out of his reach. "Who's next? Nora, you want to go?"

"Yeah," I said. "Yeah. Um—" I couldn't think, only feel my breath shuddering inside me as I tried not to cry. This was the most Grace had ever revealed.

"I don't get it," Wesley said, taking Grace's hand and having her snatch it away. "Jesus, Grace. You won't tell me anything, like at all, and then you hit me with that."

"Stop it." She scooted away from him. "You made me say it. I didn't even want to."

"Wesley," Rand said. "Leave it the fuck alone. You've got your answer."

One deep breath, and Wesley said, "Okay, Rand, I dare you to go up to the top of the cliff and look down."

"Oh, come on," I said. "Not this again."

"How ungentlemanly," Rand said. "And fuck you."

Grace had a starry look in her eyes. "Do you ever think maybe our phobias are based on how we died in a past life?" She got to her feet and pointed to a rock halfway up the cliffside. "Dare me to jump off that rock up there."

We all stayed silent as we watched her move up the rock side, her feet gaining purchase one foothold at a time. It was higher than they'd been climbing, but there was nothing dangerous about jumping from that height. Nobody had moved at all when Grace reached the rock and glanced down. "On second thought, maybe I should jump from the very top."

We all cast our eyes upward, to the highest point on the cliffside, the point where Wesley jumped two springs before.

"The lake's lower now," Rand said. "That's too high."

"Oh come on," Wesley said as she kept climbing. "Get the hell down here right now."

She rose higher and higher, bare feet finding spaces to send her up, up, up.

"I swear on this fucking lake, if you jump, we're done for good," Wesley said.

Grace laughed. "Liar."

"This is not even how you play the game, Grace," Rand said. "You don't get to create your own dare." To me, he said, "She can't make that jump."

I shook my head. "She won't."

But I wasn't sure. I'd stacked Grace's stories together like Jenga pieces, and it wouldn't take much to make the whole tower tumble down. I hadn't asked the hard questions. I hadn't made myself know her.

Maybe she'd really hurt herself—I couldn't be sure.

At the very top, she spread her arms wide. She looked like a bird with its wings open. I didn't believe she'd do it until her body lurched.

"Don't be stupid, Grace!" I shouted. "The water's not deep enough. You'll—"

She jolted backward, which made me think she was chickening out—not that she was getting a running start. Legs kicking, her body came sailing off the edge.

The splash threw a wall of water onto the bank that blinded me for a second.

The air cleared and I got up on my feet in time to see Wesley diving in after her.

I scanned the bubbling water, but couldn't see her at all.

Wesley resurfaced several feet out, rubbing water from his eyes. "Fuck. Fuck. Fuck." He slipped down again, shooting into the depths.

"She could have hit her head," I said.

"Her body would float up." Rand's eyes darted across the water. "I think."

I couldn't breathe.

Wesley shot above the surface gasping, blinking into the water beneath him, to his right, to his left, far out over the lake. He dove back down and was under for at least one impossible minute. He sprang back up.

Sobbing, Rand moved up the bank.

Hot tears rolled down my cheeks, and I wiped them away. She couldn't go this long without oxygen. She couldn't be under this long and survive.

"Nora," Rand said. "Nora." He tapped me on the shoulder. "You need to see this."

I couldn't take my eyes off the lake. "No. I—"

Rand flapped an envelope in front of my face.

The front read, *My Dearest Friends.*

I tore it open.

Hello from beyond the grave!

I am so joking—I'm very much alive, just sadly on my way back home. Something's come up and I have to cut summer short. My secret spot under the water was the best trick, perfect for smugglers and even better for me. One quick underwater swim and I surfaced on the backside of Zion Ledge. What a way to exit, right? See you in winter.

Ciao, Indoctrinates.

xo, Grace

Cheeks flaming hot, I wished Grace would come back so I could drown her myself.

"Wesley!" I flailed my arms. "Wesley! It was a trick!"

My brother crawled up on the bank, chest heaving as he collapsed with his cheek in the dirt.

Rand paced along the water's edge. "But what if she didn't make it? How do we know she's okay?"

"We fucking don't." Wesley's chest rose and fell fast. "I can't keep doing this."

Staring into the still water, imagining Grace in that old smuggler's tunnel, I said to myself, "Next winter has to be different."

And it would. We just didn't know how.

WINTER: NOW

CHAPTER 28

Everything went quiet except the wind howling in through the hole in the broken window. Our cabin wasn't just exposed to the elements now—it was a part of them.

"What the fuck?" Wesley stomped past us, eyes wild as he surveyed the damage. "We can't possibly make it through a whole night here."

"It's not that bad," I said because we needed a little hope. But I don't think I was fooling anyone, especially not myself.

"It's almost five miles to my place," Rand said. "We have to stay here."

"Wesley, stop." I put my hand on his back. "There's nowhere else to go. It's just a hole. See." I pointed at the tree punching through the glass. "We'll cover it."

I felt his heartbeat slowing between his shoulder blades. Finally, he nodded.

I stared at the damage. There was no way to lock anything up or make the cabin totally airtight, not without a chain saw and a truck with chains to haul away the hundred-year-old sugar pine poking through the curtains. "Let's get this sealed up as much as we can."

Wesley picked up the broom I'd used to trip the latch to the attic. He swept raw bits of window into a dustpan from the closet and picked up the pieces the broom didn't catch. This wasn't the safety glass they installed on newer homes. This was the ancient glass that broke into large, jagged pieces, severing an artery if it hit you just right.

"You're going to cut yourself," I said.

"So what if I do?" he asked.

I sighed.

As I stood on a dining room chair, Rand holding it steady, I removed the yellow-flowered curtains from the rods. My grandmother's, and they were in shreds. They weren't doing us any good just swaying in the wind.

Even though the freezing outside had become our inside, I was sweating from exertion, breathing air thick with everything unknown, unsaid.

Over my shoulder, I watched Wesley filling the trash can with glass. Rand backed up and bumped into Wesley's shoulder.

"Look, man," Wesley said. "I don't give fuck-all about your head injury. If you bump me again, I will put you down."

"Where is that coming from?" I asked.

"Really?" Rand said. "Really?"

Wesley dropped to a knee and went back to pushing broken

glass into the dustpan. "I wasn't the reason she left, okay? And yeah. Voices carry, asshole."

I climbed down. "We have to stop this bullshit right now."

Wearing the frown that made his dark eyebrows draw together, Rand said, "You made Grace feel isolated. And you hurt her, just for the thrill of it. That's why she ran."

"First of all, if anyone made Grace feel isolated, it was you. And second—" Wesley cringed. "There was no thrill in hurting her. But what the fuck are you even talking about? She didn't run. With all the time you're putting into this, I'd think you'd be digging into the fact that she didn't take any bags. This was Grace—nobody loved *things* more than Grace. They looked through the cabin and all her packed bags were still there."

"How do you know this?" I asked.

Wesley's finger stabbed through the air, pointing in the direction of the Honeyridge. "Because I heard everything the cops said, and her parents—those people who talked like they didn't even know her."

Grace was hard to know, *really* know. I wondered if anyone succeeded, and if that was Grace's problem or ours.

Wesley's eyes were clear and intense. "Because after we looked for her, I went back to the Honeyridge and sat there all night, waiting. Waiting for someone to find her."

Rand stepped closer to Wesley. "You owed it to her to wait. And more."

Wesley's eyes went wide. "You say what you mean or you step the fuck off."

"Calm down." Rand held his hands out in front of him.

Wesley shoved at Rand's chest. "Calm down? *Calm down?* You're trying to say that I talked Grace into running away? That I played games with her until she ran?"

"No," Rand said. "I don't think you talked her into running." That made Wesley's shoulders relax. "What you said *forced* her to run."

Wesley hit him across the face, closed fist, an impact I could almost feel, jaw burning, teeth aching.

I was on the floor with Rand in an instant. The punch had almost knocked him out cold, but he was still moaning.

All that I'd been able to hide, my sadness and my blame—my stare gave them away.

"Oh, really, Nora?" Wesley said, blinking fast. "You believe him? You think I did this too." He laughed then, and for a split second, I was worried about my brother. But he threw open the front door, snatched his coat off the rack as the blizzard blew like an upended snow globe around him.

"Well, if you think that, Nora, then fuck you too."

He was out the door.

By the time I lowered Rand's head down to floor, got my feet under me, and pulled open the front door, Wesley was a small spot where we used to be able to see the end of the driveway. "Where do you think you're going?"

"Away!"

"Wesley Tate, you get your ass back here!"

He held his coat tight against the wind, struggling to stay

252

standing. "There's a fallen tree a hundred yards from here. Died over the summer—when you weren't here. Maybe it's dry enough to burn. I might as well be warm if we have to spend all night with that shit heel!"

"Nora, leave him." The door behind me moved as Rand sunk his weight into it. "He'll get tired. He'll come back in a few minutes—it takes a lot of energy to walk in this." I hesitated and he motioned to the actual tree inside the living room. "We need to figure out what to do with this."

With hammers and ten-penny nails—because that's all we could find in the coffee can under the sink—we blanketed the gaps of air around the tree. Our barrier was thin, even with our thickest blankets, but it was some protection against the freezing wind.

While Rand cleaned his bleeding lip and the gash on his forehead that had reopened when he hit the floor, I stoked the fire. It wasn't helping. It was like lighting a match inside a freezer.

He appeared in the living room with one of my grandmother's thick, faded bedspreads draped around his shoulders. He spread his arms wide, an invitation.

I looked at him, didn't move.

"This is about warmth, Nora."

I hesitated. "Fine."

Rand paused, wrapped his arms around my waist. Something about his touch was like muscle memory clicking into place. I rested my head on his shoulder. I was instantly angry for letting myself enjoy this.

We dropped down beside the fire and waited. With Wesley gone, the only thing left to do was worry. He couldn't make it all the way to the road.

"You didn't ask me," Rand said. "You didn't ask me about being the last one to see Grace."

"I didn't ask you because you're wrong. I went to her and we had a fight."

"But after that . . . after that, she came to my place. She said she'd seen you."

I blinked and turned to face him. "Before the Honeyridge?"

"Yes. She was frantic."

I let that sink in, and more than anything, I felt relief. If I'd been the last, then this was all on me, and selfishly I wanted someone else to share my guilt.

"She showed up on my back steps asking for a place to stay for the night. Her makeup was running and she was shivering. She wasn't even wearing a coat. She wanted a place to stay, just for the night. I took off my jacket, helped her put it on, and I—I told her no. I told her to go home. I should have known she wouldn't listen."

"Why? Why would you do that, Rand?"

"Because I worried it wasn't good for her! I worried *I* wasn't good for her anymore. I kept her biggest secret. I kept it from you because I thought it was what she wanted. If I hadn't done that, everything could have been different. I didn't mean to do any harm. I thought I was doing what was best. I thought—" His voice broke.

We were all terrible friends to her, just in different ways.

We sat in silence, and I wondered if that was true. Me before him. Him before me. I didn't know if it mattered. Grace was a wreck when I saw her too.

"I'm sorry," he said. "I guess Wesley isn't the only one to blame."

"We're all to blame," I whispered.

Rand looked to the door. "Wesley may be upset when he gets back. He might . . ." He shook his head. "Never mind."

"What?"

"Nothing."

I let it go. "He's been different back home," I told Rand. "Since that night."

Rand curled himself closer to me. "Like how?"

"Angrier and more sullen. He got back together with Lauren, then broke up with her a week later. No reason, just left her crying in the hallway before first period. Then another day, a kid bumped him in the hallway. He slammed him against the lockers. My friend Bailey—maybe *friend* is too generous now—she asked for a ride to school and then tried to kiss him behind her boyfriend's back. He made her get out of his car and walk the rest of the way to school."

Wesley was my brother, and I loved him in a way I didn't love anyone else. But I hated what he'd done to Grace. What they'd done to each other. Who he'd become.

Rand stared down at a piece of the bedspread that was unraveling. "Since Grace went missing . . . We've all been different, haven't we?"

Darkness was falling hard on Donner Summit, and I thought of Wesley out there in the night, not coming back.

"I just—I wish things could go back to how they were the first spring and summer."

Rand's smile made a clicking sound. "The first spring . . . you and I asleep on the dock, under the stars, half-drunk on champagne. You talked about possibility, the universe."

A warmth filled me even though I was freezing. "Or that summer, after my accident, you and me in my room watching *Fight Club*. You almost kissed me."

He nodded. "And I told you about my parents. I'd never told anyone."

"But I didn't—I didn't ask more. I thought you were just playing that game."

"Nora, do you realize our best times together were when we were honest?"

I breathed out and he breathed in. Between us we passed a thousand memories of lake water and sun, freezing hands slipping under warm sweaters, the sway of our bodies, and the smell of fresh corsages.

"I've missed you," he said.

With my neck craning, my mouth moved closer to Rand's. We both stopped short, our lips on the verge of touching, only for a second, until our mouths came crashing together.

I slipped my hands under the waist of his sweater, hands searching for his heartbeat.

The cabin door flew open.

I scrambled to straighten myself. Rand pulled his hand out from under my top right as Wesley hauled him to his feet.

He held Rand's jacket tight in both his fists, then let go, and

Rand sank toward the floor. Just as Rand was getting his footing, Wesley punched him in the jaw again.

Rand gasped, got one knee under him to stand. "What the fuck's your problem, man?"

Wesley didn't let him get all the way up before he hit him again.

"Stop it! Stop!" I screamed.

Wesley pulled Rand close, breathing hard and his face dark red. He shoved Rand away and looked at me. "His snowmobile," Wesley said. "Absolutely pristine. It's sitting at the end of the fucking road."

WINTER: YEAR TWO

CHAPTER 29

The first night of winter break, I'd seen Grace out my bedroom window, sitting on the steps of her front porch in the freezing snow. I'd waited until she went inside to tape a Truckee Railroad Museum ticket to her door, along with a time.

Wesley and I had bought the tickets. Enough was enough. We didn't need risky adventures.

The next afternoon, I stood inside the drafty museum lobby with my hand in Rand's.

Wesley craned his neck to the door. "You think she'll come?" He tugged down the sleeves of his too-small coat. The cuffs didn't quite reach his wrists. I hadn't seen him in it since last year, our first winter, flying around the hillside on a snowmobile.

"She'll come," I said, though I wasn't sure. "You should have borrowed Kevin's coat."

Wesley had left his newer coat in the lobby of urgent care on Christmas Eve when Mom had demanded we take her for a shot of Demerol. It was gone by the time we went back for it.

We couldn't keep doing this. All through Christmas Day, while we ate Chinese food that Rand had driven up to bring us, Wesley had watched me between bites. He knew it too.

"Nah." Wesley blew a breath into his palms. "This one's fine." His hand disappeared into his pocket, came out with something silver wound between his knuckles. "Think this'll make her happy? For Christmas."

"You're giving her the moon?" Rand asked. "Quite the gesture."

It was the necklace Grace had admired that first night of summer. I didn't know if giving it to her would help push them—or us—in some new direction. I hoped it would.

"Hey," Rand said, nudging me in the ribs.

Grace strolled through the front doors. "Alive and well," she said with a smile.

As we moved through the corridors, I worried Grace would think we were being disloyal by planning our own outing, that this didn't qualify as an adventure. But she quietly took in the space while Wesley led the way and Rand and I trailed behind.

Wesley stopped in front of each and every exhibit to read the plaques. "This is what they were talking about, in the documentary," he said. "This is some Illuminati bullshit right here."

"The Illuminati?" Rand darted closer, never letting go of my hand, tugging me along. "He's serious?"

"The signs are everywhere. The triangles. The eye of providence."

Rand looked from me to Grace, then back to Wesley. "The eye of providence is a Freemason symbol," Rand said.

"Yeah." Wesley moved two feet to the next exhibit. "They're a sector of them."

"Who is they and them?" Rand asked.

Wesley sighed. "The Freemasons. They're part of the Illuminati. It's history, man." His eyes twinkled before he turned to another exhibit. "You should read more."

Rand wide-eyed blinked. "It's not *real* history. It's garbage. Conspiracy theories. It's . . ."

Grace watched them, a small smile on her lips as they bickered back and forth. I let go of Rand's hand and fell in beside Grace.

"Aren't you going to tell them you believe in the Illuminati?" I asked. "That you're a member along with Jay-Z and Beyoncé?"

"I think I like it better this way," Grace said.

Wesley and Rand continued to debate the existence of the Illuminati, and Grace and I moved outside, to the wooden bench under the OLD JAIL MUSEUM sign.

"You scared me." I stuffed my hands in my coat pockets as I sat beside her. "All of us. If you had to go home, I don't know why you had to do it like that. Never again, okay?"

She stared across the parking lot, then turned to me. "I won't do that to you again. I—I missed you more than I ever have."

"More? Why?"

She pulled a pair of gloves from her pocket and was silent as she slipped them on. "There was an emergency. Someone I love."

"Oh, Grace, I'm sorry. Are they okay?

"They didn't die or anything, but they had to go away." She said "away" like it was another continent. "And I hurt them before they left. I'm not going to see them anymore. So I guess it's kind of like they died."

"Who?"

Grace's eyes, clearer in the gray daylight, focused on me. "Nora, what about you? How was Christmas?"

I opened my mouth to tell her how we'd worried about Mom, the peaks and valleys of her addiction, the groceries she'd forgotten to buy, rent she'd forgotten to pay, work she'd had to miss. And I wanted to tell her that as much as I loved Rand driving up to bring us takeout and sit silently with me on my bedroom floor, I'd wished he hadn't needed to.

The words stuck in my throat, building until my eyes pooled. I didn't want to speak these things. But she had things too. Maybe this could be something we shared.

Grace leaned in. "You can tell me."

"I—" My stomach growled.

"Hang on," she said. "I brought snacks." She looked back across the parking lot, wiggled her car keys, and popped her trunk.

I quickly wiped my eyes. "I'll help."

"No, I've got it."

I moved behind her parents' SUV and picked up a cloth grocery bag.

"No, not that one." Grace lurched forward, but I'd already gotten it open.

There weren't snacks inside. It was a set of cuff links, a women's watch, a lacy bra with La Perla tags attached, an opened bottle of men's cologne.

"What is all this?"

"Just some things I need to get rid of," she said.

I started to hand the bag back, but I noticed a postcard with the heading *Freudian Slip* and a picture of Freud. *When you say one thing, but you mean your mother.*

"That's for Rand," she said. "For someday when he really needs to laugh. Nora—"

Only one item remained at the bottom. Wrapped in a washcloth with the Honeyridge Lodge logo was a diamond bracelet.

"Costume," Grace said. "For the right occasion."

It was actually kind of gaudy, flashy in a way that wasn't Grace.

I looked at her, watching me and faking a nonchalance that I didn't understand.

There was something there, humming like the thunder building over the mountains.

"Finish telling me about your Christmas." Grace stared at me, urging me to . . . what? Tell the truth? Make up something spectacular? I couldn't tell. And either way, it was something I couldn't give. Finally she broke eye contact and moved across the parking lot.

Turning back, she called, "The boys are probably dying without us. You know how they are."

CHAPTER 30

WINTER

Grace stood on our deck the last day of winter break, a puffy white winter coat swallowing her shoulders and sinking past her knees. "Want to go to the Honeyridge?" she asked at the door, peeking past me at the empty cabin. "I'm starving. Please, please, please."

"I'm not really hungry," I said.

"Please," she said. "I promise it'll be worth your while."

That worried me enough to know I couldn't let her go alone.

"Okay," I said. "Let me get my bag."

When Grace got me inside the hotel, she didn't go left to the restaurant. Instead she darted right and ignored me while I quickened my steps, whispering her name. At the elevator banks, she flashed a plastic room key.

I shook my head as we rode the elevator up to the third floor. All of break, Rand, Wesley, and I had planned our outings. But Grace wasn't one to let us go without a final hurrah.

She did a quick sweep of the room. Housekeeping hadn't changed the bedding or left chocolate mints on the pillows. The trash can under the desk was piled high with shopping bags and a couple of those baggage tags that airlines wrap around your bag handles at check-in.

"This is boring," I said. That was the surest way to convince Grace our time was better spent elsewhere.

She pocketed a plastic pen bearing the words *Honeyridge Lodge.* "If you're bored, then I don't think you're opening your heart to adventure."

"Where's the adventure in taking that pen? They're complimentary anyway, aren't they?"

"Maybe I'll write a check using it—people should write more checks. It's a lost art."

She made her way to the mini bar and swiped a bag of Chex Mix.

"Almost all pretzels," Grace said as she peered into the bag. "What a rip-off."

Back here, with Grace trying to make our lives bigger in a way that only made me feel smaller, I couldn't help thinking that I'd done this. She'd been close to real, back at the museum when she'd asked me about Christmas, but I hadn't taken the chance, hadn't let her in.

I sat on the bed and faced her. "When you're at home, what do you think about?"

Grace plopped down in the middle of the crisp white duvet and laughed. She unwrapped a chocolate mint and placed it on her tongue. "Being anywhere but there, obviously."

She was quiet a moment. "Sometimes I wait until my parents go to sleep and I go out to our roof. It's a great big sloping thing. Six gables across the front. It's not that hard to climb out my window and touch my toes to the ledge if I take off my shoes. On Sunday nights, after my parents are asleep and the neighborhood is dark except for the streetlamps, I like to sit on the roof until I can't possibly hold my eyes open any longer. Delaying Monday for as long as I can."

"Does it help?"

"Sometimes." Grace scooted forward on the bed, squeezing a pillow against her stomach. "It's a dark feeling, isn't it? The one that hits when you realize the fun has to end." Grace sighed and padded over to the dresser. "What else do you think we'll find?" She slid open the top drawer. "What else—"

She went silent. I knew she'd found something important because she didn't make a joke or say anything at all. She didn't breathe as she stared into the open drawer.

"What is it?"

From the dresser, she pulled out a soft pink cashmere cardigan with the tags still attached.

"Someone really left that behind?"

"Guess so." Grace tossed her sweater onto the bed and slipped on the cardigan.

I opened the closet to see what other treasures we could uncover. When the doors peeled away, I leaped back.

"Grace," I said. "*Grace.*"

A row of clothing hung from the rod, sweaters and snow suits and two pairs of boots. Beneath them were two huge pieces of luggage. I stepped sideways and looked into the bathroom. Two electric toothbrushes stood on the counter along with a mint-colored toiletry bag.

I went to Grace fast and took her by the arms. "They haven't left this room yet. All their stuff is still here."

She opened another drawer. "Do you want the sweater? Pink isn't really my color."

"You knew?"

She pulled a breath deep inside her and let it out. Then turned to me. "They took a day trip to hike the old Donner Summit Train Tunnels. They won't even be back until tonight."

"Grace! This isn't just picking up whatever they left behind. These are their things."

I threw a look around the room, and there were so many signs I hadn't seen. A pair of shoes stuck out from the end of the bed. There was a book on the nightstand and it wasn't a Gideon Bible. Then I thought of all the rooms we'd been in before. Were those things really left behind, or were they things we'd stolen?

My blue silky dress was still hanging in the cabin closet.

"Come on," I said, tugging at her arm. "They'll come back and realize their stuff is gone." I thought of the hallway outside the door—the reason we were guaranteed to get caught. "Plus there are security cameras. If they report the missing items, the hotel will watch the footage and see us. Us in the hallways, us entering their room, us leaving their room. Shit, Grace. We'll be in a lot of trouble. Like misdemeanor kind of trouble."

"Don't worry about the cameras." She twisted from side to side in front of the mirror, admiring the cardigan. "Neil's got us covered."

"No," I said. "*Grace.*"

Grace slipped out of the sweater and held it up for me.

"We can't *take* that. These are not things they left behind. These are just . . . *theirs.*" I snatched the sweater from her hand, threw it onto the bed. "We have to go. We have to go now."

I was halfway to the door when the lock clicked and the door shifted open.

My breath froze in my chest. They were back early. There was no way to explain us in their room. What would I tell Kevin? Or my mom? Or even Wesley and Rand?

The body looming in the doorway came into view.

"Hey Grace." Neil lifted his chin to me. "Nora." He moved over the threshold like he wasn't at all surprised we were there.

"Welcome." Her breath was a little shaky.

My head snapped around. Grace never seemed worried, but she was worried now.

"We got a real problem, don't we?" Neil plopped down on the end of the bed with his hands folded. "When I gave you that key, Grace, you said you weren't going to raid rooms until the guests took off. It's hours from checkout and here you are." He laughed. "Here I am."

Grace grabbed the cardigan from behind him and folded it back inside the drawer. "Time must have gotten away from me. We'll be leaving now."

She moved past Neil, but he caught her hand.

"This is how you pay me, isn't it?" he said. "Don't deny it. I know about last week. The bracelet." Neil's cool gaze went to me. "Were you in on it too?"

"Check the security footage," Grace said as she wrenched her hand out of his and backed up beside me. "You'll see she wasn't. And neither was I."

"That's the thing. You knew this place was a security dead zone that day." Neil looked at me and shrugged. "A few side businesses of mine require that. Grace knew it. Did you?"

"I don't know anything." It felt like the truest thing I'd ever said. "Except that we're leaving. Come on, Grace."

"That bracelet was expensive," Neil said. "The cops were asking questions. The woman staying in the room reported it. What would happen if I threw your name into the mix, Grace?"

"You'd implicate yourself," she said. "And they wouldn't find the bracelet because I wasn't here that day and I didn't take it."

The ground seemed to quiver beneath me. Stolen items from hotel rooms had been buying our adventures.

"You know you owe me, right?" he said. "I was on the hook for Candace for fucking months after I cut the security tapes so you and your friends could have your rooftop field trip."

She looked him up and down. "You look relatively unscathed."

He grinned, then grabbed her.

I lurched forward. Her eyes were wide as she tried to pull free.

He let her go.

Grace walked backward, stumbled, and smoothed her clothes down.

Neil had pulled something from her pocket and held it in the air. A key—the one Grace had used to get into the room. She reached out but he yanked it away.

"Mine again," he said. "It's going to be awfully boring for you with no master key."

Straightening up, she said, "Don't worry about me. I'll find something to do."

But her lip trembled.

Neil leaned forward. "You could have it back. Maybe. If you'd do something for me."

It felt like something was squirming up from my throat. I wanted to vomit.

Grace just stood there, not because she didn't seem fazed by his proposition, but almost like she thought it was inevitable. Like it was something she had to let happen.

I was moving forward before I had time to think. I grabbed Grace's hand. "We're leaving. Now." Neil tried to grab my shoulder as I moved past him, but I shrugged him off. Grace stumbled across the carpet as she glanced back at him. But she followed me, out the door and into the hallway, all the way to the elevators. The doors slid closed with us inside. My stomach lurched as the elevator lowered.

Grace, as calm as if nothing had happened at all, now leaned against the metal railing that circled the elevator, one leg crossed in front of the other.

I hit the emergency stop and we both jolted to find our balance.

"Don't ever." My hand was out, my fingers shaking. "Whatever he can give you—more wild nights through this place, whatever. It is not worth that."

"What makes you think I would even consider it? I mean, Neil." She shuddered.

But I'd seen the way she looked when he'd pried the key out of her hand. A bright shiny present, hundreds of new adventures for all of us—gone.

What Neil had up for sale were the outings Grace had contrived, adventures that topped the one before, and a great big life that didn't quite make up for something I didn't understand.

"Nora, really? I can't believe you would even—I can't—"

I slumped against the safety bar. Until moments before, I hadn't known Grace was stealing. Buying our nights. Making thieves of all of us. And if she'd steal for us, she might go further. I couldn't just let that happen.

Grace released the emergency stop and sent the elevator sinking down to earth. "I'm done with this conversation," she said. "It's over."

CHAPTER 31

WINTER

Grace's message was stuck between the pages of the book I'd been reading, replacing my bookmark with a piece of stationery bearing a cursive *G* and a meeting place.

Crumpling the paper in my hands, I sat down on the edge of my bed. I didn't want to follow this map. We'd tried so hard to end these games.

Outside, a smattering of snowflakes tumbled through the air. I was searching my closet for an extra thermal and my winter coat when the phone rang.

"They're not working," Mom blurted. "If I go back to the ER, they're going to give me a bad time again. I've told them over and over that sometimes only a shot of Demerol will do the trick and—"

"Don't go to the ER," I said, because I knew they wouldn't help her. "Try some of those yoga exercises we talked about, or take those magnesium supplements—I've read they help."

In the background, a pill bottle rattled. "I'm just going to take another—"

"Mom, stop," I said. "Don't take another. Just—" I pulled at the neck of my T-shirt that suddenly felt too tight. "Have you ever thought maybe the drugs aren't going to help? That maybe they're the whole problem?"

The door creaked. Wesley leaned against the frame with his mouth pressed in a line.

"Why would you say that?" Her voice was sharp.

Rubbing my eyebrows, I sat at the end of the bed. "It's just that meds like this are intense. You can develop a dependency, like, pretty easily."

"I'm not dependent, Nora. These are a prescription."

That she could lie so easily—it cut me deep. "That doesn't mean they're not a problem," I said. "I—I know you're hurting. But maybe if you tried to just, I don't know, cut back—"

"What would I do then?" Her voice was rising. "Not go to work? Not take care of you? Your brother?" She didn't even realize that, for years now, we'd been the ones taking care of her. "I have to go," she said. "Don't worry about me. Give Wesley a hug."

While I was still holding the warm phone in my hand, Wesley sat beside me at the end of my bed. "Confronting her like that, it's futile, you know?"

"She's—it's a bad night."

"It's a bad year," he said. "I, um, talked to that doctor at the ER a couple weeks ago. I didn't say it directly to him. I was worried about CPS maybe separating us—still am. But he said there are free programs. Like state funded or something."

A tiny bit of hope sparked in my chest. "You're talking about rehab?" I asked. "Do you think we could get her to go?"

"Maybe. But not when she's out of control, like now. We'd have to get the timing right."

I nodded. *Maybe* sounded better than what we had.

He cracked his knuckles. "The problem is us, kinda. Where to go. What, uh, would you think about moving in with Dad?"

"In Lodi?" I tried to envision it.

My imagination couldn't stretch that far.

"We've never even been to his house—or apartment. Whatever. I don't even know where he lives, how he lives."

Wesley cast his eyes in the direction of the noise from the TV in the living room. "It wouldn't be that bad. I mean, he'd leave us alone. He leaves us alone now. It's not like you and I could afford to stay in the house without Mom's check. Our after-school jobs won't cut it."

"We don't even know him, Wesley."

"*You* don't know him, Nora. There's a difference."

I didn't know what that meant. I couldn't pretend to love fishing and hiking and waterskiing just to forge some kind of relationship with him.

"He might not even want us," I said. "Did you consider that?"

"You know what?" he said. "Never mind."

"Wesley, stop. You're saying she can't get help if we don't move in with Kevin? Because maybe I could do it. If that's what it took."

"You'd hate it that much?" he asked.

"I'd—I'd do it for Mom. For you."

"But you'd hate it." He stood and moved across the carpet as if his limbs were too heavy to put into motion. "Forget it. There are other ways."

The next day, Wesley was silent the whole way to the edge of Truckee. We had only the hum of the heater for conversation.

He'd been different for months now, a faraway sadness in his eyes while he dragged between our house and school and odd jobs. I wondered if ending things with Lauren had been a mistake.

"That's them," I heard him say.

We passed a break in some shrubs lining an outer perimeter, and there was Rand, Grace, and an enclosed cemetery behind them.

When we got out, Grace, swinging an oversized wicker picnic basket, ran ahead and rattled the rusty cemetery fence. "It's locked." She raised her eyes to the top. "Think you could jump it?" she asked Wesley. "I bet you could sail right over and unlock it from the other side."

Wesley stood there with weary eyes and stared up at the fence. I didn't bother telling him he shouldn't. It had never worked before.

Grace came to stand by him. "Pretty please?"

Wesley shook out his arms, bounced on his toes like a boxer, then ran back, fifteen feet from the fence and the shrubbery below it. A deep breath and he raced forward.

He jumped for the top bar, barely caught it. Adjusting his grip, he pulled himself up. Sitting astride, he breathed hard and stared at the asphalt below.

One leap and he landed on the other side.

"Magnifique," Grace said. She pressed her face between the

bars and kissed Wesley through the gate. Then she pulled back and pushed the unlocked gate open. "Ta-da."

Wesley went red-faced under the moonlight. "You didn't tell me it was unlocked."

"And miss the Cirque show?" she asked. "You were spectacular."

"Grace, I coulda hurt myself."

Silently, Rand and I followed Grace inside.

"No, you couldn't have." She draped her arms over Wesley's shoulders. "You're my baseball man, my acrobat—I knew you could do it."

I was glad I'd never told Grace and Rand a lie like that. As much as I loved being here, telling stories, maybe I was still happiest being myself.

The smell of earth and cold filled my nose as we moved from section to section, past headstones and wiry-thin trees covered in snow, clumps of it raining down in the wind.

Grace pointed to a row of tiny buildings in the innermost section of graves. "Think we could get into one of the tombs?"

Wesley sighed, dropped the basket he'd taken from her. "It's cold. Let's just park it here."

"Here?" Grace looked left, right. "What's special about here?"

But Wesley was already opening the basket, shaking a blanket over the snowy ground.

The four of us spread out in front of the tallest enclosed tombs. Grace dove deeper into the basket to reveal different kinds of meats and cheeses. The half-moon above shone behind the figure of the angel on one tomb, casting a shadow over our midnight snack.

Rand shuffled cards as we started to eat. Poker with M&M's

275

and Skittles for chips was hard to play in the cold and dark. But we managed. Our cards played, Grace, the winner as always, scooted close to Wesley and leaned back into him. "Count the stars for me?" she said.

Wesley set his cards on the edge of the blanket. "Can you see stars from home, Grace?"

"The stars are everywhere." She sat up and scooped her Skittles and M&M's into her pile. "You know that."

"No, but I mean how well can you see them? Are they dim, like in a big city? Or bright like in the country?"

She popped a red candy onto her tongue. "I'll check, look out a window at home."

Wesley cocked his head to the side. "What kind of window is it?"

"Are you really still mad at me for asking you to jump the fence?"

"It wasn't cool."

"It's not like you would've cracked your head open on the sidewalk," she said. "Worst case, you might break an arm. I'd have nursed you back to health."

"Maybe I can't break a bone right now," he said. "Maybe I can't be laid up with a cast on my arm or leg when I go home for the rest of spring."

"Because of baseball?" Grace asked.

I squeezed my eyes shut.

He turned away from us. "Maybe I've got other reasons, okay? Maybe I've gotta work a real job and my knees have to last me into my forties, fifties, sixties. Shit. Probably longer."

Grace blew a breath through her lips like a horse. "I was just trying to make the night a little bigger, our adventure a little brighter."

"It's okay"—Wesley tossed his shoulders back a bit—"if you need that. Maybe if you had a little excitement at home, though, you wouldn't need all this."

"Do you?" Grace asked. "Have excitement at home?"

"You fucking bet."

"Hey, hey," Rand said. "Let's keep this light. Rematch?"

I gathered the cards and shuffled. "If we don't play now, we're going to devour all the candy and be out of chips."

One of Grace's eyebrows quirked. "That felt like a riddle, Wesley."

Rand and I exchanged a look.

"What, Grace?" Wesley held his chin in his hand and tapped his finger along his jaw. "You think I don't have a girlfriend back home?"

Grace's eyes met mine.

My throat felt like it was going to close, partly because I couldn't deny it to Grace and partly because I was angry enough with Wesley to punch him in the face.

Rand blew out a long sigh.

"What?" Wesley shrugged. "Nobody ever asked me not to have a life. I just wasn't supposed to talk about it. Guess I flunked that last part. Like I flunk everything else, right?"

Grace took the cards from me. "It's fine," she said, smiling at Wesley as if there were some kind of private joke between them. She gave the cards an extra shuffle. "Of course it's fine. Wesley's right—I never asked for monogamy."

"I won't be back for spring," Wesley said.

Grace tried to bridge the cards back together, but they cascaded around her.

Rand squeezed my hand. I shook my head. This was the first I'd heard about it.

Grace laughed as if this was part of some game. "And where exactly will you be?"

"My uncle—" He met my eyes. "Uncle Dan. He can get me into the house painters' union. As long as I apprentice through the busy season—spring—I'm as good as in."

The air sucked out of me hearing him say that. This wasn't some kind of a joke.

Grace looked pale. "You won't be back?" she said. "For spring. For *our* spring."

"I gotta. It's not minimum wage. It's money, real money. The kind a person can actually live on."

After what he'd said about Mom, Wesley was finding another way. This was a way to let her go to rehab. Support himself—and me too—while she was gone.

Grace smiled. "But it'll be spring," Grace said. "Our spring."

He didn't know I knew the cabin was really ours. We could cash out—sell—and still get Mom into rehab and support ourselves. But I couldn't tell Wesley. I couldn't take away the cabin, the place we both loved, the place where he could be the person he wanted to be.

"Sorry." Wesley shrugged like it didn't matter. Maybe after all the jagged edges around spring and the last summer, this place didn't matter to him as much anymore. "I can't do this anymore anyway. Have only part of you."

"But you have the best part," she said.

Wesley shifted, crunching the cards that had fallen around him. "I hope that's not true."

He didn't mean it as an insult, but Grace flinched.

"Hey." I stood and held out my hand to help Wesley up. "Let's go for a walk."

If I got Wesley out of there, Rand could talk Grace down.

"I'm good," Wesley said.

"Just go with her," Rand said, leaning in. "Break's almost over. Let's not end like this."

"End?" Wesley asked. "Like you and Nora are really going to end come Saturday night."

Grace threw a wild look between the three of us. "What the actual fuck is going on?"

Wesley sank into himself. "I'm sorry, guys."

There wasn't any way to lie around this. Besides, I was tired of lying.

I exhaled. "It's not a big deal, but Rand and I have been . . . talking back home."

"Oh," she said carefully.

Rand moved closer, reached out to put his hand on her shoulder, then pulled it back.

"Why did you hide it?" she asked. "Was it just a few phone calls?"

"Well, I've—" Rand, hands in his pockets, kicked at the grass. "I've hung out there too."

"Like how?" she asked.

Wesley sat back down, rubbed his head. "Just stupid stuff. Shooting hoops. Prom."

"*Prom.*" Grace whirled to face me. "He took you to prom?"

"It wasn't even planned," Wesley said. "He just found out she didn't have a date. So he was like, I'll be her date. Simple as that. We didn't even really have fun."

"*We,*" Grace said.

Her eyes full of tears, Grace's gaze shifted between Rand and me.

"Did your girlfriend at least have fun?" she asked Wesley. "She was there too, right?"

"Grace, come on," Rand said.

"You met her, didn't you?" Grace asked. "Wesley's girlfriend. Did she complete the three of you? Did she have red hair? Did she laugh like me?"

"Don't go down this path, Grace," Rand said.

"Did she love the three of you as much as I do?" Looking past the boys, she stared hard at me. "Rand in a tuxedo and bow tie? Your hair piled up in curls? Wearing a little tiara? Not just one of our stories, was it?"

All I could manage was: "There wasn't a tiara."

"And after?" Grace asked. "Did you see each other again?"

Rand's arms hung limp at his sides. "A few times."

"All three of you? Four of you?" She stumbled back like a deer taking its first steps. Grabbing her bag, she headed toward the parking lot. "Let's go home."

Roadblocks forced us to take the long way back to the cabins. The Jeep bounced over the potholed road that surrounded the lake, close behind the bumper of a Prius and a stream of taillights that wound up the thin road leading to our cabins.

Grace squirmed in the passenger seat. "Why is this taking so long?"

"There's a wreck or something," Wesley said, his face pressing between the two front seats. "It wouldn't be tree work this late."

Eyes locked on the road, I asked, "What's the hurry?"

"I have a night to plan, Nora."

I did a double take. "You told me—" I lowered my voice even though the boys were right in the back seat. "You told me that was over."

Grace looked over her shoulder. "You heard Wesley. Tomorrow night is the last night the four of us will be together, ever. I need to make it count."

"You didn't," I said. I thought of Neil and Grace. His hands under her clothes. Her hands under his. Then . . . "You did."

Her body was hers to do with what she wanted. But it didn't feel right. Not consensual, not exactly.

"Did what?" Wesley asked.

"No," Grace said. "No."

"You did," I said.

She opened the car door before my wheels could even stop turning.

"Grace," Wesley said. "*Grace.*"

She stumbled out into the road, wiping tears from her cheeks as she turned toward the floodlights of a close-by cabin.

"Is she drunk?" Wesley asked.

"I don't think so," Rand said.

"Fuck me." Wesley threw his door open and stepped out behind her.

From the back seat, Rand said, "Pull over. Pull over."

I veered the Jeep off the road, near the rocky shore that dropped right into the lake.

Grace, with her arms crossed, moved up the shoulder without turning as we spilled out.

Wesley fast-stepped behind her. "Just get back in the car before you get run over, okay?"

Rand groaned behind me but didn't try to push ahead. It wasn't like him to not try to comfort Grace, to rein her in.

"You're being awfully quiet," I said to him.

Wesley's hand struck out, grabbing on to Grace's coat.

"Leave me alone. Let me go home." Grace wrenched her arm away, backing up toward the lake.

Throwing his hands up, Wesley tore at his hair, then spread his arms wide. "Just *talk* to us."

Grace tried to dodge him to the right and then the left. She pressed into his shoulder, rammed her fist into his chest. Wesley didn't budge.

"I can't be with you if you're going to be this fucking crazy," he said.

Grace glanced over her shoulder to the lake behind. "You want to see how crazy I am?"

She smiled, turned around, and tromped knee deep into the lake.

"Get out." Wesley matched her pace along the shore. "It's too cold. And someone's gonna call the cops."

"Good." She walked parallel to the shore, the gridlocked road. "Maybe the cops will actually drive me home."

Wesley stomped back to the car and slammed the door.

"This is bad," Rand said. "So bad."

"Come on, Grace," I said, running along the edge of the water.

"Let me walk you home." I couldn't imagine her walking into her parents' house like this. "I could help you dry off and get into bed. I could—"

"Stop acting like this is nothing, Nora," she said. "I know what you really think of me."

I took a deep breath. This wasn't Grace trying to force Rand to be a better version of himself. This wasn't Grace forcing us on a dangerous adventure just for thrills. This was Grace spinning out.

The faces inside the cars had all turned to watch us. I looked to Rand. Bewildered, he stared at Grace, sloshing at the edge of the water. Even he didn't know how to help her.

"You need to get out of the lake, Grace. You—"

"Grace," Rand yelled. "Come on! We go home the day after tomorrow. Don't leave things like this!"

Grace froze, then faced the shore.

I shivered, pulling my coat tighter as she emerged. Her face speckled with drops of icy lake water, she said, "I never would have done that, Nora. Fucking never."

"I'm sorry," I said. "Grace—"

Clothes dark with lake water, she tromped across the road and between the trees.

CHAPTER 32

WINTER

Grace's message was folded in the bottom of my shoe when I woke up, a piece of paper with a time—10 p.m.—and a hand-drawn map both wrapped around something else: a hotel room key.

We knew she'd gotten home safe last night. Rand had trailed her all the way on foot.

Now I threw on a pair of jeans with the T-shirt I'd slept in and grabbed the Jeep keys.

For so long, I'd been worried Grace's quest for the fantastic would be the thing that got us hurt—Wesley especially—but maybe I'd been wrong. Maybe she was always going to hurt herself worst.

I stood outside her door in the brisk morning air, thinking of all the things I'd tell her we'd do next spring—just Rand and me and her. We'd make it a different kind of adventure. I was freezing by the time Grace answered her door.

She was bare-faced, every trace of makeup washed away, hair damp. "Nora." Her breath left her body in a gentle exhale, like she was both exhausted but maybe a little happy to see me. "You don't give up, do you?"

"Can I come in? I need to talk to you."

The inside of the Lombardis' cabin looked a lot like mine. Fixtures, carpets, and furniture that had been luxuries once upon a time. But a lot of the cabins in Donner were like this.

"Which, um, which one's your room?"

Grace paused, then moved down the narrow hallway toward her bedroom and motioned for me to follow.

On her dresser were packing tape and bubble mailers. Scattered next to them, items I recognized as "finds" from the hotel. That La Perla bra. The cuff links. Selling her stolen goods online—so smart, so very Grace.

Stacked all around Grace's room were duffel bags and backpacks. All bulges and straining zippers, nothing neatly packed. The end of all our vacations were like this—stacks of nicely folded clothing seemed to explode and multiply by the time it was time to head back to the real world.

"The packing's never easy, is it?" she asked.

I hadn't even started mine. I'd be up all night getting my room cleared out and my bags ready to go back to Gridley. Kevin would want to get an early start.

"Grace, please," I said. "Let me help."

Her shoulders rose and fell in a little sigh. "You better make it fast," she said. "A lot of details go into a night like this, my last night."

"What do you mean *your* last night?"

"After tonight, I have places to be that don't involve Truckee."

In the beginning, I thought Grace was the rock holding us together. Now I worried she was the one we were breaking ourselves against.

On her desk was a picture, one that she'd actually developed. I didn't know many people who took the time to turn pictures from something digital into something tangible.

The photo was of the four of us, last winter, on top of Donner Summit. Rand I were staring off into the distance down the mountain and Wesley was head-on toward the camera, taking the selfie. Grace had her head turned—her face in profile—looking up at Wesley.

She sat down next to me, eyes shiny. "Promise me you'll be okay. Promise me that once I'm gone, you'll still do wild things at midnight and look for the best sunsets. Promise me you'll make Wesley try to count the stars. Not worry about baseball or the—his girlfriend back home."

"You don't even know," I said. "He doesn't play baseball anymore. He said it to impress you. And he broke up with his girlfriend for you."

Grace kneaded her hands together. "Doesn't matter anyway."

I stood and set the picture back on the desk. "Besides, you're not going anywhere, Grace. You can tell Wesley whatever you want when we're back. Eventually he'll come back."

"It's not that easy," she said.

But I wasn't listening, not closely enough.

Beside the picture I'd set on the desk, there was another one. I leaned close, closer.

What I was seeing couldn't be real.

I snatched the picture off the desk. "Why do you have a picture of you and Candace?"

Grace's hands shook as she pulled it out of my grasp. "Because." Her voice tiny, she said, "Candace is my sister."

"No, she isn't," I said. "I saw a picture of her mom on the news. I've seen *your* mom."

"We have the same loser dad. She's my half sister."

I sat down heavily on her bed.

"Why?" I asked. "Why would you hide that from me? Pretend she was a stranger?"

I'd always known there was something there. This, I didn't expect. Maybe I should have.

"Please don't look at me like that. Fuck, Nora. I just—I didn't want to tell you how it all went down."

The seasons whirled through my mind. Frigid and sweet and scorching seasons when Grace spoke images of Candace into being: Candace on a long stretch of starlit highway, her hair full of snow flurries in an Alaskan summer blizzard, floating through the air in a plane at sunrise.

"I was really shitty to her the night she left. I knew she was going, and I knew I couldn't stop her. I was so angry at her for leaving. For leaving me. I told her I was glad she was going, that I hoped she'd stay gone. I kept going and going until she was bawling. She told me to be safe. And I—I told her that for all I cared, she could die."

I stared, and Grace glanced away.

"But why did you keep it up later?" I asked. "Season after season."

She shrugged. "The stories we told about her were better than reality."

Grace's words hammered into me. We'd stripped Candace's real story from her—all her hurt and sadness—and replaced it with fantasies that made us feel better. Nourishing ourselves to our own destruction. That's what we'd done.

"Why did she want to leave?" I asked softly.

"*Why?*" Grace stood and began to pace the small room. "Well, her mom moved a new boyfriend in with them every few months. She treated him like a king and Candace worse than a stray cat. But my shitty parents were even shittier. When she came out, they tried to send her back to her mom, like they thought she was going to rub off on me—like being gay isn't just who she is."

I sank low into Grace's mattress. "That's why she went?"

Grace nodded. "She sent me messages—I knew she was safe. It wasn't supposed to be long till she found a way for me to join her. But she couldn't make enough money." Grace turned to me. "Nora, I wasn't just stealing to buy us a few fun nights—I was socking away money to meet up with her. Someday. And now that she's back, she's living with her mom instead. When she was around, she—she loved me, she—" Grace squeezed her eyes shut. "She protected me."

"From people at school?" I asked quietly.

She laughed, but it was hollow. "Rand. Of course. He told you." Grace sighed. "It wasn't supposed to be that big a deal. Just one account where I posted what I wanted my life to be. Then another couple accounts. More. One of every kind. And then I was posting all the time." She slid down the wall till she was sitting on the floor. "They printed out every picture, taped them to my locker and every locker around. They . . . tormented me. They called me *multiple personality*. But the worst part was that I had to delete them all—the accounts, erase the girl I'd created, her perfect life."

"But you didn't," I said. "You became her. Here." I took the picture from her again, stared at Candace's incisors that I'd never noticed matched Grace's. "What did she do?"

Grace smirked. "Beat the shit out of them. They didn't mess with me after that."

A memory of Grace knee-deep and trudging through Lake Donner flashed. "You could have told us. Way before wigging out and dunking yourself in the lake in winter."

Grace turned to me, sharp. "Why? Isn't what I did the same thing you did with Rand and Wesley?"

"Us texting and talking and occasionally seeing each other, and you and me making up stories about a missing girl who I didn't know was your sister? No, Grace, it isn't the same."

"She was never missing."

"But all we ever had were *stories*."

Grace looked at the picture, set it down. "We were more than the stories."

"The problem, Grace, is that after all this, I don't believe you, because you've created a situation where I don't know *what* to believe. There were white lies and outright lies and big exaggerations, and I didn't know how to separate what was real from what was fantasy."

She crumpled herself smaller. "Some of us was real."

"What?" I asked. "Tell me."

Grace opened her mouth to say something, then shook her head.

She wouldn't let me know her. And I never let her know me either. Not really.

Shivering, I squeezed my arms tight around myself.

My phone rang. Wesley.

Before I could say hello, his voice cut through. "Mom OD'd. For real. Come home. We—"

"Oh my god. I'm—I'm coming."

I hung up as I moved toward the door.

"Where are you going?" Grace's voice, quiet, behind me. She was still sitting on the floor.

"Grace, I—" My eyes filled with tears that I wouldn't let fall. "I'll see you tonight."

She nodded as if that were true. Like always, I believed her.

CHAPTER 33

WINTER

The sounds of a life sputtering out were mundane: Endless beeping from machines. Wesley's fingers drumming against the bed's plastic railing. Murmured questions from the doctor. The click of the nurse's stylus on his tablet. Shallow breaths shuddering between Mom's lips, me grateful for every one, terrified of what would happen if they stopped, or if they kept on.

As I watched her chest rise and fall, I remembered the way we used to fall asleep on the couch watching TV when I was little and Wesley played on the floor, how I'd close my eyes and rest my head against her belly as her breathing leveled in her sleep. Pretend to be asleep myself.

I wanted her to get better. This was something she could heal from. Maybe I'd been complicit before, but not anymore. I was terrified. I didn't know how to help her. But I'd figure it out.

With every pause, every soft whir of the machines, every minute and hour, she slowly came back. Each breath more steady, she came back.

Kevin talked to the doctor. Mom needed to stay. We were told to go home.

That night, the lurches and turns of the Jeep took us farther from the hospital room we'd had to leave Mom recovering, and closer to Truckee and Rand. And Grace.

As the seat belt edge cut into my neck, I thought of how I'd left things with her.

Grace wasn't perfect. She could be frustrating and withholding and selfish. But wasn't I those things too?

Turning Candace into a fiction in order to escape my own reality was a mistake. My mistake as much as Grace's.

We'd both fucked up, trying to preserve who we were in the dark.

I owed it to Grace to make sure she knew she wasn't alone in that darkness.

String lights streamed from the rooftop door, dozens of sets of them, all the way to the edge of the roof. The night above them, out beyond the Honeyridge sign, was thick and heavy.

I clutched Grace's hand-drawn map of the road to the Honeyridge.

I needed to be here tonight, not just for the girl I'd been that first spring, who climbed those weaving stairs up here, but to talk to Grace. The urgency of it burned in my lungs.

Wesley stepped clear of the darkness, his jaw loose, and pressing his temples like he could push his hangover headache back into his head.

"It's about time. I thought my toes were going freeze off before anyone showed up." Rand shivered. We were an hour late. My phone battery was dead—I wondered if he'd tried to call. "This party had better be moving inside soon or Grace had better conjure the sun. Are we sure this is the place?"

With an outstretched arm, Wesley gestured to the spread behind him.

Honeyridge towels had been laid out beneath her wicker picnic basket, and a bottle of liquor with a blue bow tied around the neck. Even though the path marked on the map had been short, I had a sense that I'd traveled too far to end up right back here.

"Captain Morgan?" Rand shook his head as he inspected the bottle. "The Captain and I aren't on speaking terms since I experienced his spiced rum in reverse freshman year."

"You're sick, man." Wesley snatched it out of his hand. "If you can't enjoy spiced rum, what's the point of going on?"

"Do you really think that's a good idea?" I asked.

Wesley untwisted the cap and drank. "Hair of the dog that bit you."

Rand turned music on from his phone. The beat didn't quite drown out the voice in my head that told me something was wrong.

Over an hour had passed and I'd wrapped a Honeyridge towel around my coat. Rand stood under the stars, his eyes searching the rooftop. "She should be here."

Whenever Grace planned to lead us into the penthouse, I wasn't sure. Inside me churned all the things I needed to say to her.

Wesley's hands dove into the picnic basket, ripped open some fancy crackers. They crumbled against his lips. "What do you mean?"

"You really don't know her, do you?" The map Grace had drawn flapped in Rand's hand. "After all this time, you still don't know her."

"You want to explain?" Wesley asked.

"She's coming." Rand motioned to the spread. "She wouldn't not show up for this."

I moved away from the boys and walked around the rooftop. The lights from the Honeyridge Lodge sign made the white snow glisten below. Far away on the mountainside, headlights bore glowing holes into the dark. I'd watched those cars two years before, wondered where that road had carried Candace.

Now I knew one had ferried her to an unknown location where she'd work and wait for the right moment to send for Grace. But she'd abandoned that dream.

Rand looked over his shoulder at the rooftop door. "Why isn't she here?"

Maybe I knew.

Maybe Grace had left us here, brimming with so many unspoken words.

Around four o'clock in the morning, Rand walked all the way to the edge of the rooftop, staring down to the snowy ground below. I'd only seen him do that once before, the day at Zion Ledge when

Grace had threatened to jump. "This is lunacy," he said.

"She'll be here." Wesley sat on a towel, cross-legged. "Have a drink. Take the edge off."

Rand turned. "There wouldn't be this edge if you hadn't said what you said to Grace."

Wesley reached for the Captain Morgan and drank.

Another hour went by without any movement from the stairway door. Rand pulled his knees to his chest, making himself small on a towel. Wesley had his leg propped up on the rooftop ledge as he took another drink.

"Stop," I said. "You'll need to be able to stand when the police show up."

"Police?" Rand moved toward us, stopping halfway between the blanket and the end of the rooftop. "Do you really think we should involve them?"

Snowflakes blew against my face and caught in my hair as I paced across the rooftop. "Maybe we should wake up Kevin. Your parents, Rand."

"There's nothing my parents can do." Rand brushed his hands up and down my arms. "Grace will pop out of the elevator shaft or come crash-landing onto this rooftop any moment."

I shook my head. "We have to tell someone. Letting Candace go had been one thing, but we didn't know her. I mean—" I cringed.

A look passed between us.

Rand exhaled. "You know about Candace."

"You knew," I said. "Of course. All this time, you *knew*. You said we'd talk more if we were ever really worried. You watched Grace let her sister go like that. Her sister. And not say a word to any one of us?"

Rand's shoulders slumped. He stared down at the blanket beneath him.

That first morning in the restaurant, when everyone was agreeing on what to do about Candace, there'd been tension crackling between Rand and Grace. I'd read it wrong.

My lungs constricted. My anger flared for a second, then burned out. I'd kept my own knowledge of Grace from him—hotel rooms, diamond bracelets, deals and trades.

Rand said, "When I first met Grace, I'd see her around all the time, with her sister, Candace."

"This doesn't change anything, Nora," Wesley said.

I stared at him, took in his solemn expression.

"Wait, you told Wesley?" I looked between them.

For all the lies everyone had told, I never ever thought the boys might lie to me.

"You both kept this from me? Together. For how long?"

Rand sighed, defeated. "Summer before last."

I wanted to scream at them both, but we didn't have time for that.

I felt the sting Grace must have also felt discovering we'd conspired to keep her in the dark. I had to find her more than ever. I had too much to say.

Wesley smelled like rum. He swayed in the corner of Kevin's dark bedroom. It was my job to shake our dad awake.

"Kevin—our friend's missing," I said. "Grace."

Kevin wiped the sleep from his eyes, looked disorientedly between me and Wesley and back.

He threw back the covers, lurched out of bed. "You think something happened, really?"

"I don't know." Tears brimmed in my eyes and made my vision swim. "I don't know."

Bent over tying his boots, Kevin jerked up to look at me. "Nora," he said. "If she can be found, I'll find her."

All the way to Grace's, his swollen sleepy eyes were trained on the headlights pinning down the road ahead. Even though I believed Grace was choosing to be gone, there was no other option. We had to wake up everyone's parents.

Kevin threw the truck into park outside of Grace's. He rubbed a hand through his stubble and stared past Wesley in the middle seat, all the way to where I'd pressed myself against the truck door. "Have there been any creeps hanging around you and your friends lately?"

"No one," I said, but it was maybe a lie. Lots of insignificant creeps hung around us and other girls all the time.

Kevin exhaled, flung open the door. "She's probably lost in the woods."

The Lombardis were thick tongued when they came to the door.

Rand crossed his arms as he stood beside Kevin, as if he was our representative. Wesley lurked far behind me, in the middle of the icy road, watching the forest.

I stayed off the porch, in the shadow where the light from their cabin didn't splash the ground. I felt exposed standing in front of them when we'd never been a part of Grace's real life.

Grace's dad's face turned the most awful shade of green when Kevin asked if their daughter was home and explained that nobody could find her. Grace's mom wavered on her feet until her dad grabbed on to her shoulder. The gesture didn't look like comfort—more like a warning to not give anyone her tears just yet.

If Grace had shown up right then, she would have been furious to see it.

Kevin, his hands tight around a flashlight, faced the wall of white-frocked trees across the driveway. "If your girl tried to walk back from the lodge, she could have had an accident." He let the flashlight bob through the forest. "Maybe we retrace her steps from the lodge before anyone gets too excited."

A thousand tiny stings erupted across my cheeks as I called Grace's name, hurrying through the blustering white that was beginning to fall. It was strange how something that could be so soft when you landed in a heaping pile of it could also cut so sharply.

Four miles. Four downhill miles back to the Honeyridge. I lost Grace's parents, Wesley, and Rand—and that wasn't an accident. They kept turning up here and there, flashlight beams through the trees, their voices calling *Grace!* into a night that wouldn't yell back.

Grace. Grace. Grace.

I don't know how long it was before I headed back to the Lombardis' cabin by myself.

Something dark stuck up from the fast-falling white. From a distance it could have been a pine cone, but I walked toward it

298

anyway. Then I took off running, the frozen air full of knives and needles as I pulled it into my lungs.

The paper felt stiff and icy as I pressed it into my palm.

But it wasn't a note. It was that picture of the four of us.

I should have done so much more for her, and now she was gone.

And she had gone somewhere fast if she'd dropped this.

I was sure. Grace had run away from Donner. She had run away from her parents, her sister, Wesley, and us. Maybe it had been easy. All our truths exposed, our Donner existence was fading into something that sounded a lot like something we'd made up—just another story.

A couple of cops stood inside the lobby of the lodge, while the three of us sat on the edge of the stone fireplace. She'd only been missing for hours and nobody was acting panicked yet, but I knew the truth: Grace wasn't coming back.

The cops were talking to our parents. All our parents.

They'd insisted Rand drag his out of bed.

I'd seen Grace's parents now and again and Rand's dad once across the parking lot at the Honeyridge. But now they were moving like single organism while the remaining three of us—Rand, Wesley, and me—sat with our backs to the dead fire. Wesley clinging to the hand-drawn map of the lodge Grace had left for him. Rand with his nails bitten down to the quick. Me, rocking back and forth.

All at once, the adults turned their eyes toward us. Panic rose inside me, and I felt it—really felt it—what it meant that Grace was missing.

One cop, the younger one with the reddish complexion, followed the rug to where we sat.

"It'll be okay, kid. It hasn't even been twenty-four hours."

"What?" I asked.

The office squatted down across from me. It was weird, him calling me kid, because he wasn't too much older than Wesley or me. I must have looked small with the blanket around me, hands pale around a beige stoneware mug that felt too heavy to hold between my frozen fingers.

"Missing girls almost always turn up the next morning."

That wasn't true for Candace. But, like Grace, she'd chosen to disappear.

I knew what cold felt like. On my fingers, a snowball packed tight inside my palms. I knew it on my tongue and inside my nostrils, tight dry air filling my chest as I snowmobiled down the slopes. I'd never felt the cold like this, an icy fist around my heart.

As we sat there, Wesley wound something through his fingers. It sucked the air out of me when I recognized it—the necklace he'd bought for Grace. He hadn't given it to her yet.

"Ordinarily, we wouldn't even be here," the cop said. "Twenty-four hours, at least, before we'd bother with a missing person's investigation. But there've been a lot of travelers in and out of the lodge, so if we can, we'd like to rule out foul play. And with the temperatures . . ." The cop gazed out the hotel's window, where the early morning sun streamed across the icicle-covered eaves. Water dripped off the tips, warming now that the snow had cleared. "We'd just feel better—all of us—knowing the girl was somewhere with adequate shelter. You don't think she'd wander off, do you?"

The boys chimed in different versions of *no*. A lie should have come easy for me—I'd had a lot of practice.

"You remember her talking to anyone?" the cop asked me then. I wondered if I'd given him some kind of tell. "Would she have gone off with someone?"

"Did you, um, talk to that guy who works here? Neil?" Wesley asked.

I threw Wesley a look he pretended not to see.

I wondered how long he'd known the truth about Candace. If the boys had told me, maybe I could have talked to Grace, said something to lessen the pain of Candace leaving.

The cop's brow furrowed. "Neil, the kid who usually works the front desk?" He must have known him; Neil had been a suspect in Candace's disappearance. "His dad told me Neil worked yesterday afternoon, then hopped on a plane to Cabo with some friends."

"But when was that?" Wesley asked.

The cop checked his notes. "Flight took off from Reno around six. I need to talk to that kid, though. Surveillance has been down for hours. His pop says he's good with technology."

There was no surveillance all night. Nobody could know what we'd been doing, which was as good as it was bad. Just like the night Candace left.

Grace ran away, I almost blurted.

But the cop turned to Rand before I could say anything. "Kid, is your name really Rand or is that some kind of nickname?"

Rand's eyes had a bloodshot weariness when he took his face out of his hands. He hadn't tried to touch me, talk to me. It wasn't just that he'd kept the truth from me—it was that when he decided to finally share with someone, he'd chosen Wesley.

Memories of the seasons had been taking on a dreamlike transparency ever since I'd learned Candace was Grace's sister. Nothing felt real.

"That's my name," Rand said. "Full name, Bertrand Elliot."

Rand's parents looked over at the sound of his voice and moved in on us.

"Is there a reason you're questioning them?" his dad asked, his accent matching Rand's.

"Just trying to get a grasp on the timeline of the evening," the officer said, turning back to Rand. "So where were you the last few hours?"

Rand's mother whispered something to his father, but I heard it loud, pounding into my ears: "Why are we here? Rand doesn't even know them."

"I was on the roof of the lodge, for a little while." Rand nodded to us. "They were up there too. But I was only up there to look at the stars."

"The stars?" the cop asked.

"There's uh, supposed to be a comet," Rand said.

I tapped my foot against the brick fireplace, trying to get him to look at me.

Rand had grown preoccupied with the pattern of the lodge's worn-out rug. "When there were too many clouds to see anything interesting, I went back to my parents' cabin."

"And then?" the cop asked.

Rand tugged at the collar of his shirt. "I read a book. I finished it a little after midnight. It was late when these two knocked on my window and asked me if I'd seen her. The other girl."

These two. The other girl. The words ricocheted around inside me.

The cop's eyes narrowed. "So you were up on the rooftop and just oblivious to them. The spread someone laid out? The bottle of booze?" He gestured to us. "These two?"

The floor gave way beneath me. Rand's parents, their watchful gaze on Wesley and me—he was embarrassed to admit he was with us. Like he didn't even know white-hot summers, or the feel of his frozen nose buried in my winter coat. He was ashamed of us—of me.

Rand's mother sighed. "Tell the truth, Bertrand."

Like that, tears streamed down his cheeks. "We were up there together. All of us."

Rand stared at me apologetically. I looked away. The damage was done.

The cop turned his attention to Wesley. "You want to lie about anything too?"

"I'm not lying about anything," he said. "I swear."

It was hard to look at any of them after that. I was angry with Rand for lying about us, with Wesley for hiding the truth about Candace, and most of all, with myself.

A deep wrinkle had formed across the cop's forehead as he crouched in front of me. "Is there anything else you think I should know?"

Beneath the blanket wrapped around me, I clutched the photograph, the one I'd found crinkled in the snow outside her cabin.

If Grace had really run away, she'd want me to give her every chance to get out of town.

If she came back now, she'd find the three of us were no longer what she designed. The real world had bled in.

But I couldn't keep my mouth shut any longer.

My fingers smoothed the bent paper. "She ran away."

The hotel restaurant clattered with the sounds of the kitchen and the smoky smell of breakfast foods. I wasn't hungry. I'd moved away from the crowd of diners to sit at another table—the one by the window where we'd eaten lunch with Grace and Rand that first morning.

"You don't drink coffee, huh?" Mug in hand, Kevin pulled up a chair. "I don't think I did either when I was your age."

Staring at the ski lift out the window, I said, "Not like that. Not black."

"You probably like the fancy stuff." He took a sip from his cup. "You've known Grace a long time, huh?"

"Sort of, yeah," I said, keeping it simple.

"I only really met her once. Your accident. That girl, damn. She was off the back of the boat, in the water before I turned the ignition off. Could have been mangled by the propeller."

I pulled my knees into my chair, held them to my chest. "I don't know why she did that."

"You would have done the same thing for her, I think."

Warm tears cut down my cheeks.

"Come here," Kevin said. He came around the table, sat in the chair next to me, and pulled me into a sideways hug.

I sank into it, this comfort I shouldn't take. We wouldn't

have even been here, in Donner, if not for my grandmother's will forcing us back into his life. I pulled away.

"If you need anything, Nora, you just tell me. With this or . . . or with your mom. I heard she's better now. More stable."

I nodded. It was a small consolation. "We do need something. We need a—little help. To sell the cabin."

"Oh," he said. "I didn't know you'd made a decision."

I sat back in my chair. "We haven't. Wesley probably won't agree."

His scruffy chin in his hand, Kevin cocked his head to the side. "When you turn eighteen, it's pretty much your call. If Wesley doesn't want to sell, he'd still have to. Or come up with enough to cover your half of the inheritance. Buy you out."

I turned sharply to face him. "So I would force him."

"It's not like that. This isn't about hurting him—it's helping him make the right decision. He might be pissed, but you'd be doing it in his own best interest."

I nodded. "Why are we talking like this now? After everything?"

"We should have before," he said.

"You tried," I said. "I didn't always."

Kevin met my eyes, blinking fast. "I didn't always try very hard either. I figured you two would just do the things I used to do—fishing, hiking, waterskiing. We know how that last one turned out. Sorry I fucked this up."

What he'd done had been trying—in the backward, awkward way of his. I was the one who had made a conscious decision not to try. Maybe I'd made that mistake before too.

And now it was too late to save Grace.

WINTER: NOW

CHAPTER 34

These boys I loved, I couldn't trust them. Rand and Wesley, who'd helped create an existence from snowmobiles cutting through powdery drifts, sunscreen slick and warm on our skin, damp pine-flavored air in our lungs, and wild nights that had defined and destroyed us.

So many secrets. How could we be us with so much withheld?

Now Wesley's hand was tightening around Rand's throat. White-hot panic seized me. "Let him go," I said, prying at Wesley's fingers.

"You're still on his side, Nora?" Wesley asked.

"I'm not on anybody's side except mine and Grace's."

Wesley yanked forward, then back, arm shaking with effort. The back of Rand's head thudded against the wall, and he flinched. "This lying piece of shit didn't even have an accident."

"What are you talking about?" I said, at last getting Wesley to ease up. "The gash. Rand, if you didn't have an accident, then how?"

Rand gasped, blood trickling from his split lip. "Self-inflicted."

"What? Why?" I asked.

"Yeah," Wesley said. "Motherfucking why?"

Rand wouldn't speak or fight back, just lolled his head against the wall, not looking at us.

Wesley's grip tightened again, and he shuddered. The snow on his jeans and coat had melted. He was soaking wet in the ice-cold cabin.

I was afraid of what they'd do to each other. What we'd already done to each other.

"Wesley, you have to stop," I said. "Go change into something dry before you get frostbite and lose your fingers and toes."

He didn't let up.

I gestured at the snow billowing in through the still-open front door and the darkness beyond. "Look out there. Even if the snowmobile is running, he still can't make it home."

Wesley's hand slowly relaxed.

Rand slipped down the wall toward the floor and curled his knees to his chest.

"She loved you the most," Wesley said. "Fuck you. Fuck you."

The whole house rattled as Wesley walked over and slammed the front door, sealing us in for the night.

I heated the last can of chicken noodle on the gas stove.

Wesley had gone out to the woodshed, gathering some of the probably-too-green wood he'd chopped that afternoon. We'd make ourselves sick breathing in all that sap and smoke once we lit it. But sick was better than dead.

We were going to make it. But first we were going to get very cold.

Rand was in the bathroom, pressing gauze to his wounds. He needed stitches, but I couldn't do anything about that.

All I cared about was that the cabin was finally silent except for the trees thrashing against the house, the wind snapping the blankets we'd used to tape off the window, and the bubbling pot of soup.

Wesley had attacked Rand with questions that still screamed throughout my head: *Why would you lie? What the fuck, man? What happened to your face? The snowmobile is pristine, so what, you kicked your own ass?*

Behind me, the fall of footsteps.

Even if I hadn't known Wesley was outside, I would know who stood behind me just from the sound of his breaths.

"I found these way in the back of the cabinet." Rand slid an unopened box of oyster crackers across the kitchen tiles.

"He speaks," I said without turning from the stove. "I don't know who to trust, Rand."

He hopped up on the kitchen counter beside me. "Ask me anything."

"You'll lie to me. You'll lie just like you've been lying since you showed up on my doorstep today. Like you've been doing for I don't even know how long."

He flinched. "This is just us. I won't lie. Ask me anything and I'll give it to you straight."

I reached into the drawer for a spoon, slammed it shut. "Whatever you tell me, I won't be able to believe you."

"Yes, you will," he said. "You'll believe me because you'll absolutely *hate* the answers."

I faced him. "Okay, why did you pretend you were in an accident? Why would you . . . *do* that to yourself? Why would you want to end up stranded here?"

"Because I needed to get inside and I knew your dad installed that alarm system after Grace's disappearance. I figured you'd only let me in if something bad had happened."

Heat rose up from my chest and settled in my cheeks. "Well, you weren't wrong, were you?" I was angry and embarrassed that he was right. "But why?"

"This is the one place I hadn't been able to look for some hint of where Grace had gone. I'd—I'd already checked the wood-shed."

My heart dropped into my stomach. "No," I said. "No, you didn't."

He exhaled. "I only broke the lock to see if there was a note inside. When I came back to fix it last week, all the wood was gone. Someone else stole it. I'm so sorry, Nora." He looked through the kitchen to the living room, hazy with gray smoke from the uncured wood, the tree branch lying like a dead thing on the rug. "Believe me."

"You're the reason we might freeze to death."

"I'm fully aware. I'm the one who made a bad situation entirely worse. That's one of the reasons I knew I couldn't leave you both stranded like this."

"Don't tell Wesley," I said. "Did you find anything? Anything anywhere?"

Rand's eyelids were heavy with disappointment and fatigue. "Absolutely nothing."

We moved all the bedding into the upstairs hallway, away from the tree that had fallen.

"We need more blankets," I said, getting up and pointing myself toward the attic.

I gave a hard tug on the rope connected to the trapdoor. Instead of the ladder dropping down, the rope fell with a soft thud to the floor, the frayed end still hanging above.

"No big," Wesley said. He wedged a foot against the banister and heaved himself up toward the ceiling, balancing on the rickety railing. With one hand holding on to mine for balance, he reached across the ceiling. Even straining, his fingers were at least six inches short of the latch.

Rand stood back, eyes moving from the railing to the attic door and then to Wesley. "You could jump for it, catch the door, and pull it down."

Wesley squinted down at us. "And hurt myself. You'd love that, wouldn't you?"

Rand walked a slow circle. "I'm not trying to injure you. But I've seen you scale a graveyard fence, monkey-bar a ski lift."

"I don't know," I said.

"No, wait. I can do this." Wesley let go of my hand, steadied himself against the wall. His heels balanced against the outside of the banister, he leaped.

His fingers just missed.

He smacked down, one foot landing square on the landing,

the other slipping out from under him. His knee banged into the hallway wall. He groaned.

I took an involuntary step forward to help him.

Cradling his arm, he said, "I'm okay. Just gotta rub some dirt on it, yeah?" he said, getting to his feet too fast. "Okay," he said. "I'm going for it again."

One leap, a grab, and the ladder stairs came tugging down. As the first section of stairs unfolded, Wesley let go and landed, this time softly.

"Yes!" Rand clapped once, loud.

Wesley smiled up at the open attic and Rand nodded back.

I hoped the truce would hold.

Wesley hurled an armful of blankets at us when we he came back down. I was still holding my mug in my hands, even though it was no longer warm. I'd wanted so badly to find a letter from Grace somewhere, like that day at Zion Ledge—the first time she'd disappeared.

Then I could go back to being mad at her again. The anger was so much easier than this.

"Wesley, Grace didn't leave you letters, did she?" I asked. I wished we'd been closer over the last year. I wished I'd asked sooner.

"Letters? No, never." He shrugged. "Why? You still looking for evidence she ran? How did she run away if she didn't take anything with her, Nora? All her bags were still packed inside the Lombardis' cabin. She would have needed clothes and cash and stuff."

"But Grace could get things," I said. "She had ways."

Wesley picked his mug up off the carpet and turned it in his hands. "What about, like, some pervert or something? There are psychos out there who would have wanted to take her. Grace was"—his voice caught, and when he looked back up, his eyes were shiny with tears—"lovely."

Rand sniffled. A deep breath shuddered out of me.

"Maybe," Rand said. "But according to her parents, the cops said none of the guests fit the bill. No serious offenses. No violent felonies."

"Vineyard Vines? I never liked how he looked at her. Cops said he was on a plane, but—"

"He really was on a plane," Rand said. "I confronted him. Well, punched him."

"What?" I asked.

Wesley laughed. "No, you fucking did not."

"No, I did. Hit him right in the mouth, split his lip open. I was aiming for his cheek, but that was good enough."

Wesley's eyes went wide. "What did he say? What did he do?"

"I don't know." Rand laughed. "I ran like hell. Didn't look back."

I laughed. Even Wesley grinned.

"Or—" Rand stopped and waved his hand dismissively. "Never mind."

"What?" I asked.

Rand tipped his head back against the wall. "Or after all the horrible awfulness of that day, zero hope we'd ever all be together again, all the family shite she had going on, she decided to end things . . . permanently."

I exhaled, long and hard. I didn't want to think like that. "Nobody ever found a body or any signs or any note. Grace didn't kill herself." But how sure could I be?

Wesley zipped his jacket up to his chin and wiped his nose on his sleeve. *"Zero hope we'd ever be all together again.* Any way you look at this, it's my fault, huh?"

"I didn't mean it that way—" Rand started.

Wesley rubbed his eyes, digging his fists in them before he looked up. He stomped toward the stairs. "I'm going into my room because if I'm going to freeze to death, I'd rather do it the fuck alone." He slammed the door so hard, I felt the reverberation in my teeth.

The realization hit me slowly and then all at once. If Grace wanted a permanent end, she knew this land—she'd know how to make sure she was never found.

Rand and I turned off our flashlights to conserve battery power— the batteries were old and we didn't know if they had minutes left or hours. Alone with only the cold dark pressing down, I remembered that Nietzsche line that Rand had quoted—staring into the abyss so long, it looked back into you. After all the significant and insignificant ways we'd hurt each other, maybe the abyss was inside us.

A cloud built over me. It sucked up all the air in the room and then dove down inside me searching for more.

"What are you thinking about?" Rand asked.

I took a deep, shaky breath of cold air. "The abyss."

"Oh, just that." Thumping his flashlight against his thigh, he laughed softly. "The good old abyss."

"Do you think Grace ever knew you weren't actually into Nietzsche?"

"Maybe she didn't." Rand reached past me to pull another blanket over us. "She knew I liked philosophy and somehow we kept going back to Nietzsche. The dark stuff. Like my dad."

"Why do you think he believes in all that?

Rand settled against the wall next to me. "With all the horrible things going on in the world, I guess he settled on one school of thought—existential nihilism. Heavy shit. He doesn't think people should procreate. He thinks everything would be better if we stopped multiplying, like so many species before us, just walked into extinction."

"Well, that's . . ."

"Dark? Depressing? Take your pick. Either way, it's been miserable. My life, I mean, since he came to his big"—Rand formed air quotes—"*realization*. He doesn't just believe people should stop having children. He believes it's actually highly unethical. So how am I supposed to take that? Sit there at dinner and ask him to pass me the sweet potatoes while I know that having me was the greatest ethical stumbling of his life."

"He tells you that?"

"Yes. No. Well, yes and no. I read between the lines."

"You should tell him his theories are bullshit," I said.

Rand looked up, laughed. "Well, that would make for lively dinner conversation."

"Really, you should," I said. "This is why he and your mom fight?"

"Eh, kind of," he said. "She can't keep living like this. His depression is like a black hole that's going to swallow her if she doesn't get out—I heard her say that on the phone to one of her friends. That was when I called you. Before prom."

"When you said you were trying to prove you deserved to exist, this is what you meant."

He nodded.

"Why didn't you ever tell me this?"

"Whenever it came up, we found a way to distract us—which I liked. But also"—he shrugged—"sometimes I wanted you to ask. Or I wanted me to be braver, to risk saying more."

I pressed my shoulder deeper into his, not only because I was cold but because I wanted to be a fraction of an inch closer to him. "I'm sorry."

"I am too."

The day Grace led me to her trunk, and I saw where she kept all her stolen stuff, I wondered if she wanted me to ask. I wished I had. Maybe it could have mattered.

"All I can think about is Grace," I said. "The three of us hanging out between the breaks, talking, laughing. We kept ourselves from her. She was the one who may have needed our friendship most."

"You're right," he said.

The wind whining above gave way to a splintering sound. Our eyes went to the ceiling and then to each other.

Rand glanced up. "Whatever that was, it doesn't fill me with the greatest confidence about the rest of the night."

The Sheetrock overhead cracked, a rushing line that ran from the front wall of the house, upward to the slanted roof that ran over the staircase.

The possibility of what might happen built within me.

"The snowfall's too heavy," I said. "I don't know if the roof can support—"

Another wail of wind and Sheetrock rained down. We covered our heads, closed our eyes.

The stuff coating us was too cold, too powdery to be all Sheetrock. Something struck my leg. The sound of the impact faded away. Heat radiated from my shin.

Lost to the falling white, I felt Rand's warm hand in mine.

As the debris settled, I opened my eyes.

"Wesley," he said. "He was in his room."

Our feet pounded the floor, me in front of Rand.

"Wesley!" I yelled.

Littering our path were clumps of snow and papers from the attic and shingles and pieces of roof. I went still, looking up at the damage.

Above, through a space at least as tall as me and a dozen feet wide, I could see the black night speckled with thick falling snow. The spinning sky rained into the house. Snow already powdered the stair treads as Rand and I rushed—stumbling and tripping—up the landing.

"Wesley!" We'd lost our flashlights. They were buried somewhere under the carnage. "Wesley. Wesley. Wesley!"

In his doorway, his shadow appeared.

He stepped into the moonlight. A dark trail ran from his hairline, down his cheek. Teeth red with blood, he swayed on his feet.

* * *

We stuffed the fireplace with pieces of moving boxes. We'd moved back downstairs—it was safer here but not by much. We were already out of wood. Cardboard ignited and burned red hot for only a few moments until it disintegrated to dry ash.

We did it again and again. It barely cut the chill of the wind rushing in through the blankets we'd used to seal off the front window, let alone the gaping roof above.

Wesley'd been unsteady on his feet when he'd tried to stand. Rand and I sat him in front of the fireplace beside us, where we could keep an eye on him. We all checked our phones again. No service.

Rand fed the fire, his nose bright red and his lips peeling. "We're not going to make it until morning. Maybe we could seal ourselves inside the bathroom."

My toes were numb inside my boots, and my ankles tingly and painful. I didn't want to tell the boys. "We wouldn't have the fire. It's barely big enough for one person to turn around."

"We could try to build one," Rand said. "Maybe in a pot. It could take the chill off."

I shook my head. "With the way things have been going, I wouldn't be surprised if we burned what's left of the house down."

Rand moved into the kitchen, cranked the oven up, opened the door. "This is gas, right?"

Wesley held his hand to his hairline, pulled back to look at his fingers. Through the firelight, they were shiny and sticky with blood. "Yeah, but man, that's dangerous too.

"It's something." Shaking, I watched snow tumbling softly

down from above. "That roof. We have to close it up somehow."

"How high—" Wesley's lips moved as he stared at the ceiling— I realized he was calculating distance. "Maybe Dad has an extension ladder out there."

"That would have come in handy for the attic door," I said dryly.

Wesley got halfway to his feet, swayed, and balanced his hand on the wall. "I'll see if it's there."

I got to my feet, knees a little shaky. My leg was still throbbing, but I didn't think it was fractured. "No way," I said, grabbing his arm as he moved past me. "You're hurt. You can't."

He shrugged out of my reach. "Don't tell me what I can't do. You're always criticizing me for something."

I blinked. "I—is that true? I don't mean to do that at all."

"For not being around, for not fixing stuff right. What do you want from me, Nora?"

"What do I want from you? I don't even know what that means."

"When I'm gone, it's to try to help you. And Mom."

"Wesley." I exhaled. "That's never what I wanted from you. I just—" I thought back to Wesley mowing the neighborhood lawns for extra cash, trying to fix broken appliances, working at the mechanic shop, taking the job for our uncle. "I know you did all that for us, me."

His eyes were wet. He sniffed and straightened up. "I tried. It never felt good enough, though."

"You didn't have to be good enough," I said. "I just wanted you . . . *there*."

His arms circled me, his chin pressing down on my head. "I'm sorry I wasn't."

Snow dusted my cheeks as I sank into his hug.

Rand cleared his throat. "Nora," he said. "Wesley. Not to break up this beautiful moment, but I have an idea."

Duct tape and wall-to-wall carpet that we ripped up with X-Acto knives wouldn't have been the tools I chose, but Rand swore they'd work, and about this, I trusted him.

Outside, Wesley held the ladder against the house, his teeth chattering. "You say the word, Nora," he called, "and we'll stop."

"Or I could try to do it," Rand shouted up to me, not for the first time.

"No," I said. The boys were in pieces and I was the only one who was somewhat whole. I would be the one to climb up to the second story and patch the roof. Rand freaking out halfway up the ladder wouldn't help any of us. "Just go inside. You know what to do."

The higher I climbed, the more the ladder seemed to waver. I glanced down at Wesley, his fists around the ladder rungs.

"You're good," he called.

I trusted Wesley, his judgment and his hold. The ladder itself was a rickety piece of equipment that was the only thing standing between me and a twenty-foot drop.

My fingertips finally found the edge of the frozen roof. I pulled myself up, breathing the cold inside me, then belly crawled across the frozen shingles. I stayed on my stomach, not only because I was afraid I would slip, but because I was worried about the already snow-heavy roof being able to support my weight.

It was worse off than I could have imagined. The shingles I could see should have been replaced years ago. We already would have had to redo the roof before we could pass a home inspection.

My down coat worked up around my middle. I winced at the scrape of my exposed belly against the icy roof, and followed the light shining up through the hole. It spotlighted the falling snow-flakes and almost looked beautiful against the night sky.

When I reached the splintered void in the middle of the cabin, Rand had his flashlight pointed into the space to light my way.

He stood halfway up the stairs, and his shoulders sunk with relief when he saw me.

"See," I said down through the hole. "Everything's fine."

"Just please hurry." Rand tossed the first large piece of carpet up to me.

My knees slipped as the weight of it hit my hands.

Sliding, I heard him cry out.

I splayed myself wider, grasping for splinters and rot. The knee of my jeans ripped, but I finally stopped.

"I'm coming up there," Rand yelled. "I'm coming up!"

"No." I sighed. In the dark, a black bead of blood formed on the tip of my finger. I sucked it into my mouth.

From the waistband of my jeans, I took out the hammer. From my pocket, a couple nails.

Behind Rand, Wesley appeared in the shadows. He would be back outside after I had the carpeting nailed to the roof and the hole covered. He'd hold the ladder steady against the wind as I climbed down.

His breaths came in short gasps. "You're doing good, Nora. Nice and steady. Slow and careful. You got this."

The boys braced themselves against the stairwell, blinked against the falling snow as I nailed each piece down hard into the crumbling rooftop.

"Another," I said, and Rand tossed up a fresh piece of carpet.

This was working. It wasn't waterproof, but it could hold until morning.

The more pieces I patched in, the less I could see into the house below and the less space remained for Rand to shine light on my work. I had my own flashlight in my pocket, but I couldn't hold it plus a hammer and nails. If I set it down, the high pitch of the roof could send it rolling to the edge and tumbling to the ground below.

But I was almost done.

A corner of the carpet was stuck on something and draping into the hole in the roof below. I needed to pull it closer to nail it in place.

"Can one of you get something to push this back up?" I shouted down to the boys.

Rand picked up the broom we'd used earlier. He propped the end of it against the carpeting. One push and the handle snapped in half.

"Shit," I heard Wesley say. "You broke it."

"I don't think my technique was the issue," Rand said. "What else do you have?"

Their voices moved away.

"There's a set of snow skis in my room, back of the closet," Wesley said, muffled.

"Hang on, Nora," Rand yelled.

The cold throbbed in me. With all the exertion, I was breathing too hard, sucking in too much frigid air. I pressed my cheek to the carpet I'd already nailed down and closed my eyes. In the soft haze of falling snow and my slowing breaths, I waited. I don't know how long.

A crash below jolted me alert. "What's happening?"

There wasn't an answer, only a thud and a pop and Wesley's pained voice.

"Shit, man, you hit me. Why'd you fucking hit me?"

My hands clawed at the carpet edge. Through thin gaps, I could see slices of the room below.

The scuffle of shoes. The fall of a body. A gurgle of breath. Rand heaving his arm back, swinging. Wesley's eyes wide and wild.

"Stop it!" I beat my fist on a shingle that came loose, tumbled down. "What the hell are you doing, Rand?"

He had Wesley against the stairwell wall, his forearm bearing into Wesley's throat. Wesley's feet were barely touching the slick, snowy floor beneath him. Rand had snapped.

"All this time," Rand said. "All this time and you hid it from us."

Wesley, grip tight around Rand's wrists, said through his teeth, "You had no right. That was mine. *Mine.*"

"What are you talking about!" I screamed.

Rand shook a loose sheet of paper in his hand. "He has a letter, Nora. A letter from Grace."

From Grace. *From Grace.*

Wesley gurgled something and his face turned blue. Rand let up.

Wesley got out: "And it's my private business. Between me and Grace."

Roofing beneath me crumbled. Shingles tumbled, carpets gave way, fabrics ripped. I fell into the space below, braced for impact.

But I was caught, the back of my coat on a sharp piece of board or a nail.

The boys broke apart.

Rand ran up the stairwell, reaching out. I stretched, my fingertips grasping at air.

A loud rip sliced through the night. I dropped.

The impact came first, then the pain.

It felt like my body splintered into a million pieces when it hit the staircase. But under all that hurt, there was an eerie, peaceful calm.

SPRING AND SUMMER: YEAR THREE

CHAPTER 35

I didn't go back to Truckee that spring or summer. I stayed on at the pizza place and told Kevin they required me to work the summer if I wanted to keep the job through senior year. I couldn't go back to Donner. Summer was Rand, Wesley, and Grace.

But Grace was gone and it felt like Rand had left right behind her. He was just as absent from my life. Wesley wasn't going back for the summer anyway.

He drank and he fought. He helped my uncle out two days a week until he got into it with another guy at work and my uncle fired him. In the living room where we both slept, he kicked a basketball-sized hole that might as well have been my heart.

One morning, he left.

He didn't tell me where he was going, but he took the duffel bag he carried for every break.

Donner was his now. He could have whatever remained of it for as long as we still owned it—springs, summers, winters, whatever. I didn't want it anymore.

I didn't look at social media. I'd connected with Rand before, and I didn't want to see him now. I didn't want to know if he was applying to colleges or letting the music of a live band thrum through his heart or falling in love with someone who wasn't me.

My story was in my top desk drawer, and I ripped it in halves, then quarters, and more and more until my words were confetti.

I was too old—too *something*—for stories anymore. That kind, at least.

All summer long, when the pizzeria would close for the night and I had a good eight hours to kill until morning, I drove up through the foothills. I wound and wound my car through the twisted, tree-draped hills, spinning and searching for a sensation I couldn't quite describe but also couldn't find.

Music blasting through speakers, ringing inside my ears, I felt a little less alone.

But the quiet always came. It enveloped me in a cool darkness that could have only been fixed by air that smelled of pine, and friends that lifted me and laughed, and adventures that lasted through the night and carried me into every bright, new season.

When the foothills left me feeling empty, I traveled the dry, flat valleys, hoping for a fissure in the earth to swallow me up. I just wanted to feel some of the excitement summer was supposed to bring. The adrenaline rush that summer had always brought, before.

I was cleaning out old binders one hot August Saturday, getting them ready for the new school year, when Mom padded into the kitchen.

She sat across from me at the kitchen table as I pulled out a half-page story I'd written last year while the history sub showed a movie.

Her eyes were sunken a bit, dark smudges underneath, both making her look older.

A bottle of pills sat between us. She focused on it and looked away.

I tensed.

Her hand reached out, but she moved it past the pills, toward my binder. "You should have a new one."

"This one still works. Mostly. One of the rings is a little bent."

"I wish you could have a lot of new things," she said, her eyes distant, then homing in on my story, smiling. "I used to write stories like that too."

"I don't write stories anymore." I crumpled it, tossing it into the trash along with last year's history notes.

"Yeah, I stopped too. I wish I hadn't. I even had one published. Just in the local paper, but still."

I blinked. I hadn't known that.

"Do you still have it?" I asked.

"Oh, somewhere. Probably buried in an old yearbook or something."

I stared at her, this mother I barely knew. Her eyes were dark like mine. Her nose freckled like Wesley's. She used to write stories. What else did she do? What else had she lost?

"Don't stop writing them, okay?" Mom sighed, then her eyes drifted to her pills. "I haven't had any today. And this headache . . ."

She popped one onto her tongue.

It wasn't me she was lying to. I could see that now. It was herself.

"I hope you feel better," I said. And I meant it, deep in my bones.

WINTER: NOW

CHAPTER 36

Wesley's shoes crunched up what remained of the snow-covered stairs as I caught my breath. He looked me over. "Are you hurt?"

I shook my head.

He knelt next to me. "Can you talk?'

"Yes." It came out as a wheeze.

He turned, ripped the letter out of Rand's hand, and wiped his tears on his sleeve. "She meant this for me. Only me. Not cool, snooping through my stuff."

Rand, on his knees at my side, brushed his thumb over my lower lip.

"I'm fine," I said.

Rand turned to Wesley. "When I grabbed the skis, I knocked the shoebox down. I couldn't stop myself from noticing Grace's handwriting."

I sat up slow, looked at Wesley, and asked, "When did you find it?"

Wesley refolded the paper along the creases Grace had scored the year before. "Back home. A couple days after Grace went missing."

"Can I?"

Wesley stared at my outstretched hand. He sighed. "Fine."

Wesley,

You're back home now, hopefully finding this letter in your dirty clothes before you washed them. If not, I hope I'm soggy but legible. Your feet are twitching for summer-hot dirt that's never going to make it between your perfect knobby toes. And you're sad because of me—who wouldn't be? (Haha. Also, don't be!) But I want you to know that while you're painting houses, I hope you laugh, and I hope you love someone (yes, even if it's not me—see how I'm being the bigger person here? It blows.), and never forget what I told you about the stars. You're not going to paint houses for long. Those maps! The curls in your cursive! Someday you'll make something big and beautiful. You owe it to the universe. And I hope you're not going to keep boring yourself with baseball. How mundane. All those rules and regulations and ugly pants. You were meant for better.

Yours (Sort of. Wherever I am, I'm still mine.),

Grace

"How could you hide this?" Rand shook his head. "Knowing what it shows. Proves."

"What does it prove?" I asked.

"*Wherever I am* means she didn't kill herself." Rand's forehead crumpled as if he was thinking something awful. "Unless she's talking in some kind of spiritual, New Age way. I guess that would be very Grace."

"What are you saying?" I asked. "That this is a suicide note?"

Wesley sniffled as he took the letter back. "She'd never left me a letter before. Just this one time. Maybe she still meant to show up on that rooftop or maybe she meant to disappear. But I think she didn't want me to feel guilty. Or maybe that's just what I hope. I've had a lot of time to think about this." Wesley smoothed the damp paper and laughed. "But I don't know why she added that part about baseball."

Rand had asked if we were beyond secrets, and maybe I was.

"The day she went missing, I told Grace you never played baseball," I said. "And I told her you had broken up with Lauren. It wasn't to hurt you or to expose you. It was just something that spilled out."

"It's not your fault," Wesley said into his chest. "Look, it's mine, okay? I saw her again. That night."

I blinked.

Wesley crossed his arms. "I was the last to see her."

"What time?" Rand asked. "Was it that night?"

Wesley looked up. "What?"

"We both saw her too," I said. "Me first—that morning. Then Rand." All the details of the hours before Grace vanished came spinning into the light then.

When we finished, Wesley said to Rand, "It was after you. Had

330

to be. I met her out in the woods. It was fucking freezing." He looked at me. "It was after we got back to Truckee. After we left Mom. Grace—she tried to tell me about Candace. But I already knew, and as soon as she realized that, she took off." He scrubbed his hands over his face. "Maybe if I had told her sooner I knew the truth, maybe . . ." He shook his head.

"Grace's state of mind that night." Rand shuddered. "I didn't help her when I could have. When I *should* have."

"I was with her when I got the call about Mom. If I hadn't kept all that truth from her for so long, if I hadn't worried what she'd think of me, it would have been so easy to explain that morning. Leaving wouldn't have been walking out on her. I didn't ever let her know me, and because she didn't know me, she thought I was abandoning her."

"But I saw her last," Wesley said. "I could have fixed it."

"No, you couldn't have," I said. "Whatever happened that night, it doesn't matter. It wasn't one night that pushed her to do whatever she did. It doesn't matter who saw her last, who said the final cruel thing. It was two years of not letting her in. That's on all of us."

Wesley stood. He exhaled hard, tears streaming down both cheeks. He didn't say where he was going, but as he moved up the stairs, picking his way hurriedly over the debris, he carried Grace's letter as if he couldn't wait to put it back where it belonged.

After Wesley was gone, Rand said, "You're right. We all wronged Grace. In a million little ways. With our silence as much as our lies. If I'd ever thought any of this could happen, I never would have kept you in the dark about Grace's secrets."

"I know," I said. "I do. I kept things from both of you that I shouldn't have. And I kept things from Grace. And she kept things from us."

"Do you really think we didn't know her?"

"Yes," I said. "And no. I did know her. I know she loved sno-cones and stories and living big and feeling big and giving gifts, and she loved us. I didn't know what it felt like to live in her home, with her parents. I didn't know she had a sister she loved, who'd left. I knew she was hurting sometimes but I rarely knew why." I swallowed. "She was supposed to be one of our best friends. I should have known what to say. What to do."

"Maybe." He sighed. "The three of us weren't the only ones who kept secrets."

"There were so many things I didn't know, Rand. There were a few times—near the end—when I felt like maybe she wanted me to ask. And I didn't. I just took from her—I took all the stories and let them fill me up."

I thought back to the conversation with my mom, how knowing that little piece of her from before—how I couldn't even be angry anymore. How anger was too simple an emotion.

Imagine if we had all just known Grace a little better. Maybe it wouldn't have saved her. But maybe it would have.

Rand rubbed his eyes. "I didn't ask either. I didn't because I thought I had enough pieces of the puzzle to know why Grace did the things she did. I thought it was better for her if I didn't force her to have those conversations. And I was afraid the real truth would ruin things here, stop me from seeing you and Wesley." He looked at me. "Do you think that's normal?" he asked. "Never asking those questions?"

"I never asked you either, did I? I never— The real situation with your dad. I—"

"Nora, it's fine—"

I stood up, paced. "But it's not."

Those times with Sasha and Bailey, when they were talking like they knew each other—because they *did*—I didn't ask them either. Chase, in his car, playing that song he loved, I didn't ask him. I never really tried with any of them.

Blinking fast, I turned to face Rand. "In the restaurant at the Honeyridge, I asked Kevin why after all this time he was *trying*. But really, he tried more than I ever did. I blamed everyone for the fact that I didn't really know them—Sasha, Bailey, Kevin, and Grace too—but it wasn't entirely their fault, was it? It was partly mine. They could have asked, but I also didn't try."

I tried to smile, but my voice cracked. "This is why I don't have other friends."

Rand squeezed my arm. "Just because you made a mistake doesn't mean you're going to keep making it."

Waiting for dawn was all we had left to do. I handed out extra pairs of socks. We wore them as mittens over our gloves to get through the night. We were exhausted, our bodies, minds, hearts.

Wesley looked at his cell phone. "It's one a.m. A little after. The roof's better than it was, at least. Sunrise is in six hours. All we have to do is avoid freezing to death till then."

He clanked some things around in the kitchen before showing

up holding half a fifth of Kevin's whiskey he'd taken from the top of the fridge.

"This is kind of a last night," he said. "The three of us here. Together. Let's do what we do on last nights."

Kevin wasn't much of a drinker. He wouldn't notice it gone. He wouldn't be too mad, anyway, I didn't think—we'd never made him too angry. And I wanted to feel that warm burn of liquor in my chest. I wanted some part of me to not be cold.

"It's definitely a last night," Rand said. "No matter what happens, we'll never be together like this again. Even if we want to."

Wesley unscrewed the top and drank. "I'm not going to want to be together *like this* again. Guarantee you."

Rand took the bottle next. His face was a bruised and bloody roadmap of the last twenty-four hours. "You said something that's been bothering me—you said she loved me the most."

Wesley peeled back the label on the bottle. "It's wasn't really an exaggeration."

"But it's not true. I remember Grace talking to you, telling you to try to get closer to your dad—go fishing, skiing, whatever. That she believed it would make you happy or fix a problem. Something."

I looked up. "I never knew that."

For all Grace's complaining about Wesley being away with Kevin, it was her own design.

Wesley shrugged.

"She did love you. She loved all of us." Rand sighed and stared up at the snow blowing through the ceiling. "I'm sorry, Wesley."

Wesley lifted an eyebrow as if he thought Rand was tricking him. "For what?"

"That I blamed you for chasing Grace away. Before she left or—before Grace disappeared, she wrote you that letter. Obviously she didn't blame you. I shouldn't either."

Wesley looked up at the ceiling, then back down to Rand. "It's okay, man." He squeezed Rand's shoulder, sniffling a little. "No big."

My eyes burned as I took the next drink, only a little bit.

We'd spent three years of our lives together for short spurts of time. Ten days after Christmas, a week at spring break, three months of summer. Our tragedy, I guess, was that in all that time, we did everything we could to not know each other.

But somehow we did know each other, better than we'd thought.

Wesley, with his split open lip and half-swollen eye as he tipped back the bottle, was my brother. I lived with him twenty-four/seven. We devoted our days to keeping up the lie that our mom was okay—at least to the outside world.

We didn't know everything about each other, and I wanted to know more. I wanted to try. "Wesley, what do you want?"

He smiled. "Not to freeze to death."

"That's not what I mean. After you graduate, for the rest of your life, what do you want? You really think you would have been happy in the house painters' union?"

"School's not easy for me like it is for you." He lifted his eyebrow at Rand. "Or you. Nora, you may not be any valedictorian, but you never ever study, half the time you don't even turn in your homework, and you can still pull A's and B's. You know how hard I'd have to work for an A?" He took the bottle back, but instead of taking a drink, he just untwisted the cap and twisted it back. Again and again. "I like the idea of building things, even if I'm no good at the actual building. I like drawing out sketches of how to make them. I guess I'd be an architect. But it's a lot of math—"

"You could learn the math," Rand said. "With tutors. You're smarter than you think."

Wesley could draw maps to scale and he knew how things worked and fit together. He just didn't learn the way I did.

"Grace knew you didn't want to be a house painter," I said as I thought about the letter. "And I know it too. But the counting the stars thing." I smiled and rolled my eyes. "So Grace."

Wesley blew on the lip of the bottle until it sounded like the ocean. "Grace thought it would ground me. Give me something to do to make me forget. She said there were enough stars to make me forget." He laughed. "She was right. I couldn't count ten of them before whatever I was freaking out about—Mom, money, Laura, Kevin—faded for a minute."

"Grace was wrong about some things. Not everything," Rand said. He pressed his fingertips into the corner of his eyes. "I miss her."

"I miss her too." Wesley sniffed as his teeth chattered.

"I always will," I said.

Wesley smiled to himself as he turned the almost-empty bottle in his hands. "That night on the ski lift, I was having too much fun to care that she almost killed me."

Rand hiccupped, then laughed. "Sorry," he said. "I'm a sad excuse for a lush."

The three of us told stories about Grace into the darkest part of the night. The good and the bad. The temperature kept dropping to the point where we were too cold to talk but afraid to go silent. We talked to stay warm, to remind ourselves we were alive.

I woke up with my nose in the crook of Rand's neck and Wesley's head on my leg. I hadn't remembered falling asleep. My throat was dry and raw from talking almost all night.

At first, I wasn't sure if it was morning or nighttime again. Blankets tacked over the windows and the heavy trees outside blocked the light, keeping the cabin dim.

Then I saw the snow coating the stairs, at least a foot deep. And it shone bright in the sun streaming down.

Past Wesley's shoulder, his cell phone sat on the edge of the blanket. Four solid bars.

In the bright, red-sky dawn with the snow stacked against the cabin and hanging in the trees, we could see the blizzard had blown through. Emergency services and Caltrans were working around the clock to get the roads clear.

We called everyone who needed to know we were okay, Kevin and Mom and Rand's parents. They weren't letting any cars through at the highway, and even if they could get in, until a snowplow blasted away all the snow, there was no road to travel.

When I got off the phone with the 911 operator, the boys were sitting in the daylight streaming into the freezing kitchen, talking about what to do.

Holding my phone in my hands, I leaned my forearms onto the counter. "If we were really hurt or something, they could move us up the priority list. But since we're not in too much danger of freezing to death in the daylight, but we can't stay here another night, they said they could get a rescue team in here before nightfall."

"Doesn't sound promising," Rand said. "When's everything going fully operational?"

Wesley slid onto the barstool beside me, his eyes bloodshot and his laptop open.

"That works?" I asked.

"It was under my bed," he said. "Internet's back. Weather's getting better. We should be getting out of here tomorrow."

"I'll head down the road and check on the snowmobile soon," Rand said. "If it's not buried, maybe we can use it to get to my place."

Wesley looked up from the screen and cleared his throat. "You wanted to know what the Lombardis' place sold for. I'll Zillow it."

Maybe Wesley had finally resigned himself to the sale. Letting this place go was starting to sink in. It felt like losing a part of myself.

Wesley held his tongue between his teeth. With his eyes narrowed at the computer, he said, "Strange. Um, Grace's parents sold the cabin in June."

Only six months after her disappearance. But that made sense. "After what happened, they must have wanted to get some distance from Donner," I said.

"No, it wasn't a normal sale."

"What do you mean?"

Wesley wouldn't say, just stared at the screen.

Rand flipped the computer around. "It was a foreclosure."

"A foreclosure?" I asked. "Why would Grace's parents let that happen? They were rich."

"What are you talking about?" Rand asked. "Grace was anything but rich."

I looked at Rand as he stared right back at me. "You thought Grace had money?" he asked. "Nora, no. Not by anyone's definition, really. Her mom worked as a cashier at a discount grocery store and her dad was on disability. They lived in an apartment in Henderson."

I couldn't speak. I thought back to all the things she'd stolen and sold. I assumed her parents just didn't give her a lot of cash, not that her family was broke.

"I thought you knew. The life Grace invented for herself, that was part of it," Rand said.

Grace was a trick, an illusion, a stretch of my imagination. She'd designed herself to be exactly that. And the more I learned of her, it seemed there was more I didn't know.

"In foreclosure since October," Rand said. "Grace had to know before winter break."

"She knew that when they came back for spring break, it would be the last time." I pushed away from the laptop. "Wesley, when Grace got so angry, it wasn't until you said you weren't coming back in spring, right?"

"I think so," he said. "What does that have to do with anything?"

That was the turning point that miserable night, when Grace lost it—when Wesley mentioned there wouldn't be a spring.

Rand's eyes widened. "The foreclosure would process after spring. She probably had an idea just how long her parents could keep up the payments. How long they could hang on."

Wesley blank-faced blinked at me. "Guys, I'm, like, lost here."

"All that talk about the last night wasn't just Grace deciding to leave. When you told her you weren't coming back, she realized that night was actually our last night all together."

All of us, vacationing in these boxes in the hills, it was easy to assume everyone had money. Grace's parents—just like me and Wesley—didn't really have anything except the cabin itself.

Both Grace and I were dreaming about the same things, a life that everyone around us seemed to be living. We wanted it so bad—the exact same thing. I spent every season never knowing she was chasing the exact same fantasy.

CHAPTER 37

WINTER

Sore and beat-up and frozen so cold, we couldn't remember what it felt like to be warm, Wesley and I each went to the crumbled places our rooms had been to gather some clothes, our toothbrushes, our nerves. We could wait out the clearing roads at Rand's cabin with a running heater, hot showers, and food. His parents weren't due back from Reno for days, not that they could get through to Donner if they wanted.

I dropped my backpack outside Wesley's open door and peeked inside his room.

He stared up at the sky showing through jagged Sheetrock overhead. "You think this place'll fetch a few more bucks with the new skylight? It has a certain *quality*, don't you think?"

I brushed the snow off his bed and sat down. "Insurance will take care of it. Eventually." As I kicked my shoes through the six inches of white coating the carpet, I wondered how long the repairs would take. "Are you still mad at me and Kevin for selling this place?"

Wesley crossed his arms as he stared up at the sky, then stuffed his backpack with socks and a pair of dry shoes. "I was never mad at you. That wasn't the feeling."

"I wasn't trying to take the cabin away from you."

"I know," Wesley said. "All I've been trying to do for the last year is think of a way to take care of Mom and take care of you. Something that wouldn't mean losing the cabin. And I worried—" His nose turned a brighter shade of red and he wiped it on his sleeve. "I worried she'd kill herself. Not on purpose. An accident. And with me gone, you'd be the one to find her."

I squeezed my eyes shut. "Those state-funded rehab programs, do you think they're still in the cards?"

"Even if this place sells for top dollar, it won't be enough for us while she's away."

I sighed. "Kevin would let me live with him, if I asked."

Wesley looked at me like my words sucked the air out of the room. "Just the two of you after I go to college? You'd do that? You said you wouldn't before, and that's when it was both of us. You—you don't really even like him, do you?"

Kevin couldn't have been more understanding that winter night at the Honeyridge. And in spite of his love for Donner, he was the one who found a way for me to sell it, because he thought it was the best thing for me. For us.

"The problem isn't that I don't like him—I just don't know him. And that's partially my fault. But I want to know him."

Wesley squeezed my shoulder. "You're sure?"

"Yes," I said. "I want to try."

Rand knocked on the open door. "Snowmobile is fine—I can take you one at a time."

"Okay," Wesley said. "You go first. I want to get some things."

He grabbed a shoebox out of the closet, and as he tucked it inside his bag, I asked, "Is that where you hid Grace's letter?"

He took the lid off, flashed the inside. "Yeah, that and some other things I've been collecting over the years. Grace things." He passed me the box. "Here—go for it."

My fingers slid over a slim rock they'd skipped at Zion Ledge, a brochure for the jail museum, ticket stubs for *E.T.* we'd found on the ground, stacks and stacks of notes and maps, and the necklace he'd never had a chance to give her.

A thick soup of summers, winters, and springs slowed me down—Wesley monkey-barring the ski lift, Rand's skin slick with sunscreen, and Grace's toes in the murky Zion Ledge waters. All I could feel, in spite of everything that had gone wrong between the four of us, was a deep, inexpressible kind of love for Grace and our friends.

Rand reached for something and held it high. Morning light reflected off a silver dollar.

My breath slowing, I asked, "What's the date?"

Rand smiled. "You know the date."

Wesley shrugged. "It's from the ice cave. You remember—"

"1983," I said. "Of course I do."

There was something incomplete about the way she'd left the rooftop of the Honeyridge Lodge. Grace had a flair for the spectacular and there was something strangely mundane about a bottle of Captain beside a wicker picnic basket on a blanketed rooftop.

"No way," I said. "No."

"What does this mean, guys?" Wesley asked.

"It means Grace was going back to the ice cave without us," Rand said, "who knows how many times. Grace told Nora to leave the coin in the cave. Now here it is. She went back for this, for you. Or she did at least once. Getting there on foot would have been a journey in itself after that last winter storm."

"Do you really think that would have stopped her?" I asked.

Rand and I stared at each other. We were starting to piece together what went wrong that last, cold night—a horrible, terrible thing to understand.

"Maybe it's not what we're thinking," I said. "She could have left something for us—"

Wesley nodded, covered his mouth with his hands and gave me a look I couldn't read. "Or a clue. A hint."

"Wesley, what?" I asked.

He only shook his head.

I got up from the bed, paced through the snow. "We have to try. To know."

Rand took me by the shoulders. His hands squeezing me, I felt his urgency, how badly he needed to know where Grace disappeared, that she didn't just vanish into a snowy Donner night.

We should have waited another day, waited till the next morning when the roads were clear. But we didn't.

Rand stood in the garage of his cabin, moving ice chests and boxes away from his parents' second snowmobile. "We should have thought to go there sooner."

"I didn't think of it," Wesley said, slipping an axe into his backpack. "I would have never thought to check there. I should have, but I didn't."

"The ice cave wasn't safe outside of summer," I said. "Maybe not even then."

"We shouldn't be going there now," Rand said. But he kept clearing a space to pull the snowmobile out. We had to go.

Bringing Grace home was on us. After all, we were the ones who had lost her.

"You really think this is the place?" Wesley turned away from the shadowy, brush-covered hillside and blinked at the bright whiteness beyond.

We'd bundled into as many layers as we could fit under our down coats. Rand had borrowed an extra pair of pants from Wesley. They were too big in the waist and a couple inches short, but he'd forgotten to change them at his house.

Hats, gloves, and scarves formed barriers against the bleak atmosphere. With my boots ankle deep in powder, I pushed back a branch and clawed at snow until I found an opening only slightly wider than my shoulders.

Rand touched my back, fingers spreading. "Are you sure you want to go in?"

If the ice cave was the last place Grace had gone, then maybe it held the last clues of where to find her.

"No." I slipped inside and looked back. "But I have to check."

A few steps and I came across a wall of frozen water, an unmoving waterfall that sealed off our entrance.

"Damn," Wesley said. "The blizzard sealed this thing up good."

"Here." Wesley passed the axe to me. "Demolish it."

A few of my swings and the ice crumbled, giving way to a dark hole that echoed our footsteps. Rand ducked in behind me, but the space wasn't quite big enough for Wesley.

I looked back into the daylight. Wesley pulled back the axe to widen the opening.

A howl made our eyes shoot upward. A gentle crack that escalated into an avalanche.

Crumbling ice and rock rained down over us.

"Back! Back!" I tugged Rand deeper into the cave just as a wall of snow sealed our exit.

The world around us went still, and I squeezed Rand's hand.

"Nora. Rand." Wesley's voice sounded muffled and so far away.

"We're—" Yelling made dust particles fill my chest. I coughed into my scarf. "We're okay!"

Rand clicked on his flashlight and scanned it over my face and body. "How do you feel?"

"Rattled."

"No joke."

Wesley, his voice a dull echo, said, "I'll get help. Stay safe."

Rand knocked on the rock wall. "I hope we don't run out of oxygen."

I thought of my call to emergency services. They were suffocating under the weight of calls of those snowbound and car-wrecked. Saving us would be a hundred times harder but hopefully not take a hundred times longer. "Oxygen won't be the problem."

Rand sighed. He was shining his flashlight over the cave wall where we'd carved our names into the slate over a year ago. "It's still here."

"Of course. This is supposed to be here a hundred years after we're all gone." I traced the *G* in Grace's name and shone my flashlight into the void. The air still felt like only we could breathe it. Air that had been made especially for our fourteen-, fifteen-, and sixteen-year-old selves. "We're going to be down here for at least a few hours. We might as well look for what we're trying to find."

Dodging under a row of icicles, I made a hard right turn.

Up ahead, I spotted a square shape looming. A box. I skimmed my fingers over the outside that Grace had decorated with snapshots of the four of us. The dampness from the cave had made the photo paper crinkle. Rand stepped back to give me room. I opened the box, thumbed over the three gift tags. *For Rand. For Wesley. For Nora.*

This was the missing part of the rooftop goodbye at the Honeyridge. Grace had known her parents were losing the cabin, and she'd taken the time to collect gifts for each of us—Wesley's announcement about spring had bumped up the timeline. And her own departure.

"Rand," I whispered, wiping my wet face with my gloved hand. "Look in the box."

Rand took a knee in front of the box. He held the postcard and laughed as tears streamed. It was the postcard with the *Freudian Slip* heading and that picture of Sigmund Freud. "*When you say one thing, but you mean your mother.* I love it. I wish she knew. But why did she get this for me?"

"This was the end," I said. "She'd been collecting things all along for us. Our last vacation where we'd all be together, and she wanted to leave something for all of us."

For Wesley, she'd left something long and papery, rolled into a tube. We should have saved it for him to open first, but we were greedy for any new piece of our friend.

"A blueprint." Rand let it unspool and smiled a little as he inspected it. "Of the gazebo at the top of the Donner Pass. This is rare, I bet."

She knew. She knew Wesley secretly wanted to be an architect, where I didn't know that until last night. "Maybe all along Grace knew us better than we knew her."

Rand sniffed into the sleeve of his coat. "Obviously."

Last, I took out the gift with the tag that said *For Nora*.

"I don't get it," Rand said as I peeled back the paper.

Faux diamonds sparkled through my tears. I wondered how long she'd been holding on to it for me.

"It's for senior prom," I said. "I think in some way she was giving us her blessing."

I closed the box and got to my feet, staring off into the shallow, darkest recess of the cave, the deeper part we'd never tried to venture.

My eyes focused. And I sucked in a jagged breath.

I reached out a hand to steady myself.

Down into the darkness, I pointed the flashlight.

It shone on Grace's purple glove, then the long arms of her charcoal down coat, then the shiny copper of her hair. Grace's boots, her gray suede booties, were half-covered in snow, but they were the same ones she'd been wearing that day. Her eyes were closed as if she were sleeping, except tiny snowflakes dotted her lashes. Her lips were blue and parted as if she were pulling in one last breath.

Grace had her knees to her chest and her coat bunched around her throat.

Inching away, I pressed my back against the cave so hard, my spine ached.

It was her, but it wasn't.

She was Grace, but also just a shell that used to hold her bubbly laugh and the flash of a new idea bright in her eyes.

Rand saw, and moving fast to my side, crushed me to him. He held me, my face pressed into the chest of his coat.

I pulled back and looked up at him.

Tears ran like rivers down his cheeks.

He pulled back and pressed a hand to his mouth. "The entrance must have caved in last winter." He sobbed, then whispered, "Sealed her in. She came here, to leave something or to get something, and she couldn't get out."

"To get these things for us," I said.

Under all that clear ice, a few feet away from Grace, Rand and I curled together. The freezing temperatures of the night before in the cabin felt balmy compared to being trapped between those slick stone walls.

Hours passed, us trapped in the ice cave beside what remained of Grace. I wished I had something to cover her with. It felt wrong leaving her out in the open. Exposed.

She'd finally frozen to death in this space, and by the way Rand went silent and pressed my hand to his heart, I wondered if he thought the same fate awaited us.

People get warm before they freeze to death. They say it's a euphoric feeling, heat spreading like sparks of light all over your arms and body. Then they get so tired, they go to sleep.

As the soft glowing warmth radiated from my chest, down my limbs, into my fingertips, I thought about stars Grace would never see, sunshine she'd never feel, stories she'd never tell.

CHAPTER 38

WINTER

A ribbon of light cracked through from above. Sunlight spread like an overturned cup onto the cave floor.

"Rand." I shook his shoulder. "Rand."

He didn't wake up, only slumped forward, his freezing cheek grazing my hand. I shook harder and he jolted awake, blinking at the light beaming down.

"You're okay." I squeezed his gloved hand tight. "You're okay."

He looked off into the dark part of the cave, Grace's body. "I thought this was all a dream," he whispered.

"No, it was a nightmare."

He shook his head. "At least now we know."

They pulled Rand and me out of the deep cold darkness and into warmer air that felt like knives inside our frozen lungs. A part of me wanted to stay under, trapped in a world where Grace still wore gray suede boots and kept a secret burial ground of treasures all to herself.

"There's a body in there," I heard Rand say. "Our friend."

The EMT turned a shade of gray. "What?"

"Grace Lombardi," I said. "She's been in there all this time."

"Grace Lombardi," a woman whispered.

Grace, the girl who vanished once into the cold Donner night, was infamous. The media reported about a girl who disappeared just like her sister, everyone waiting for her to return alive. A story, but not the kind she'd wanted to become. Now all the myth surrounding her dissolved into hard truths.

They gave us thin metal blankets that looked like something you'd use to cover the windshield of a car in the heat. With it tight around my shoulders, I felt the glow of warmth finally travel through my veins.

I showed the paramedics my injured leg from the night before while they bandaged Rand's forehead. They said they'd order X-rays at the hospital.

Wesley, small in the distance, straddling the road, broke into a run. As he darted around the corner, I glanced to Rand, being examined by a paramedic. Just out of earshot.

Wesley's arms closed around me, pulled back, tears streaking from his eyes.

Kevin emerged from behind the thicket of emergency vehicles and came running.

He yanked me into a hug that knocked the cold air from my lungs. "You scared me to death." We stayed like that until his pocket buzzed, and he pulled away to look at his cell phone. "Yeah, yeah," he said into the phone. "She's fine and I've got her. I'm here with her now . . ." He pushed the hair back from my face while he was talking, like he had to see me, really see me. "Yes, she's fine. She's fine . . . Okay. We'll—we'll be in touch."

"Who was that?"

He cringed. "Your mom."

Something about the way he said that told me she wasn't okay. "What happened?"

Kevin deflated, sat on the bumper beside me. "She's not great. It's a bad time for her right now. I—Nora, I know. I know now."

Over Kevin's shoulder, my eyes caught Wesley's. He gave me a little nod. He'd told him.

"I'm sorry, about everything, Nora," he said.

"What's going to happen to her now?" I asked.

Kevin turned his phone in his hands. "That depends a lot on your mom. In the meantime, it's probably not a good time for you to head home. Your uncle says he's got an extra room until your mom's back on her feet, if that's something you'd like to do."

"Or maybe we could stay with you?"

He winced. "Well, the cabin's out of commission. It'll be months until we can even get it on the market."

"What if we stayed with you in Lodi?" I asked.

"You'd want that, really?" There was a brightness in Kevin's smile that I hadn't seen before. "Um, yeah. Of course."

His eyelids hanging heavy, his arms moved around me again, careful not to hurt anything bandaged, and he gave me a squeeze so tight, I wondered if he was trying to make up for the dozens of hugs I'd never had.

His ringing phone broke us apart again.

"The hospital," he mouthed as he stepped away.

Rand loomed closer with a slight limp and a bandage on his forehead. He sat on the bumper beside me.

They brought Grace's body out into the blinding whiteness. She was wrapped in a black cloth body bag, but they hadn't zipped it up when they carried her into the daylight. From our perspective, Rand's and mine, sitting in the back of the ambulance, we could only see her amber-colored hair swaying in the blowing breeze.

I started to cry and so did Rand. His were soft gulps that turned into hiccups, but mine were the quiet, running-fast tears of a girl who'd made a lot of mistakes.

SUMMER: NOW

CHAPTER 39

Our cabin we'd once loved now in pieces and our mom in rehab, we spent the last of winter, spring, and summer in Lodi with Kevin.

He bought a new sectional for his apartment so we'd each have a place to sit around the TV, and he filled a couple backpacks with things from the back-to-school section at Target. We cooked real food that wasn't always grilled, and asked real questions.

The answers that weren't easy to give or hear were the ones I cherished the most.

Back home, I searched for every news report I could find. They felt like breaths of fresh air, a way to keep Grace alive a little bit longer. They were frequent the first couple of days and weeks, and tapered off as the months warmed.

First, I started writing stories about my mom, her picking out outfits for herself and then buying ones for me to match. I'd fill page after page each time I visited her, committing every detail about her life to paper. Next I started writing about Candace. With each email we traded, I added pages to my journal about her life back home and what she'd do each day to make it a little better. Finally, I started writing about Grace, but it wasn't easy.

I felt guilty for being here when she wasn't, and I owed her this—her real story. Somehow maybe writing it would take that feeling away.

Girls went missing every day. Sometimes they turned up the next morning, sleep-wrinkled with confetti still hanging in their hair. Sometimes they turned up a year later. A lot of the time they were never found. Even when they were, the flashiest of stories were the ones the public wanted. Kidnappings and girls found alive in storage units in the backyard and girls found buried in shallow graves.

The stories the media told had never felt wrong to me before. But now I wanted to know the real stories about those girls, girls like Candace and Grace. I wanted the world to know Grace's real story so badly that the feeling seemed like it would swallow me whole.

We might have found her body sooner if only we'd talked to each other instead of shutting each other out.

We knew Grace's family had acquired their cabin similar to the way our dad ended up with ours. The death of a distant relative and the idea of having somewhere to get away from it all. They held on as long as they could, until property taxes and a reverse mortgage drowned them in debt.

They told Grace they'd let the banks take it by early summer.

We knew that somehow, even as she tried like she did to not let us know the real her, she still found a way to know us.

We knew when she came to Donner, Grace could be our hedonistic ringleader, the queen of let's do this to forget and live for the moment. Grace liked dusky red sunrises against freshly fallen snow, expensive things, wind picking up her auburn hair and pulling it toward the stars.

Even if we didn't know everything, we knew more about her than I'd realized at first—we knew enough to love Grace.

Three weeks after the recovery of her body, her parents had a small funeral in Henderson, Nevada. Wesley and I drove up from Lodi and met Rand outside.

He wore a shirt with Freud on the front. "For Grace," he said.

I hugged him. "She'd love it."

"Added bonus," he said, "my dad hates Freud. I'm trying this new thing where I argue against his bullshit philosophies. Dinner conversation has never been so lively."

I smiled slowly. "I'm proud of you."

Only two other people our age followed us into the church—a girl with short cerulean-blue hair who told us she hated the way the bullies tormented Grace but she didn't know what to do about it, and a doe-eyed, skinny boy who lived in the apartment next door to Grace's.

He said Grace would climb onto her fire escape after her house went dark every Sunday night. She'd stare up at the moon. He'd never tried to speak to her. He wished he had.

Candace was there too, but she sat in the back away from her dad, alone. Her sobs were the loudest when the pallbearers carried out the casket.

After it was over and the remains of the congregation scattered, Wesley went off to find the bathroom while Rand went forward to say something to the priest. Candace stood by a picture of Grace.

A girl with dark, cropped hair came up beside her, slid her hand into Candace's.

I recognized her from the first night at the Honeyridge. I smiled just a little. Maybe Candace had a little bit of happiness now.

"I'm sorry," I said. "I'm so sorry for your loss."

Slowly, she turned, her bleary eyes brightening a little as she focused. "You're Nora."

I opened my mouth. Nothing came out.

We'd only emailed. I didn't expect her to know me.

"She told me about all about you, you know," she said, brushing the hair out of her eye. "Grace. She told me about you and Wesley and Rand. Your seasons. They were"—she smiled back at Grace's picture—"everything to her."

Her girlfriend stepped away. "I'll be outside."

"I wish they could have been even more," I said. "For Grace, especially."

Candace nodded. "I wish a lot of things could have been more for Grace." She glanced to the side door by the church's organ, where Grace's dad motioned for her to follow. "I guess I've gotta go. But I'm glad you came."

"Me too."

Candace took three steps away, then turned back. "Hey, Nora," she said. "If you go back there, try to remember the good things too. Grace would want that."

I smiled. "There are a lot of those to remember."

I sat down in the front pew after Candace was gone, staring up at Grace's smile that showed her sharp incisors and her perpetual bedhead. The heat of my tears seared my cheeks as I sat there, trying to memorize her cheekbones and the patterns of her irises.

I realized nothing really could make up for what I'd done and hadn't done. All I had left to give Grace was to honor her in the next season and every one to follow, in the spaces between the seasons, and the everyday kind of days that all ran together.

Grace deserved all that. And more.

FALL: NOW

CHAPTER 40

Insurance covered most of the repairs to the cabin, but it took months for the checks to come through and the repairs to get done.

Escrow would close in late October. It was a sacrifice we had to make, for Wesley's future and my own.

I sat on the bed in my room at the cabin, blank white-ruled lines spread out before me. It was time to finish my story.

I wrote for hours, filling pages with Grace's sharp incisors, her whoop that could echo through the night, the way she could touch your arm and send an electric shock right through you, the sadness that filled her after Candace left, the hopelessness she felt when Candace returned.

Kevin knocked on the door that afternoon. "You doing okay? You need anything?"

I capped my pen, closed my notebook. "I'm—I'm good."

He started to step away, but I said, "Hey, are you and Wesley taking the boat out later?"

"Um, yeah." His shoes shuffled across the carpet. "We were going to try our hand at catching dinner, but we could do something else. If you wanted—"

"No, let's go fishing," I said. "I'd like to try it at least once."

After Kevin shut the door, I padded across the freshly laid carpet. I planted my feet on the windowsill, curled my toes around the molding. I could still see sunlight pouring into the cabin Grace's parents no longer owned. I imagined her there, waving back at me wearing a know-it-all grin. My heart heavy, I looked toward the lake, near the water, where a trail of gray smoke rose from a distant chimney.

Orange and red fluffy leaves rained down like confetti as I pulled my sweater tight and walked down the trail with my flip-flops slapping my feet.

I knocked on the front door, but behind, a car door slammed in the driveway.

Rand had his hands in his windbreaker pockets as he ambled toward me at the front door. "I thought I'd like to see what this place looked like in the fall."

"The leaves remind me of Grace," I said. "Her hair."

He looked up, blinking at the sky. "She would have loved them."

"We could take them to her," I said. "I'm visiting the cemetery tomorrow."

Rand plucked one off the ground and held it up.

After all those bright summers, heart-pounding winters, and promising springs, I wished Grace could have all the days in between too—boring, lazy, quiet, ordinary, and even sad, full of the hard questions, uncomfortable truths, and the most authentic of stories.

We had to live those days for ourselves, and for her too.

A gust of wind made another avalanche of leaves pour down. I said, "Let's make sure Grace has fall."

Jessica Taylor is the author
of the critically acclaimed
A Map for Wrecked Girls.
She adores atmospheric settings,
dangerous girls, and characters
who sneak out late at night.
She lives in Northern California
with her husband, their dog,
and many teetering towers
of books.

jessicataylorwrites.com
 @JessicaTaylorWrites
 @JessicaTaylorYA